✳ GRAVITY
vs. the girl

RILEY NOEHREN

Forty-Ninth Street Publishers

ISBN 978-0-615-26165-2

First Forty-Ninth Street Publishers edition 2008

TO DAVE & MARY

I carelessly wrote about illness and hospitals and Seattle, not realizing that I was daring them to happen. From now on I will only write about finding buried treasure and eating ice cream, I swear. Thank you for everything.

✳

Chapter 1

TODAY

TODAY IT FINALLY HIT ME: I have worn nothing but jammies for one solid year.

Today I remembered that Jello is not an appropriate breakfast food, and that three o'clock in the afternoon is not an appropriate time to eat breakfast.

Today I figured out that the crazy lady upstairs thinks *I'm* the crazy one. Sure, she's a sociopath, bears a strange rash on her neck, lives with no less than five hundred Pomeranian dogs and works out to 1980s aerobics videos on her mini-trampoline, but *I'm* the crazy one.

Today I realized that the crazy lady upstairs is absolutely right.

It all started when that little girl approached my bedside and poked me in the arm until I woke up. It was the most awake I had been in weeks, but I played dead right there under the covers, hoping she would just leave. I mentally replayed my routine from the night before and was sure I had double-checked the locks on the front door. I always double-check the locks, even those days when I never had reason to unlock them in the first place.

I was sweltering but had goosebumps. I thought I could hear my own heavy breathing, only it wasn't mine—it was hers. She was inhaling through an open mouth as little girls are prone to do, wheezing almost, despite the fact that she had no reasonable need for air. I supposed it was like locking locked doors: force of habit.

After five minutes, I assumed I had worn down her notoriously short attention span and she was about to give up and go home (wherever that was), so I opened one eye a slit. Instead, she just started poking me harder.

"Go away," I mumbled. "I'm trying to sleep." My voice was surprisingly hoarse when I said this. It had been a long time since I had said anything out loud.

It was noonday but the blinds were pulled. I could barely see her crooked hair in the dim light—a mangy set of braids done with a side part so that hair from the left side covered up a choppy section on the right that was forever growing out.

She was the only little girl I knew with a comb-over. She didn't belong in my room. She didn't belong in today, for that matter.

"Grown-ups aren't supposed to take naps," she stated authoritatively.

"It's not a nap," I said. "I haven't gotten up for the day."

"Why not?"

I rolled over while I contemplated this. In my slumbered haze, the pull of the bed on my body seemed unbearably strong, and this simple movement felt like trying to sprint in a swimming pool. She was only six. How on earth could I make her understand?

"Gravity," I said.

It was a dirty trick. Anyone who had ever spent ten seconds with this little girl knew that she considered gravity her mortal enemy.

"What?"

"The incessant pull of the earth on my body, forcing me into a supine position. I just can't fight it anymore."

But now she was on the other side of the bed and in my face again. She crossed her arms defiantly. "I don't believe in gravity," she huffed.

"Yeah well, I don't believe in ghosts and yet, here you are, poking me."

"I'm not a ghost."

"Oh, really? Then how did you get here?"

I stumped her with that one. She clearly couldn't remember, but she was never one to shy from fibbing her way out of any predicament.

"I rode my bike."

"The Strawberry Shortcake bike?"

"Yes!" Her eyes brightened at this. "You remember."

"You rode that little bike all the way from Commerce, Oregon?"

"Yep."

"That's like 150 miles."

"I know." Her yarn-spinning momentum was building now, and she leaned across the bed towards me, resting her dirty elbows on the rumpled comforter. "It was a really long ride. I had to bring a sleeping bag and camp out on the way. I ate lots of hot dogs."

"That sounds like quite the adventure."

"It was, but I wasn't scared, even in the parts where I had to sleep alone in the woods in the dark."

"So how did you jump the gulch on your bike?"

"Uh, what gulch?" she stalled.

"You know exactly what I'm talking about."

"Oh yeah, *that* gulch. I tied a million balloons to the handle-bars and I flewed right over it."

"That sounds an awful lot like your favorite movie."

"No, it was different, because Elliot had E.T. and I just had some balloons and my bike doesn't even have a basket but Daddy said he'd get me one soon."

"If your bike doesn't have a basket, then where did you keep your sleeping bag?"

Her mouth turned downwards and she pulled away from the bed, dragging her chubby hands across the duvet cover as she did so. I felt a little bad. I should have remembered she was only six regardless of the fact that she was so rudely haunting me.

"Be that way," she said. "I don't want to play with you anyhow."

And with that she was gone. From my bed I looked through the doorway down the empty hall and thought about checking the locks.

On any other day I would have pulled the covers over my head and slept until I convinced myself this little girl's visit was only a bad dream. On any other day I would have turned off my worries by noting that it was impossible to have dementia when you were brain-dead. On any other day I would have recited the words to songs I used to like until I lulled myself back into a self-induced coma.

But this was not any other day. It was today.

Today I put "shower" on my to-do list. Today I admitted I was broke. Today I felt sunshine in winter creeping through the slits in the blinds. Today I wiggled my toes under the covers, figuring one has to start somewhere.

Today I longed for laughing. Today I thought about thinking. Today I considered crying.

Today I wished for tomorrow to be set apart.

"I figured out why you're so sleepy," the little girl said. She was back and had resumed poking me, this time in the neck. Apparently any comments about the implications of missing bike baskets were forgiven.

"Why is that?" I asked.

"You stayed up late with all the grown-ups for the countdown with the disco ball."

"Huh. That sounds like a decent excuse."

Today is New Year's Day, you see, and I have but one resolution:

To get out of bed.

Chapter 2

SOMETHING WORSE

I SAT CROSS-LEGGED on the cold wood floor and surveyed the situation. I was in the living room. *This is progress*, I thought, nodding to myself. *It is what the RPP would do*—that is, if he left his bedroom for the first time in a month for anything other than using the restroom or checking the locks.

Then again, the RPP would never spend an entire month in his bedroom in the first place. That's just not his style.

"The RPP" is law-student speak for the Reasonably Prudent Person. If you went to law school (like I did), even if you graduated six years ago and yet the experience seems like a past life (like mine does), then you surely remember that the Reasonably Prudent Person is he by whom all of our actions are judged, at least from a legal standpoint. And if you didn't go to law school, let me just warn you that if you are ever so unlucky as to find yourself in front of a judge or jury regarding a particular decision you have made, the question will surely be asked, "What would the Reasonably Prudent Person have done in the exact same circumstances?"

After making his acquaintance, I tended to critique my behavior by the RPP's excruciatingly high standards. It was an exercise in losing, for the problem with the RPP was that he was so consistently prudent and reasonable while I, on the other hand, was not.

For example, the RPP always looks both ways before crossing the street. He checks his rearview and side mirrors anytime he puts his car in reverse, even if it is just to back out of his own driveway, even if he has backed out of his own driveway a million times and not once was there a car behind him because he lives at the end of a private street.

I looked around my living room and questioned whether the RPP could even bear such surroundings. The designer furniture was wearing blankets of dust. The coffee table was littered with empty plastic cups that once held Jello snacks. The floor was turning the bottoms of my feet black. I envisioned the RPP furrowing his brow.

You see, the RPP mops up spills in his grocery store the minute he discovers them. He fixes creaky steps just in case they are rotting. He replaces light bulbs the minute they burn out. The RPP does not keep wild animals, explosives or dangers attractive to children on his property. He does not store barrels of flour next to open windows. He never takes parcels of firecrackers to train stations.

As a plumber, the RPP always observes the plumbing code. As a doctor, he checks twice for missing sponges before stitching his patients back up. As a rancher, he does not trespass and neither do his cattle. As a therapist, he keeps your deepest, darkest secrets—unless, of course, you confide you are planning on killing someone, at which point he politely calls to warn them.

If the RPP has an epileptic seizure—even one—he will give up driving for life. If the RPP's dog bites someone—even once— he will have the dog put down.

The RPP should put me down, I briefly allowed myself to think. It was an indulgent thought—as sweet and decadent as a stolen

Godiva truffle to a recovering chocoholic. Then again, I was in the living room for the first time in a month. This was progress.

"Why don't you sit on the couch?" that ghost of a little girl asked. For whatever reason, she had decided to stick around.

The white leather sectional was once my prized furnishing; now it seemed too much like my bed. The couch was methadone, but the floor was cold turkey. It was safer to stick with the floor, but I didn't want to admit this to the little girl. Instead, I just shrugged my shoulders. "I like it here."

"Why don't we go walk the dogs?" she asked.

I shook my head. "I already told you, not today."

She sat down on the couch herself and eyed me with all the resignation a six-year-old could muster. "What happened, anyway?" she asked, shaking her head. "You're a real mess."

Her observation torpedoed my resolve. *What happened?* It was a question I hadn't allowed myself to ask for a year. However, I had spent a good part of the previous six months answering it, in lieu of doing anything else.

What happened?

Something bad happened, of course. It happened at work. Well, it mostly happened at work. It also happened on the way to work, on the way home, going to the grocery store, crossing asphalt, walking concrete, waiting in lines, on the escalator, up the elevator and in the dressing room at Nordstrom. It happened at the gym, it happened on the phone, it happened in a panic in the middle of the night. It happened up and down. It happened to and fro. It happened in the meantime and in between.

And the something bad that happened was . . .

Nothing.

"Nothing happened," I told her. "That's the whole problem."

"I'll say."

It was particularly difficult to explain the weight of nothingness to this little girl. She rode her bike through the Oregon wilderness, after all. She picked up bunnies and frogs and daddy long-legs in the afternoon and in the evening she would eat dinner without washing her hands. She was constantly surmising on ways to outwit gravity—namely, how to cross the chasmal gulch that separated her hometown of Commerce from the rest of the whole wide world where, she was convinced, a host of adventures awaited her.

This little girl felt that doing nothing was synonymous with lackluster or tedium. She wasn't old enough to appreciate its true menace.

By contrast, the RPP extracts the safety nothing has to offer and embraces it. The RPP always shows up on time for work. The RPP has a grocery list. The RPP is neither bored nor defeated by the monotony of life.

The RPP would never quit his job and forget to find another one. The RPP would never put on jammies and forget to take them off. The RPP would never sit on the living room floor and spend six hours plotting his next move.

"Let's go walk the dogs," the little girl pleaded with me as she stood in the bathroom door.

"Not this week," I said, only it didn't come out quite that way, as I was in the middle of flossing my teeth and attempted to talk by pushing my tongue against the right wall of my mouth.

"But I can hear them barking," she whined. "I think they want to go for a walk."

Of course she could hear the dogs barking—the crazy lady upstairs had five hundred of them. "They never stop barking," I explained. "But you'll get to the point where you don't notice it anymore."

She sat down on the toilet, crossed her arms and pouted. She repeated this gesture about every five minutes. I suppose it was sort of her signature move. "It's boring here," she whimpered.

"Then leave."

"Only if you come with me."

"Stop rushing things. You're not giving me enough credit."

"Credit for what?"

"For this," I said, waving the floss at her. "For all of this," I said, motioning towards the toothbrush, the toothpaste and the mouthwash. "*This* is progress!"

"Brushing your teeth is progress?" she asked. "I've been brushing my teeth since I was a baby. You're a grown-up who's too fraidy-cat to even go outside."

She was right, of course. I looked down at my floss. It didn't seem like such a milestone anymore.

"But I can't go outside," I said.

"Why not?"

"It's freezing out there." It was mid-January in Seattle. "And I don't even know the lady who owns the dogs." This was also true. Although the crazy lady lived just upstairs, I had only exchanged passing comments with her at the mailboxes on a few occasions until I realized she was a sociopath who was always scratching her neck, at which point I would fake a cell phone conversation each time I saw her just to avoid making small talk or catching whatever it was she was clawing. "Anyway, I don't have anything to wear."

The little girl gave me the once-over. "Well, you can't wear those jammies, that's for sure," she said. "They're disgusting."

I looked down at my frayed pajamas. I envisioned the RPP agreeing with the little girl. In my mind, the RPP is always wearing a starched oxford shirt, but no tie. He wears a white crew-neck undershirt for decency. He wears khaki slacks, but they look nice, because they have a crease pressed down the front of each leg. If it is cold, the RPP dons a cardigan or maybe a windbreaker. He does not accessorize but for a watch and a belt.

But the RPP would similarly disprove of the little girl's attire, which could be best described as Punky Brewster chic. "You're not one to talk," I told her.

"What do you mean?" She looked down at her outfit defensively. I happen to know she picked it out herself.

"For starters, you're wearing magenta corduroys with rainbow patches on the pockets. Those haven't been in style since 1983."

"But all the kids at school—"

"And the pants totally clash with that bright yellow shirt."

"No, they match because they both have rainbows on them."

"You have to match *colors*. You can't match rainbows to rainbows."

"Yes you can!" I had to smirk at her indignity, knowing that one of her other favorite outfits was a cacophony of plaid and stripes that was matched according to the inclusion of teddy bears on each item. At times, I felt her father should be incarcerated for ever letting her leave the house in such an ensemble.

I leaned across the countertop and pointed at the grass stains covering both her knees. "To top it off, those pants are filthy."

"Well, I got that when—"

"I know how you got it."

She crossed her arms and pouted again. "At least I have a life," she said.

There are few things more humbling than the realization that a ghostly six-year-old does, indeed, have more of a life than you—even if it is of the hopscotch and dress-up and imaginary-friend variety. Hopscotch was an excellent defense to nothing.

But this little girl knew nothing of nothing. No, this little girl could not understand that nothingness force-fed middle-aged women into airline seatbelt extenders. This little girl had no idea that nothingness begat anger in suburban schoolboys—anger so strong that they loaded their backpacks with bullets instead of books. This little girl would never know that nothingness invented online dating.

"Listen," I said. "I'm just not ready for the dogs. But in a couple of days I'll be completely out of food and will have to go to the store. You're welcome to come with me then."

"Really?" she asked.

"Yeah. And if you're embarrassed to be seen with me, I'll go find some clothes in the closet."

Her eyes grew wide at this.

"No, don't go in the closet," she pleaded, her voice lowered.

"Why not?"

"Because there's another one in there, and she's a lot scarier than me."

"Oh." I sat down on the floor, still gripping the floss, devastated by the realization that I was crazier than I had first estimated. "You've seen this ghost?" I finally asked.

"Yes," she nodded gravely.

"What does she look like?"

"Kinda like you. Only a whole lot prettier."

I nodded. "I suppose she's wearing a business suit?"

"You mean like something fancy ladies wear to work?"

"Yes."

The little girl nodded again. "She's real mean and nasty. And boy, is she mad at you! That's why you shouldn't go in the closet. She'll scream at you until you cry, and then you'll go back to bed and we'll never walk the dogs."

I put my head in my hands. It was a bad habit I inherited from my father. Whenever I saw him do it, I thought it looked pathetic, like an ostrich sticking its head in the sand. Despite my aversion to it, I had never been able to break the habit myself. As a lawyer, I had to grip the underside of the table during an intense negotiation in order to prevent myself from doing it. If it got really bad, I would take a bathroom break and sit in the stall with my head in my hands until I got the urge out of my system.

Once more, I thought of the RPP, shaking his finger at me. Of course, the RPP would never go so mad that he would begin talking to ghosts. And even if he did, the RPP would surely act with sufficient prudence to avoid royally pissing one of them off.

The RPP also wouldn't subsist on soda and nonperishable snack foods for the better part of six months. When I ate my last Jello cup three days later, I had no choice but to keep my promise to the little girl.

"How old are kids who fit in the front seat of a grocery cart?" I asked her the following afternoon.

"Only babies sit in the front seat," she shrugged. Her insufferable Big Girl pride was always getting in my way.

I was standing in the grocery store and looking at a small boy sitting in the front seat of his mother's cart and I just *had* to know how old he was. He reminded me of a time when I was similarly proportioned. I don't know how old I was, but I do know I was small enough to fit in the front seat of the grocery cart. If I thought I could get away with walking right up to him and inquiring as to his age, I would have done so.

But I was wearing my jammies, a college sweatshirt and rain boots, and I remembered enough about the real world to know it was poor form for adults to approach children they didn't know and ask them how old they were, particularly when the adult in question was dressed like a homeless person. As a result, I never figured out how old I was when I was his age, just that I was equally small.

The grocery store in my parents' town would play easy-listening music over the PA system. Small me wouldn't know the words, but that didn't stop her from singing along at top volume, writing her own lyrics along the way. She would swing her feet to the rhythm, jostling the shopping cart in the process and her mother would absent-mindedly throw her hand back to steady it while she mentally debated the price of peas. The other shoppers smiled at the small girl as they rolled by—in praise, she assumed, of the fact that her lyrics were so superior to the original. The smiles only encouraged the singing, and if she weren't so imprisoned by the metal cagery and that surprisingly strong strap, I dare say she would have hopped into the back of the cart to add some hand movements and a little hip-wigglin' to the mix.

I now realized that they were all laughing at her. I blushed with embarrassment just thinking about it. Yet I was caught between wishing the singing never happened and wishing I could go back and relive that moment just to see what it felt like. I never sang anymore. Before my year in jammies, I would occasionally sing along to the radio in my car, but even then it was only at night, with the top up and never at intersections. Even then I turned the radio volume up so loud that I couldn't hear my own voice.

At that moment, I would have sold my left rain boot for a copy of those impromptu lyrics. I hoped they would contain astute observations on the carefree nature of childhood and the meaning of life in general, but I had been around kids just enough to know that if I was in the cereal aisle I was likely singing about cereal and if jam was in sight, I was probably singing about jam.

But *what* did I sing about jam?

I was thirty-one years old. I no longer fit in the front seat of the grocery cart. I was overwhelmed at the thought of getting dressed. I had stopped looking forward to . . .

Anything.

So there I was, standing in my jammies in the grocery store, staring too long at a stranger's child and feeling consumed with the desire to turn around and retrace my steps so that I could understand just exactly how I got there. But like Hansel and Gretel, I apparently left breadcrumbs for markers and the blasted birds ate them all while I was preoccupied with living.

I shifted my attention to the little girl ghost, who had picked up a box of Count Chocula. She shook the box with disdain. "They changed it! It used to look different."

I couldn't figure out if she was a breadcrumb or a bird.

The small boy's mother rolled him away. I looked down at my own shopping cart. It was full of things I didn't want to eat, because none of them were Jello. I left the cart in the middle of the aisle and walked away.

"Wait! Where are you going?" the little girl called after me.

"Home," I said.

"But you don't have anything to eat!"

"I'll come back tomorrow," I said, increasing my pace as I headed for the door.

"But it took us so long to get here," she whimpered.

"I know, but now that we know what buses to take, it will be easier tomorrow."

"But *this is progress!*" she cried, as I moved further away.

She was right in the sense that just getting to the grocery store had been a monumental accomplishment. Armed with information about the other ghost, the little girl and I had sidestepped the closet all week. The only clothes I had in my bedroom dresser were underwear and pajamas, so we decided it wouldn't be the end of the world if I went to the store in pajamas so long as I wore an old college sweatshirt and my hair in my face and tried to pass for grungy and nineteen. Still, all my shoes were held hostage in the closet but for the pair of rain boots I kept with the coats by the entry. They were meant to be worn over shoes, and therefore were a little big on my bare feet, but I managed to drag them around on the slick streets without falling.

It took half a day to determine what series of buses I needed to take to get to the store. It took over an hour to travel the same distance by bus that I used to drive in ten minutes without appreciating the convenience.

I knew that, after all that work, it was a step backwards to leave empty-handed. I could feel the little girl's disappointment. I could sense the shadow of the RPP tracing my steps, tsk-tsking my cowardice.

But you know what? The RPP is far from perfect. He makes a terrible party guest. He doesn't have much of a sense of humor as he takes things too literally. Sarcasm is pretty much lost on the guy.

At the bus stop, the little girl caught up to me. She sat down on the bench, crossed her arms and pouted. "You were doing so good," she said.

"I know. But it will work better with a shopping list."

She swung her feet, drawing shapes in a puddle with her sneakers. I thought about all that perishable food, perishing away in my abandoned cart.

It figured that guilt would be the first emotion to come back.

Once we were on the bus, my head began to clear. Again, it struck me that this little girl was impervious to nothing. This little girl proudly matched rainbows to rainbows. She didn't care a whit about her horribly crooked hair. She wore a bright pink princess costume to her own mother's funeral and fancied herself the center of attention at a marvelous gathering of her parents' closest friends.

I realized I had been hard on the RPP as well. You probably wouldn't want to date the RPP. You might prefer the company of the quasi-employed drummer you met at a club last week. But you would want the RPP to be your friend, your neighbor, the guy next to you on the freeway when you looked down at the radio dial for a second too long. Your very life depended on it.

"You didn't used to be such a fraidy cat," the little girl observed.

"I didn't?"

"No. At least not back when you were me."

She was absolutely right. There were no grass stains on my jammies, there were no holes from climbing trees or running so fast and carelessly that I fell down—just the general wear and tear one would expect from staying in bed an entire year.

What happened?

I used to be a lawyer—a successful lawyer. Now I was a recluse talking to one ghost, hiding from another and hyperventilating after a single excursion outside. I was waiting to ride the bus in my jammies and rainboots.

Something bad happened and the something was nothing.

But the nothingness of now was something worse.

Chapter 3

500 POMERANIANS

"Hi," I SAID.

"Hello," she scratched.

"I'm your neighbor from—"

"Downstairs, I know." The crazy lady clawed at her neck some more and frowned. "I heard you were ill."

"Uh… I'm not sure how you heard that, but yes, I suppose I was."

"You're better now?"

"I'm recuperating."

"Not contagious, is it?"

"Not that I know of."

She looked me up and down with squinted eyes. "You're thinner. It suits you." With that, she turned around and disappeared into her apartment.

"Where'd she go?" the little girl asked after a few minutes.

"I'm not sure. Maybe we should just leave."

"But the dogs—"

The crazy lady cut her off with the most horrible hacking cough I had ever heard. "Well, come inside already and close the door," she barked at me. "It's no wonder you took ill."

The little girl and I rushed into her dark unit and shut the door behind us. I was immediately overwhelmed by that *Twilight Zone* feeling one gets when they visit a neighbor whose home has the same floor plan as their own—the bones are the same, but the difference in style and arrangement is otherworldly. Of course, the most obvious difference was that her unit reeked and roared of dogs, while mine did not, but there were other noticeable contrasts. My unit was minimalist, while hers was packed to the hilt. She had tons of furniture, most of it upholstered in floral chintz. There were stacks of women's magazines all over the floor, but they weren't even good women's magazines—they were the kind that are sold right next to the tabloids and the gum when you're waiting in line at the supermarket, full of an odd combination of fad diet advice and dessert recipes.

She had apparently banished her five hundred pups to the bedroom in an effort to keep them from storming me, but I could still hear them. I sat down on one of the floral couches and turned my attention to the opposite wall. A theme immediately emerged. It was covered in pictures, plates, cross-stitch pieces, little spoons and thimbles—all commemorating a wedding. Sadly, it was not her wedding.

When dealing with a crazy person, you always reach that sticky point where you have to strategize whether to (a) avoid mentioning the craziness like the proverbial elephant in the room, or (b) start a dialogue about it, as if to suggest it were not crazy. As I was mulling over these options, I noticed the crazy lady had stopped scratching and was staring at me. It was then that I decided to go with choice (b) out of desperation for something to say.

"I see you're a fan of The Wedding," I said.

"Yes," she nodded, "it was a magical day."

"It was," I agreed, looking at each item on the wall.

Her demeanor instantly brightened and she resumed scratching. "You remember it?" she asked. "I assumed you were nothing but a child then."

"Oh, I was," I said, still nodding. "But that made it all the more magical." She smiled. The little girl nudged me in the ribcage with her elbow. "Listen," I said, hoping I had laid a sufficiently buttered-up groundwork, "my doctor has advised me to start taking afternoon walks as part of my, uh, rehabilitation."

"He has?"

"Yeah, you know, fresh air and all."

"I don't think cold January air is good for anyone, especially someone who's been sick."

"Okay, I will be sure to take that up with him at my next appointment. In the meantime, I believe you have several hundred dogs—"

"I have two."

"Yes, I meant two."

"They're Pomeranians."

"Yes, I meant two Pomeranians."

"So?"

"So I was wondering if any of your two Pomeranians need walking right now. I think the company would assist my recovery."

She stopped scratching again. Strangely, her overall demeanor was more disconcerting when she was not scratching. I found myself holding my breath until, slowly, her hand started up to her neck again.

"Normally I wouldn't allow it," she said. "These are my babies, after all, and I barely know you. But I am a firm proponent of animal therapy, and you look as though you could use a touch."

By that point, I wanted nothing more than to tell her that she looked as though she could use an entire bottle of calamine lotion, but I politely resisted the urge. "I believe you are right," I offered. "If this works, I'll tell everyone about it."

"Including your doctor?"

"He'll be the first."

She looked quite satisfied with this barter. "Very well then," she said, "you can take the babies for a walk. Of course, I assume you'll be donning proper warm attire first."

That's right—in dealing with me, the crazy lady had also opted for choice (b) by pointing out the midday jammies but acting as if they were normal—or at least that they were normal for making social visits but somewhat less normal for walking "the babies." If it were any other person, I would have simply said "No, thank you," and made my way back home. But I had worked too hard in the past three weeks to be out-maneuvered in a game of *Who's crazier?* by none other than the crazy lady upstairs. My jammies were freshly laundered. The blanket of dust in the living room had been removed. There were perishables like produce and dairy in my refrigerator. Call it pride, but I refused to let my precious produce be defeated by third-rate women's magazines.

"Of course I'll be changing my clothes," I said. "I wouldn't dream of walking around outside in this."

The little girl's jaw dropped. As for the crazy lady, my calling her bluff sent her into a scratching frenzy. She turned towards the hallway and snapped her fingers. "Charles, Diana," she called, "come to Mommy!"

As we headed back down to my condo to change, the little girl grew panicked. "Can't we just go to the store and buy you some new clothes?" she begged.

"No," I said. "I'm broke and it's ridiculous to buy new clothes when I have an entire closet full of them. Besides, the crazy lady is expecting us to come right back."

"But you don't know what a bully she is—"

"It's two against one," I said. "And you do want to walk the dogs, don't you?"

I tried to maintain this feigned confidence as I entered the condo and walked down the hall towards the bedroom. It was a wonderful closet, I reminded myself—cedar-lined and with a designer storage system. It even had an island of shoe racks in the middle and a little upholstered bench to sit on while you buckled your Mary Janes. But with each creaky step towards the closet, I could sense the ghost's budding anticipation at our arrival.

I stopped in the bathroom and smoothed out my hair. When had it gotten so long? I removed my sweatshirt and kicked off the rain boots. Perhaps the ghost would think I had just gotten up? No, she was far too smart for that. I paused for a moment at the absurdity of meeting one's neighbor in one's jammies yet grooming for a ghost—but this ghost had excruciatingly discerning tastes.

The little girl held my hand as I swung the closet door open and flipped the light switch. It even smelled like her in there.

We took a cautious step inside. I was struck by the enormity of the closet and the contents therein. I didn't remember purchasing the five million pairs of shoes lined up on the rack, but once I eyed each pair individually, the memories came flooding back. This pair was on sale, that pair had been a splurge but worth it and those others gave me incapacitating blisters and I couldn't figure out why I had held on to them. Business suits lined the entire left side of the closet—twenty suits in nothing but black, navy and dark grey. Silk scarves and belts hung from hooks on the far wall. Sweaters, shirts, casual pants and dresses were on the right. On the top shelf, far out of reach, designer handbags were lined up like displays in a museum case.

I reached out to touch a scarf, but something cold smacked my hand.

"Boo!" the ghost said, her mouth incredibly close to my neck.

I jumped back. The ghost crossed her arms and started cackling.

The little girl hid behind my leg, but she fought back hard. "*Boo-hoo!*" she taunted. "We already knew you were in here."

The ghost and I stood there for a second, sizing each other up like the two Haley Mills in *The Parent Trap*. She was wearing a navy business suit—the very best one in the whole closet, naturally. I could have fed myself for a year on the cost of that suit. She wore nylons and a pricey pair of heels. Her hair was pulled back into a fat bun at the nape of her neck, and she wore a pearl necklace and matching earrings. Her makeup was meticulous.

She was clearly overdressed for an extended stint haunting a walk-in closet, but I didn't point it out. I feared inviting a response that I was clearly underdressed for traipsing about Seattle.

Our differences were many, but neither of us could ignore the fact that we were wearing the same face.

We made eye contact and hers narrowed to slits. Her structured frame started to shake.

"You sold my car," she spat, her voice low.

"I wasn't using it," I stammered. "I needed the money."

"It wasn't yours to sell," her voice lifted. "It wasn't your money to spend."

"I—"

"I bought that car! I earned that money with *hard* work!" She looked me up and down again, this time openly seething with disgust. "How dare you?!"

She lunged at me, pinning my neck against the hooks and the belts, squeezing hard.

"Stop it!" the little girl screamed, but the ghost didn't listen. I started to choke.

"If you kill me, you'll die too," I gasped.

"I'm already dead," she smiled as she tightened her grip on my throat. "As for you, it's a mercy killing. My conscience is completely clean."

I pulled at her arms, but my bed-weakened body was no match for her gym-honed strength. I started to choke.

"I said *stop it!*" the little girl cried. She moved to the isle of shoes and began throwing them everywhere, banging their $400 heels against the shelves. In the process, a few of them chipped.

"*What are you doing?!*" the ghost shrieked as she released her hold on me. She rushed over to the little girl and flung her out of the way.

I pulled the little girl off the floor and held her close to me to protect her. But the attorney ghost paid no heed to us. She squatted over the tiny leather carcasses on the floor.

"My shoes," she moaned, as she tenderly picked each one up and inspected the carnage. She looked back at the little girl like a wounded animal, clutching an ankle boot to her chest. "How could you do this to my shoes?"

The little girl's chest puffed up at the realization of her own power. "I'll do it again if you don't be nice to us. I'll wreck them all."

"And I'll let her," I said.

"I'll set fire to this whole closet!" the little girl puffed, taking it a tad too far in my opinion.

"But this closet is all I have left," the attorney trembled. Slowly, she placed each shoe back in its designated place on the rack. "The two of you already took over the rest of the house. You ate red Jello on my white leather sectional. Do you even remember how much that cost?"

"I do," I nodded. It was more than the gross national product of some developing nations.

"All I wanted was the closet," the attorney sighed. She curled up on the floor, still clutching one of her shoes.

"We didn't spill any Jello on your couch," the little girl said, sweeter this time.

"We'll let you have the closet," I offered. "But I need to ask a favor."

"What's that?" the attorney mumbled, entirely defeated.

"I need to borrow some jeans."

Ten minutes later found the three of us looking in the mirror together. The designer jeans I was wearing were a tad loose due to my recent Jello-cup diet. The attorney ghost was envious of this as she was always trying to lose ten pounds and exercised like mad in an effort to do so. As I tightened my belt, she pulled the bottom of her suit jacket over her hips.

The t-shirt and sweater combo were not as hip as the jeans, and neither were the athletic socks and battered running shoes I was wearing, but altogether everything was comfortable. I put on a knit scarf, a knit hat and a winter coat, hoping the combination would suffice for the crazy lady upstairs.

I turned around and looked in the mirror again. It wasn't the world's cutest outfit…

But I was dressed.

The attorney crossed her arms. "It's okay for lounging around the apartment, I suppose."

"No way," the little girl cried. "We're going to walk the dogs."

"What dogs? The crazy lady's dogs?"

"Yes," I replied.

"*Outside?*"

For such an over-educated ghost, she could be a little dense. I motioned to my knit cap. "Yes, outside!"

"Not without me you're not!"

Charles, Diana, the two ghosts and I dashed southeast through Belltown towards Pioneer Square. Although Pomeranians are small, this regal pair had me panting to keep up as they dragged me through the neighborhood at whip-speed. They seemed delighted to have a break from their overbearing mommy, most likely because I allowed them to hug the gutter and sniff all sorts of stuff that they were surely not permitted to do when she held the other end of the leash.

"This is a travesty," the attorney gasped, struggling to keep up with the rest of us while running on the icy streets in her heels. "I cannot believe you are you are out-dressed by a couple of dogs."

"They're Pomeranians," the little girl corrected.

Indeed, the crazy lady had outfitted Charles and Diana in hats, woolen capes and little knit booties. The capes were personalized: Charles' was embroidered with a metallic crown, while Diana's bore the initials "H.R.H." Although I was wearing thick mittens, their bejeweled leashes hurt my hand as the dogs pulled on them.

The little girl was underdressed in her yellow rainbow t-shirt, but she didn't seem to notice the cold. She skipped ahead in the street, waving her hands. "We're playing *outside!*" she exclaimed. The smile on her face was uncontainable. It was also contagious. My cheeks, already chapped by the crisp air, were pained by smiling so hard.

"This is so embarrassing," the attorney said. Sure, the outlandishly dressed dogs and their gleefully smiling handler had attracted a few stares, but nothing more than that.

"Go back to your closet if you're embarrassed," the little girl suggested.

"It's Seattle," I assured her. "Nobody will remember us once the next oddball comes around."

We headed east on James Street and north on Fifth past the smaller boutiques and towards the big shopping malls. Everyone slowed down a bit to look in the windows including, it seemed, Charles and Diana. The attorney paused at a shop where she had purchased many of her business suits.

"The cuts have all changed," she said. "The jackets are shorter." She looked down at her own beautiful suit. "Mine is a little dated now."

Charles and Diana had us backtrack west towards Pike's, where the odors that I personally found a little nauseating apparently put them in some sort of doggie euphoria. We went around to the back of the market and looked out over the Sound.

"Hey, it's the ocean," the little girl said.

"Not exactly," the attorney mumbled while wrinkling her nose.

The little girl put her hands on the glass. "You could go any-where from here," she said.

"If by 'anywhere,' you mean Bainbridge Island, then yes, you can," the attorney said. She looked up and away from the water for the fifth time since we had been on the walk. Something was calling her east. I had an uneasy feeling I knew what it was, but I avoided bringing it up. I didn't want to get in an ugly argument with a ghost in the presence of Charles, Diana, some fishmongers and every tourist in Seattle.

But once we were on the street again, I realized she also avoided bringing it up. She thought she was so conniving, but she forgot that, having once been her, I had the distinct advantage in predicting her every move. She led us toward it and Charles, Diana and the little girl haplessly followed behind. I wanted to object, but I couldn't yell at them out loud in front of all these people. I was rendered mute by my own psychosis and the threat of its being discovered.

Up the street we went and east again, then south towards the library and the large buildings. The little girl and the two Pomeranians were just building momentum, but the attorney and I stopped dead in our tracks the minute we saw it. Charles and Diana nearly yanked my arm out of its socket when we did so.

"What's wrong?" the little girl asked.

I couldn't answer.

"The tall black building," the attorney offered, "It's where we used to work."

The little girl recognized the trick and narrowed her eyes. She turned to me. "Does this mean playtime's over?"

I nodded and turned the dogs around. "Let's go home," I said, pretending I was talking to the Pomeranians.

We took a few steps north, but the attorney didn't follow. She sat down on a stone bench in the plaza fronting the office. She put her head in her hands. For a minute I forgot she was invisible, and I was embarrassed for her.

She looked up at me. "Don't you miss it at all?" she asked.

"It was terrible there," I muttered defensively.

"No, *this* is terrible," she said, motioning towards the dogs, towards the little girl, towards me. "I miss it. I miss being Samantha Green, Esquire."

Have you ever woken up in the morning, showered, gotten dressed, driven to work, began your day and, hours later, said something to a colleague only to find yourself choking on your own words? After you cleared your throat, did it occur to you that you were hoarse because you spent half a day before ever saying something out loud?

That's exactly how it felt when I heard my own name spoken for the first time in several months. It never occurred to me that it hadn't been spoken until it finally was. At that point, it was too late to undo the damage.

"I miss everything about it," the attorney said. "I miss a full calendar, I miss having a contacts file, I miss the colleagues, the income—"

"Then why'd you go off and quit?" the little girl asked.

The attorney dismissed her comment with a hiss. She turned back to me. "I miss being *alive*." She stood up and walked towards me, her voice gaining strength as she advanced. "You worked so hard to be me—everyone was proud of you. I was never meant to be a memory, a ghost of the woman you used to be."

"You've got it wrong—" the little girl said.

"Shut up! This is between her and me." She gripped my shoulders. "Do me a favor." She winced at her own words. "Strike that. Do *yourself* a favor. Resuscitate me. Call up the firm. Tell them you had some family problems. Tell them you just needed to recharge your batteries. Tell them whatever you want, but leave out the part about the pajamas. Things like this happen all the time in the profession. You know how desperately they need women on partnership track. They will take you back in a heartbeat."

I looked up at the looming skyscraper.

The attorney sensed my doubt. She was pleading. "I know it seems strange now, but you've got to trust me: in six months' time it will seem as though the last year never even happened."

"She's tricking you again," the little girl warned.

The attorney sneered. "Banish the inner child were she belongs—the distant past. Be a grown up. Cope."

Was it possible? Could I just make a phone call, put on a suit and report for duty on Monday? I racked my brain but couldn't pinpoint just what had been so horrible about the job in the first place. I remembered being overworked yet under-challenged. I remembered the pain of complacency. Yet my year in jammies had put those things in sharp perspective.

"Don't do it," the little girl begged.

"Why not?" I whispered, beseeching her to answer for me.

"Cause that big building will make you be her again. She's mean and she's sad and she never wants to play. All she cares about is her stupid high heels."

I looked between the two ghosts. I felt like someone on an eighties' sitcom faced with temptation—you know, where the angel appears on one shoulder and the devil on the other, and they both instruct Kirk Cameron to do different things. But for Kirk it was clear which of two the bad influence was. These ghosts were not dressed in red or white. How could I know which one to trust? They're always misleading you on TV.

"Don't do it," the little girl repeated. "Call up Daddy instead. There's lots more fun stuff to do at home. We can go ride bikes."

"Don't listen to her," the attorney spat. "She's a child for crying out loud. I'm an adult. I'm the most successful you've ever been. I know what's best for you."

"You'll just be sad again if you go back to work."

"You'll end up wearing pajamas for life if you move back home."

"She's lying!" the little girl cried. "Don't believe her tricks."

"What tricks?" the attorney asked. "Getting a job is what grown-ups do. 'Riding bikes' in Commerce, Oregon is for children and people whose drivers' licenses were revoked."

The little girl grabbed my free hand. The dogs swirled around her feet. "But you *have* to remember," she implored.

"Remember what?" the attorney asked.

"That *she* is the one who made you get into bed. I am the one that GOT YOU OUT!"

For a very split second, I had an out of body experience. I saw myself from the perspective of all the passersby—a disheveled thirty-one year old woman with two outrageously dressed Pomeranians, looking up at a skyscraper, frozen in fearful though. They couldn't see the ghosts. They were not privy to this war being waged in their midst. To them, the ghosts were nothing more than the slight exchange of expressions passing across my face.

"Sam?" a male voice called, snapping me back to my own frame.

"Oh my gosh," the attorney gasped. "It's Alex Martin."

A gaggle of her former coworkers had just exited the building. It was lunchtime—the wrong time to be hanging outside your old office if the last thing you wanted was for your former coworkers to see your unbrushed hair and your crazy neighbor's regal canines.

Across the plaza I met eyes with Alex Martin for a split second. He seemed to be the only one in the bunch to notice me, but he was blinking incessantly, as if he wasn't absolutely sure of my identity. Although we were yards apart, I could tell his eyelashes were as long as ever.

"Samantha?" he asked again, as he moved forward with his crowd.

I never answered. Instead, I turned and fled the scene. Charles and Diana quickly got the hint and took off like a couple of greyhounds, their tiny bootied feet nothing but a blur. The little girl ran to catch up. Eventually, the attorney reluctantly followed.

Six blocks passed in six seconds. Somehow, the two Pomeranians, the ghosts and I all ended up crammed into a dirty telephone booth. If you haven't used a public phone in a while, I would caution you that they have only gotten worse since all the normal people got cell phones. I hadn't placed a collect call since junior high, so it took a few tries—especially since I refused to take off my mittens.

Jack accepted the charges. Of course he did.

"Sam?"

"Hi Dad."

"Sam, where are you?"

"Don't freak out. I just went for a walk. I'm about a half mile from my apartment."

"Do I hear dogs barking?"

"Yes, I took the neighbor's two Pomeranians for a walk."

"Sure sounds like more than two."

"I know."

Jack had been waiting for this call for over three months. It was only now that I was actually making it that I realized how cruel it had been to withhold it for so long. It was sorta like not realizing you hadn't spoken all day until, in fact, you had: by the time you figured out your error, it was too late to correct it.

"About your offer, Dad—"

"I'll be there as fast as I can drive."

*

Chapter 4

150 MILES

FOR THE PAST NINE YEARS, Alex Martin and I had lived identical lives and yet we barely knew each other. Indeed, there were days when it seemed as though Alex and I were the only students in our law school class, or the only associates at Wallace and Kennedy or the only young single professionals in the greater Seattle area. Regardless, we had spoken to each other on only three occasions.

In law school, Alex Martin was all boy. He was tall and lean and effortlessly muscular—a natural athlete as opposed to a gym rat. His olive skin had faint freckles due to spending too much time in the sun, and the way his dark, curly hair was cut gave away the fact that his roommate owned a set of clippers. Alex's college wardrobe was constituted as follows:

- 0.5% professional wear,
- 5% white socks,
- 8% nylon basketball shorts,
- 10% sweatshirts,
- 10.5% stuff that begins with "cargo,"
- 12% blue jeans,
- 14% sneakers, and
- 40% free t-shirts.

In fact, looking at Alex Martin's free t-shirt collection was like reading his diary. There was the one from the bank, when Alex opened up his checking account. There was the one from the student film festival, where he had volunteered at the ticket counter. He had one from the car dealership documenting his promotional test drive. He had t-shirts from countless 5K charity runs and the like—the kind that are dripping with corporate logos. Alex had free t-shirts evidencing each of the many co-curricular clubs he participated in as an undergraduate. And yes, as a law student, Alex still occasionally sported the "Class of" t-shirt from his high school graduation. He went to a huge high school. I know because I sat behind Alex Martin during many a dry class period that would make Socrates himself attempt suicide by hornbook were it not for the soothing process of reading the alphabetized names of a thousand people who, as far as I was concerned, only existed because they were so memorialized in cotton.

But despite his horrific fashion sense, there were two things about Alex Martin that gave him a supernatural ability to make a good first impression. The first was the fact that you could tell just by looking at Alex that he was good at things. For some reason, that had always irked me.

The second was the eyelashes. Although Alex Martin was all boy, he had these amazingly long eyelashes—feminine eyelashes, even, although they were stick straight. If you ever had occasion to discuss Alex Martin with other women, the eyelashes *always* got a mention. Some women claimed that Alex had batted those eyelashes at them. I, for one, had seen him blink repeatedly when he seemed to be focusing particularly hard on something, but I never witnessed anything that would qualify as "batting." I think the batting camp was making that up.

But like I said, I barely knew the guy.

Such were the thoughts infiltrating my spinning head as Washington dissolved into Oregon through the passenger window of

Jack Green's pickup truck. I thought if Jack drove fast enough, he could outrun these thoughts, outrun my memories, outrun the ghosts. But the ghosts had hitched a ride in the back of the truck with all my stuff, the same way those ghosts hitch a ride in your car at the end of the Haunted Mansion ride at Disneyland. There was the little girl, sitting on a duffel bag, smile bigger than China, crooked braids flying in the wind. Then there was the attorney, perched in her suit and heels atop a banker's box, all slit-eyes and frowns.

"It's a step backwards," she yelled at me earlier that afternoon as I hurriedly stuffed clothes into the duffel bag.

"No," I defended myself. "I'm not doing well on my own here. It's reasonable and prudent."

She snickered at my reference to the RPP. We both knew that the RPP would never, at age thirty-one, call his poor father and say "Retrieve me in Seattle. Bring me home. Ask me to wake up every day. Call my creditors. Settle my accounts. Pick up the pieces of me and then pick up the tab."

Now *she* was the lost one, looking at me through the window. She sat there helpless, watching Seattle—watching herself—fade into the distance. She created a life there, her whole life, her entire existence. Every mile closer to Commerce raised the ticket price of her getting it back.

It was all Alex's fault.

The first time I ever spoke to Alex Martin, we were both waiting in line for an on-campus interview with Wallace and Kennedy. The interviewers were always running behind, and that day was no exception. Alex, a top-tenner in rank and in spirit, began playing mind games with me. First, he reviewed his notes on the interviewer in my presence. I pretended not to notice.

"So what practice group are you interested in?" he asked.

With the exception of five lonely minutes, I hated Alex Martin from that moment forward.

You see, it was a trick question—the trick being that Alex was coaxing me to mention a practice group preference in my interview. But I was also a top-tenner and had done my research. I knew Wallace and Kennedy did a rotational summer associate program and wouldn't be responsive to specific requests.

"Technology commerce," I responded, hoping to give him a false sense of security.

Alex got called up first. When he came out, he and the interviewer were shaking hands and laughing like old friends. I knew it was a performance Alex had choreographed for my benefit.

That interview netted me another interview, which in turn netted me an offer to summer at Wallace and Kennedy after my second year of law school. I turned them down and went to the Los Angeles branch of an east coast firm instead. It was a lonely summer; my drummer of a boyfriend, Mickey, had stayed in Seattle to sleep in and otherwise trash my already trashy apartment. Yet I missed Mickey the same strange way that I missed the rain. It made me sad that it was always so sunny in L.A.

"Here we are," Jack said as the truck pulled into our long, wooded driveway. He said it as if I didn't know the way to my own childhood home. He said it as if we had been gabbing the whole trip.

Once we pulled to a stop, the little girl straddled the side of the truck and stood on the rear tire. "We're here!" she beamed as she looked at the house.

I looked at it, too. It always seemed smaller than I remembered. My memory of the house was frozen from the little girl's perspective—several feet closer to the ground. Reality couldn't compare.

The attorney stood up in the truck and smoothed out her hair. She looked in disbelief around the semi-shabby front yard. Her face remained static, but she kept clenching and unclenching her right hand into a fist.

I turned to help Jack with the bags, but then the little girl let out an "Oh, brother."

I followed her gaze up to the second story of the house just in time to see a figure dart away from the window.

The attorney saw it, too. She smirked.

"What's the matter, Sam?" Jack asked.

I shuddered. "I think this house is haunted," I blurted out, before I remembered that I should really work on self-editing. Jack looked at me alarmed. "I'm sorry," I stammered, desperately backtracking.

"You mean to tell me that after living here most your life, you just barely realized that?" he asked.

I didn't answer. He shrugged, picked up the banker box and headed into the house.

The second time I ever spoke to Alex Martin was at a bar in Seattle at the end of our second year of law school. Mickey's band was playing at the bar—Mickey's band was *always* playing at that bar and, as a result, it was *my* bar. Alex wandered in with a few fellow members of the young cretin's club, or whatever they were calling themselves back in the day. We exchanged awkward hellos, but Alex started telling his friends all about me as if we were better acquainted than the truth would suggest. His friends weren't from law school, they wouldn't understand how law school works—how you could know everything about everyone without really knowing anyone, at least within the top twenty percent.

Alex's buddies bought the act, and, unfortunately, Mickey bought it, too. One of the only reliable things about Mickey was the fact that he didn't care who his girlfriend was talking to unless it was in front of Mickey's own friends, at which point Possessive Mickey came bursting out of his Dickeys like the Incredible Hulk. So when Alex made the mistake of chumming it up with me in front of the band, Mickey came and put his arm around me and nibbled on the back of my neck like it was habit or something when it wasn't, when he usually wouldn't stand within two feet of me, especially on a night he was drumming. Mickey didn't want to look too attached. Yet Mickey wanted me to look very attached. Such was the enigma that was Mickey.

Alex seemed surprised—surprised to realize that a top-tenner like me was dating a tattooed drummer like Mickey. As it turned out, surprise was Alex's Kryptonite. He backed down and it felt good to watch him back down. I never saw him in that bar again.

"You moved the furniture," I said to Jack upon walking in the front door. In twenty-five years he had never moved the furniture.

"Yeah, about six months ago," he said, clearly embarrassed. "I needed a change."

"Ten bucks says Sarita moved it," the attorney mumbled, as she wiped a finger across the living room side table to check for dust.

"You needed a change?" I asked. "That sounds like something Aunt Sarita would sell you on before moving your furniture without asking."

The corners of Jack's eyes cracked into a silent smile. "Something like that," he said.

"I don't like the new way," the little girl said with disgust. Indeed, moving the furniture only made the fact that it had gone so long without being moved more noticeable. The fawn carpet was striped like a circus tent now that the formerly unexposed areas were visible next to those worn deep brown by the pattern of traffic. There were huge divots in the carpet around the room— places where the furniture used to be.

The divots in the dining room were the worst. In the corner of the dining room laid stacks of dishes where my mother's china cabinet used to be.

"It was falling apart," Jack explained. "I got tired of reinforcing the screws, so I gave it to Goodwill. I keep meaning to get something new, but I haven't gotten around to it."

"Maybe I can help you pick something out," I offered.

His eyes lit up, but he feigned indifference. "Maybe."

In law school, it's all about that second summer. Choosing where to spend your second summer is your only voice in your own destiny, and I blew it by summering in a city I didn't want to live in at a firm that didn't have an office in the Pacific Northwest. I frantically interviewed at other firms the next fall, but a third year who summered elsewhere is damaged goods in the legal profession. So I called up the recruiting coordinator at Wallace and Kennedy, reminded her who I was, explained the Los Angeles debacle, laid several references and effigies at her feet and generally begged for mercy. The firm hired me on as an entry-level associate. I was enormously grateful, but was also sad to discover that the only classmate who would be going there with me—indeed, the only person I would know on my first day at work, on my very first day as a certifiable adult—was none other than Alex Martin.

The third time I ever spoke to Alex was the summer after graduation. Because we were in the same associate class at the same firm, we were also in the same bar review class at the same time, because that's the way Wallace likes it. Every day, Alex and I would leave the office at four o'clock in the afternoon, get in our separate cars, drive to the bar review course in tandem, park next to each other, walk half a block to the street light, cross the street, walk another half block back up to the bar review building and attend the class without ever talking.

Until that one night, the night we were reviewing torts, which necessarily involved an extensive discourse on my old khaki-panted friend, the RPP. After four hours of hearing the RPP's many virtues extolled, Alex and I and a few hundred of our fellow future jurists were standing at the street light waiting for the signal to change so we could cross. The light took forever. It was a busy street during the day, but at nine o'clock at night the traffic only came in spurts.

At that particular moment, there wasn't a car in sight. And yet we all waited. I stood there trying to figure out if we were waiting to be reasonable or to be prudent—but I was pretty sure it wasn't both.

A guy laughed. It was Alex Martin. He was looking at me and laughing.

Alex put one foot in the street and turned to me, his hand extended.

"Shall we, Samantha?" he asked, as if he were asking me to waltz.

I couldn't help but smile as I answered him.

Jack and I ate TV dinners on TV trays in the family room, just like we always had. We watched *Law & Order* reruns while we ate, just like we always had. I once heard that, at any given moment, the Beatles' "Yesterday" is playing on a radio somewhere in the world. Similarly, I would wager that at any given point, an episode of one of the *Law & Orders* is playing on television. It's funny how you can watch a sitcom you liked ten years prior and it's so dated that it's almost unbearable; yet *Law & Order* never gets old. I guess that's because haircuts and humor go in and out of style, but murder never does. Murder is like the little black dress.

As I dipped into my cranberry crumble, I tried to reconcile myself with the fact that I had woken up in Seattle ready to take on two Pomeranians and that I would go to sleep in Commerce with a belly full of Salisbury steak. Somewhere in the middle of it, Alex Martin had called out to me. I had lived twenty years in just one day. It was definitely twenty years—not twenty hours.

Needless to say, my split-second decision to come home was beginning to reveal some unforeseen drawbacks. For one, I had forgotten to pack any shoes other than those I was already wearing—the old sneakers. For another, there was a new ghost hiding out in my childhood bedroom, under the bed no less. As patient as Jack had been with me, I was pretty sure he'd put the looney bin on speed dial if his adult daughter whined that there was a ghost camped out under her pink gingham bed skirt.

The endless supply of ghosts was becoming a bit of a drag. It was only that morning, after all, that I had narrowly escaped suffocation by the attorney. I was perennially baby-sitting the little girl. Who knew what issues this latest poltergeist would present?

Just like the rest of the house, Jack had never redone my bedroom. Yet unlike the rest of the house, it had escaped Aunt Sarita's furniture-moving renovation. I assumed Aunt Sarita was a little scared of me—and by "me," I meant old me, the attorney. I never thought I would say it, but I could actually sympathize with Aunt Sarita. I was scared of "me," too.

The bedroom was still furnished with the same ivory children's set that the little girl had marred with stickers. There was a four-poster twin bed with a pink gingham canopy and matching bedspread, with contrasting floral pillows. A beat-up, one-eyed stuffed bunny rabbit took center stage on the bed. There was a white six-drawer dresser with a mirror, and a coordinating desk with a hutch. The desk was obviously built before the computer age—even a small laptop couldn't clear the bottom shelf when open. Today's six year-old would never put up with it. She'd be all, "Where's my docking station supposed to go?"

The hutch was filled with beat-up paperbacks that had never been returned to the library and some porcelain dolls from Grandma. The little girl was not supposed to play with the dolls, but that didn't stop her from covertly switching around their clothes and brushing their hair once in a while. Naturally, some shoes were lost, some buttons were burst and some hair was ruined in the process. As a result, my one shot at being one of those people making millions off their childhood collectibles was completely blown.

Upon our arrival at the house, the little girl marched into the room like she still owned the place. But looking around upset her.

"Brother!" she said after Jack had dropped off the suitcases and left with an awkward assurance that there was no hurry to unpack or . . . do anything.

"I agree," the attorney said, as she disdainfully sat on the bedspread. "A *little* pink is okay, but this—"

"I like pink!" the little girl retorted. "But look," she said, pointing at a poster of The Coreys on the closet door, "She keeps putting her stuff in here."

"Oh, shut up!" shouted a shrill voice. It came from under the bed.

The attorney and I exchanged glances, eyes wide.

On closer inspection, I began to see the things that didn't belong to the little girl—they belonged to someone much older. In addition to the picture of Messrs. Haim and Feldman, other Tiger Beat centerfolds graced the walls. A pair of pom-poms hung over the back of the chair. A high school yearbook lay open on the desk; the page was covered in very large, bubbly handwriting.

I opened the top drawer of the dresser. It was littered with cheap makeup in ghastly jewel tones. It looked as though a child's colored pencil set had been dumped out in a drawer—but I'm afraid those teals and purples were actually eyeliner. There had to have been five tubes of Maybelline Great Lash mascara in there. Just the sight of the pink and green tubes reminded me that the former occupant of this room had once read that Madonna swore by Great Lash and that the former occupant of this room swore by Madonna.

"This room is like a museum," I said.

"No," the attorney corrected. "It's a tomb."

Shall we, Samantha? The "me" who smiled at Alex Martin's mischievously-posed question was woven of the final rebellious strands of the career student I used to be. But the smile faded the minute the student turned into the corporate attorney. The student scoffed at the RPP, but the attorney's livelihood depended on him. You see, the student who smiled at Alex Martin ceased to exist the day she pulled her hair back in that bun, put on a suit and raised her right hand in front of a judge.

The playful Alex Martin who dared to ask *Shall we?* disappeared as well. Alex and the student were no longer overconfident yet under-responsible students. They were lawyers. They owed duties of confidentiality and loyalty and care to persons and entities not of their choosing. They had billable hour quotas to meet. They were stuck on the associate train known as "partnership track." The train ride was over a decade long and had no stops. Not even for a bathroom break. Not even if they got motion sick.

One time the attorney sat two seats down the gargantuan conference room table from Alex at an associate's luncheon. She admired his nice shirt and thought back to the free t-shirt wardrobe of times past. It was the first time she realized his career had either forced him or enabled him to stop wearing them, and yet she still considered Alex Martin a free t-shirt kind of a guy. That's the problem with first impressions—they are very territorial.

The meeting was predictably dull and the attorney found herself fixating on Alex Martin's wardrobe the way the student had fixated on the names of his high school classmates. She tried to visualize him going shopping to purchase the dress shirt he was wearing, but she just couldn't do it. In her mind, Alex went shopping on a Sunday afternoon and so he was naturally wearing a free t-shirt, the bank one to be exact, and that one pair of faded jeans and running shoes. Of course, the employees of the fancy store where the dress shirt was purchased would have never given a guy wearing a bank t-shirt sufficient attention to help him select it. *A girl must have bought it for him*, she told herself.

Unfortunately, the associate lunches were always heavy on the salt and a high sodium content never agreed with the attorney. As a result, she recklessly allowed her mind to wander further and she tried to imagine Alex ironing that shirt, because it was ironed very crisply. But again—she couldn't picture him ironing and she couldn't picture him owning an iron or purchasing an iron or shaving, eating breakfast, brushing his teeth, making his bed or getting dressed for work. It all seemed impossible.

And what did he do when he got home? Was his house clean? Did he have a housekeeper? Undoubtedly, he ate dinner in front of the television, but what kind of dinner did he make for himself? Did he squeeze produce at the grocery store or was it all frozen burritos and takeout? Alex Martin was hard to figure that way. The attorney had known him yet not known him for far too long to answer any of these questions. On the one hand, she couldn't fathom any person who owned nylon basketball shorts doing anything domestic. On the other hand, he did seem fairly health-conscious. He had run in several 5Ks and competed in triathlons and such—at least that's the story the t-shirts told.

"Are you awake?" the attorney asked. She was crunched up on the window seat, heels and all, looking out at the night sky.

"Yeah," I said. It was the first time in a very long time that I could remember struggling with sleep. It was difficult, what with the ghost under the bed constantly sobbing and all.

"What are you thinking about?" the attorney asked.

"I'm thinking about you, actually," I said.

"I'm thinking about Alex Martin," she fumed. "Of all the people—I'll bet he told everyone at the office he saw Samantha Green dressed like a homeless marathoner out walking a couple of dogs that apparently ride unicycles in a small circus."

"Remind me, why do we hate Alex Martin so much?"

"Ugh," she sighed. "He was so cocky—treating the partners at Wallace like his own personal fan club. And don't get me started on how he was always flirting with the staff. You know, the firm was his turf because he summered there and we didn't and, boy, he never let me forget it."

It was true. Wallace and Kennedy was like Mickey's bar in reverse, where Alex had the advantage. And so we did hate Alex Martin, we hated him for all but five minutes of our life.

I shared the attorney's curiosity regarding Alex's reaction to seeing me today. I thought back to *Shall we?* and that free t-shirt collection and realized that Alex and I had watched each other grow up without intending to do so.

It was embarrassing to accidentally play such an important role in somebody else's life.

✳

Chapter 5

BEAUTIFUL FAILURE

THERE WAS THIS GIRL. Her name was Starene. I'm pretty sure it wasn't her given name, but it was the most fabulously appropriate name that has ever been uttered.

Starene was a contender in a televised Karaoke spectacle that I watched with my cousin Libby two weeks into my new life in Commerce. Already Jack, the ghosts and I had settled into a bit of a routine. It involved lots of gardening and television. It involved very little talking, with the exception of the little girl asking me when we were going to go "ride bikes" every five minutes.

During the extensive time I recently spent in bed, I had forgotten what a marvelous companion one's television can be. It's funny how when you're at a dinner party and you get stuck talking to a guy named Charles Likenblatter about the problems presented by modern waste management, you can get so bored you consider impaling your own forehead with a salad fork in hopes of passing out from the pain, yet a four-hour televised documentary on the same topic can be riveting.

The same is true of Karaoke. Karaoke has always been a spectator sport for me and a painful one at that. I'm no boxing fan, but I would rather watch a live boxing match *to the death* than a bunch of tipsy friends or colleagues do Karaoke because I have a weak stomach and boxing obviously involves less bloodshed.

But have you seen all the Karaoke they have on television these days? You can't peel your eyes off it. I suppose that, technically, it's not Karaoke, it's a certifiable singing competition of sorts. I also suppose the reason it is infinitesimally more enjoyable than live Karaoke is that, rather than looking at the floor to avoid eye contact with your coworker, who is painfully warbling his way through "Piano Man," you're actually cheering for the crash and burn performances because you have the voyeuristic luxury of watching them in total anonymity.

Libby, for one, reveled in these shows. As we watched, she had *two* cell phones handy, ready to call in a double vote. The little girl also seemed to enjoy the program—but she actually considered most of the singing to be skilled.

Starene had a bad perm. Starene also had a bad bleach job with roughly two inches of roots. The harsh chemical combination of bleach and perm solution gave the lower half of Starene's mane the texture of yak fur.

Starene wore a bright pink t-shirt with, naturally, a bunch of rhinestone stars on the front. Perhaps "half a t-shirt" was a more accurate description, as it did not quite reach her waist.

Starene was an "apple" rather than a "pear." Indeed, she looked like an upside-down gourd with two toothpicks for legs. Starene capitalized on her slightly smaller lower half by stuffing it into a pair of skin-tight low-rise jeans. The button at the waist appeared to be under a tremendous amount of stress.

Fortunately, when Starene stood perfectly still, her ample stomach folded over the waist of the jeans and concealed all evidence of the strain. Unfortunately, Starene rarely stood still. In fact, as she sang, she jutted her upper body forward in a repeated motion that looked somewhat like a disaffected chicken. Perhaps it was a professional technique intended to assist her in keeping the rhythm while she "auditioned" acapella. If so, it was definitely not working.

"She's terrible," the little girl noted with a face that looked as though she had just eaten an entire lemon, and she was absolutely right. Starene was perhaps the worst singer I had ever heard, that is, if the unmelodious warble coming out of her mouth could be called "singing."

Libby found Starene hilarious. She keeled over laughing on the couch, despite the fact that she had apparently seen a thousand ads promoting Starene's downfall, despite the fact that she hit me quite hard in the arm the minute Starene made her debut and said, "This is the one!"

Libby had black hair with crazy-cut bangs. She was thirty-three years old but was currently going through that "goth" phase most awkward people experience as teenagers. Good for the Goths, I say. I had never been one, but I imagined it was healthy for awk-ward teenagers to embrace their awkwardness, band together, challenge the social structure and then wear tons of black eyeliner to scare off anyone who would challenge them.

Sadly, the Goths would never give Libby the time of day. Call them hypocrites, but don't blame them. You see, the Goths were all about mystery and manufactured angst. By contrast, if there were one word to describe Libby, it would be "obvious."

Libby liked graphic novels. Libby liked role-playing computer games. Libby had been lucky in love in the sense that she had en-joyed more internet-based relationships than most, but she had been unlucky in love in the sense that those relationships always ended with the guy choosing his own mother over Libby.

Libby would always narrate television shows while viewing them with others. "Watch," she would say, "He's going to fall in love with that girl he's talking to . . . He's going to miss his plane . . . He's going to slip on a banana peel . . . He's going to save the business at the last minute . . . He's going to buy an identical hamster for his girlfriend and hope she doesn't notice it's not the same one he accidentally killed while she was on vacation." As far as Libby was concerned, history had never known a television character named anything other than "He," "She," "Her Friend" or "the Little Robot Guy."

Even worse, Libby would recount something that just happened, something that she should have realized you were privy to, because you were standing right beside her.

"Did you see that?" she'd ask.

"Yes, Libby, I saw it. I hope he's okay."

But it was as if she had you on mute the whole time. "That guy just walked into that light post," she'd say.

"I know. I saw it. I just told you I saw it."

"Oh," she would say, disappointed.

Life was constantly disappointing Libby.

But don't blame Libby for her Libbyness. Blame Sarita, her mother—Aunt Sarita to me. Sarita was the proverbial tree from whence the apple fell, but she would never fess up to it. She spent her life bossing everyone around, but particularly her husband Stanley, her brother Jack and her daughter Libby.

Sarita was the last of a dying breed—the commando housewife. You never needed a doctor, psychiatrist or government leader when Sarita was around as she had the answer to all of life's problems (whether requested or not).

"Brother!" the little girl exclaimed upon hearing Jack tell me that Sarita and Libby would be joining us for dinner. "Why do *they* have to come over?"

"I hate to agree with the child," the attorney said, yawning, "but in this case I absolutely do."

"Don't blame me," I said. "Dad's the one who invited them over."

"Don't be a fool," the attorney retorted. "They invited themselves."

I wondered if the omniscient Sarita would feign the solution for my poltergeist conundrum. "Just rub them with a little club soda," I imagined her instructing while pantomiming a rubbing action. "That'll get those ghosts right out."

Libby I could handle, but I had secretly seethed at Sarita for the past two weeks and I feared my feelings would get the best of me once I saw her in person. I seethed at her every time I walked past the dining room and saw that china stacked on the carpet.

"Who's Mickey?" the little girl asked me one day as I sat on the dining room floor, staring at the teacups.

"What made you ask that?" I said, more than a little startled as I had just been thinking of the idiot myself.

"I was just talking to someone about him," she shrugged, as if she was always chatting it up with one person or another. "Is it Mickey Mouse?"

The attorney caught the little girl's words as she walked down the hall. "No, dear," she laughed. "He was a mop-headed drummer, not a cartoon mouse." She looked at me with wry accusation. "They were all drummers, weren't they?"

"I don't know," I responded. "You would remember better than I would."

But I did remember Mickey, of course. Mickey was the empty half of the tiny closet in my law school apartment. Mickey was the vacant space on the counter. Mickey was the pillow case that stayed clean, no longer dirtied by his many grease-based hair products.

Mickey just up and left one day. I was relieved he was gone and sad he was gone at the same time. I was also a little mad I didn't beat him to it. Before my year in jammies, I was blessed with a healthy dose of competitive spirit in work, sports and relationships.

Three days before he left we had been in a firestorm of a fight, which was not unusual at that point. I was about to take the Washington Bar Exam. I was pacing the tiny apartment, rapidly running through memorized lists of the elements of assault and what happens to a childless widower's property when he dies intestate.

All the while, Mickey was drumming.

I told him the bar was important to me. He said it was bourgeoisie. I reminded him the bar-study stipend from Wallace and Kennedy had paid both our bills for the past two months. He told me he had a potential gig in New York. He asked me to move there. I had been studying for the *Washington* bar exam for two solid months and he asked me to pick up and move to New York.

I told him to grow up and ditch the rock star fantasy. I packed a suitcase and checked into a hotel for the duration of the bar, so I could have some peace and quiet in which to study (and think, and sleep).

I took the exam. I passed the exam. I knew that my upcoming lucrative career as an attorney would eventually make the hotel room charge on my credit card no longer seem like the most frivolous expense in history.

But when I returned to the apartment, he was gone. Half the closet was empty. He stole my grandmother's good blender. There were divots in the carpet where his drum kit used to be.

I was really mad about the blender. Every morning I would use that blender to make a yogurt smoothie. Mickey slept until noon, yet he was always whining that the blender woke him up too early—as if a guy who played drums three hours a day had any right to complain about thirty seconds of blender whir. The neighbors never called about the blender whir. The cops never showed up due to the blender whir. Eviction had never been threatened as a result of the blender whir. The same could not be said about the drums. Regardless, the blender became a great source of contention, and to this day I am convinced that Mickey took it out of spite.

Within two days of his departure, I realized I missed the blender more than I missed Mickey. Out of habit, I would walk into the kitchen and pull out the yogurt and fruit and turn around and see the empty counter and mourn its loss all over again. Purchasing a replacement was out of the question. My grandmother's blender had like 300 horsepower. It didn't draw haughty distinctions between "liquefy" and "mix." It had only one button and only one setting: perfect.

In the end, I switched to toaster pastries and gained five of the ten pounds the attorney ghost was still hauling around.

The attorney spent every minute in Commerce mourning her apartment and designer furniture. As much as it was my prison for a year, I sometimes missed it, too. I looked at the imprints in the dining room carpet and wondered if everyone missed things more than people—if everyone missed blenders more than Mickeys.

Of course, I already knew the answer, at least as it applied to Jack's household. Mickey was a drum kit, but my mother was a china cabinet, something heavy, something where a quarter of a century could pass and there would still be imprints on the floor. Poor Jack Green was still looking at the imprints—he couldn't look away, he couldn't pretend not to notice the stacks of fine dishware all around, surrounding the spot where the china cabinet used to be. It would take at least two lifetimes for the air to fill the fibers and raise that carpet back up. It would take at least two lifetimes for the china to find a new home. Unfortunately for Jack Green, he only had the one.

"You should get a new china cabinet," Aunt Sarita told him. "You've worked hard for your money. You deserve to have furniture that's not falling apart." Sarita had proven on many prior occasions that she wasn't the best reader of persons. And yet I still seethed at her for not understanding Jack.

"Those were Mommy's plates," the little girl said.

"I know."

"She died. She had cancer."

The attorney raised her eyebrows. "I see you're still milking that one for all the attention it's worth," she said.

I was in my bedroom with the ghosts when the doorbell rang, announcing Sarita and Libby's arrival. I looked down at my attire, suddenly realizing I was overwhelmingly underdressed. It was the dog-walking ensemble, a variation of which I had worn every day since I had been home: the oversized sweater, the designer jeans and the running shoes. As you know, I packed my bags rather hastily, and this was the nicest outfit I brought with me—mostly because it was the only outfit that included footwear.

The attorney looked at my sneakers and sighed.

"Do you think I should put on a skirt?" I asked her.

"It's a nice thought, but *no*. Right now you look like a slob. However, if you wear those shoes with a skirt, you'll look positively bananas, and I'm afraid our dear relatives are just dying for you to look bananas."

"But I've worn these shoes with a skirt three times since I've been here."

The attorney rolled her eyes. "I know. But trust me tonight: it's better to look like you don't care than to look like you can't care."

"You should listen to her," cried the shrill voice from under the bed. The attorney and I paused for a second before silently agreeing to let it pass unacknowledged. Although the attorney and I didn't always get along and she had previously tried to kill me, we were at least familiar with each other. The same couldn't be said for the unknown entity under the bed. We had learned to sleep through her incessant sobbing every night. Eventually we would learn to tune out the spoken outbursts that were growing more numerous each day.

But the little girl wasn't sensitive to our silent exchange. "Shut up!" she shouted, while kicking the bed frame. And she wasn't even allowed to say "shut up."

Through the heating vents of the old house, I could hear Jack making small talk with the two women as they carried in dish after dish.

"Watch that, Jack. The potatoes are hot," Sarita barked.

The little girl's eyes grew wild with excitement. "Did you hear that? She brought the cheesy potatoes."

"Don't you dare eat them," the attorney growled at me. "They're nothing but starch and fat and sodium." She looked me over one last time, straightening the sweater. "This will undoubtedly be the happiest day in Libby Billingsley's life," she mumbled.

As I descended the stairs, the ongoing conversation grew louder.

"Libby, you left the sheet cake in the car!"

"I only have two hands, Mom."

"So where is she, Jack?"

"She'll be down in a minute"

"Well, I just want to know if there are any buzzwords or topics we should avoid. You know how Libby always manages to put her foot in her mouth unless she has ample warning."

"I'm not sure about any 'buzzwords'—is that how you put it?" That was how she put it. I paused on the stairs with the two ghosts, all three of us anxious to learn what my buzzwords were.

"What I'm saying is, should we steer clear of mentioning things like 'depression'—"

"Or suicide?"

"*Libby!* I told you in the car not to bring that one up!"

"You said in front of Samantha."

The little girl furrowed her brow. "What's *sooey-side?*" she asked, tugging on a braid. The attorney just laughed.

"Samantha's fine," Jack said in stern voice. "She's just not very responsive to questioning right now, so if you'll talk about yourselves rather than giving her the third degree, I'm sure we'll have a pleasant evening."

The attorney laughed again. "This is going to be a fun night."

Even the little girl doubted this. "At least she brought the sheet cake," she said, still tugging on her braid with more than a little worry plastered on her face.

The attorney closed her eyes for a second. "Sarita does make a mean Texas sheet cake," she offered, before turning to me, finger pointed. "Don't eat any of it!"

The first thing Libby noticed was the running shoes; the whole evening she couldn't take her eyes off them. Even once we were seated at the table, she found excuses to steal a peek at them: a slipped napkin, a dropped fork, an itchy ankle. Finally, in the middle of a forced conversation between Sarita and Jack regarding the goings-on of the Commerce School Board (of which Sarita was a longtime member), Libby couldn't take it anymore.

"Have you been jogging?" she asked.

"No," I said.

"It's just, you're so skinny."

"I'm only back to my college weight," I shrugged, suddenly aware that I had been picking at Sarita's funeral potatoes for an eternity. The little girl *loved* Sarita's funeral potatoes as they were a welcome break from her fast-food diet, but after a year of eating Jello cups and two weeks of TV dinners, I felt as though the potatoes were gluing my insides together with cream of chicken soup.

"How did you do it?" Libby asked. I wanted to tell her that staying away from funeral potatoes was a start, but Libby was the last person on earth to need diet tips. The woman had so much nervous energy that she had been rail-thin her entire life, much to the doughy Sarita's chagrin.

I opened my mouth, but no words came out. I couldn't mention the Jello. I couldn't dish on the stay-in-bed-all-day workout regimen. It wouldn't be fair to Jack.

"Sam's been walking a lot lately," Jack filled in. "Takes the neighbor's dogs out, isn't that right?"

I nodded my head in agreement. This was how it had always been at dinners with the Billingsleys—Jack and I in silent concert. "Two Pomeranians," I managed, forcing the words out of my throat, which felt starched shut. "Charles and Diana."

"Like the royals?" Sarita asked.

"Yes," I said, grateful for the frivolous topic. "My neighbor in Seattle is obsessed with them, especially their wedding. She still has her original recording of it on VHS, and she has commemorative plates and spoons decorating her living room."

Sarita gasped. "Doesn't she realize they're divorced? That the Princess died? That it was one of the most tragic marriages of all time?"

"No, I don't think so," I said. "At least she prefers not to realize it. I don't think she realizes it's not 1986 anymore, for that matter."

Libby laughed out loud. "Her neighbor doesn't realize it's not 1986!" she reported to her mother.

"I heard her, Libby," Sarita said with characteristic exasperation. "It *was* a beautiful wedding," she offered by way of condolence. For a moment, everyone thought of that two-mile train as they picked at their dinner.

"So Libby," Jack said, clearly fearful of whatever power an extended silence might instill in Sarita, "I heard you got a promotion at work."

"I did!" she exclaimed, as if she had just received the news at the dinner table. Turning to me, she bragged, "I'm the new assistant swing-shift manager at the call center." Since high school, Libby had worked at a call center that handled the customer service for several major companies, most of them computer-related. Thus, if your computer breaks down and you call the 800 number in the manual, I am afraid you are most likely not talking to a computer expert; rather, you are talking to someone with an associate's degree in psychology from Blue Mountain Community College such as my cousin. Then again, you probably figured that out during the call.

"That's great," I said with as much enthusiasm as I could muster, which, admittedly, wasn't much. Jack shot me a glance that said *try harder or we're both in trouble*. "You should really feel accomplished," I added, with a little more sincerity.

"We're all very proud," Sarita said. "Not as proud as if she found a husband and gave me some grandchildren—"

"So how's your job going?" Libby asked, eager to change the subject.

There was an awkward moment of silence. "Here we go," the attorney ghost sang across the room.

"I quit my job," I said.

"That's what you said last Christmas."

"Libby—" Sarita warned.

"Yeah, I haven't gotten a new one yet."

"In over a *year*?"

Jack smiled. "Fortunately for Sam, her last job paid very well and she was a good saver."

"I suppose your ample savings is paying the rent on that high-class apartment in Seattle?" Sarita asked, apparently believing that since Libby had opened the door, she was free to barge right through it.

"It's a condo," I corrected. "I pay a mortgage, not rent." I looked down at the table, waiting for Jack to give me permission to lie. But as much as he tired of her, he was incapable of standing up to his older sister. One only needed to glance at the stacks of china littering the room's perimeter to know that.

"I've just started helping out," he offered quietly.

"I see." Sarita was talented like that. By raising her eyebrows and enunciating in a particular way, Sarita could give a two-hour lecture on one's personal failures with the shortest possible complete sentence: *I see*.

But Sarita was a liar. She didn't see; she never saw. If she did, she would have realized that Jack clearly didn't want the new china cabinet. He never ate in the dining room anyway—he ate in the family room on a TV tray using a melamine plate. And if he was going to give away the cabinet, he should have given the china to Goodwill, too. Better yet, he should have thrown it in the ground right after her.

"If you need some money, you could always come work at the call center for me," Libby offered.

I suppose Sarita couldn't see the two ghosts that swung down on me like vultures at the sound of this, one an attorney and the other a little girl.

"Don't even think about it," the attorney sneered.

"They have a huge turnover rate at the call center," Sarita advised, oblivious to the danger she created with every single word. "They're always hiring."

"I can't imagine why," Jack said.

"The pay starts at eight dollars an hour," Libby said, "but you can earn extra if you meet customer satisfaction quotas or if you sell the caller additional services."

The attorney snickered. "Your bonus at the firm was more than your annual salary would be at the call center."

"Maybe you should do it," the little girl offered, "just to get some spending money. Then you won't have to go back to the big scary building."

"It's a complete waste of your education!" the attorney retorted.

"But it sounds really easy," said the little girl. "If Libby can do it—"

"It's really easy," Libby said. "That is, if you know how to type and read good."

"I don't think she would have made it through law school without knowing how to type or read," Jack mumbled.

The attorney's hands were dangerously close to my neck. I wondered if she would try to strangle me again. In a way, it would be funny. The authorities would undoubtedly assume I died from the nagging or possibly as a result of starchicide.

"The hours are very flexible, aren't they Libby?" coaxed Sarita.

"No," Libby said. "Usually they start you off on graveyard, but since we're related, I think I could pull some strings to get you on my swing shift."

"She just got here," Jack said. "We haven't worked all of this out yet."

The Billingsleys temporarily dropped the subject and the two ghosts receded. But forty minutes later found Libby and me watching televised Karaoke in the den while our parents resumed the battle in the kitchen under the guise of doing dishes.

"Jack, she's thirty-one years old," Sarita said. "She can't expect her retired father to pay her extensive bills while she takes her sweet time figuring out life. You're on a fixed income."

"I've got plenty of money, Sarita, and it's mine to spend as I please. Besides, don't you think those are strong words from a woman whose own adult daughter has never moved out of her house?"

Libby pretended not to hear this, but I could feel her bristle on the couch next to me.

"Libby doesn't have a *condo* somewhere else. She doesn't have pricey student loans. She's had a steady job for the past fourteen years."

They were both right. I was thirty-one years old, and Libby was thirty-two. We were adult women—we should have been the ones in the kitchen with the dishes while the elders tended to their grandchildren. Instead, we were both single, childless and apparently helpless, relegated to watch a show targeted to preteens while our parents sorted the dinner mess and attempted to sort out our lives.

"The student loans were an investment," Jack explained. "If I could have paid the full tuition price and saved her the hassle, I would have."

"I'm not suggesting she abandon the law, Jack. I'm just suggesting that she work a monkey's job in the meantime while she figures things out."

At the mention of monkeys and their employment, Libby turned to me and said with false cheer, "So have you seen Melissa since you've been home?"

"Melissa Matthews?" I asked, shaking my head. "I haven't seen her in years. We sort of lost touch."

Libby's jaw dropped, as if losing touch with Melissa Matthews was a cardinal sin. Growing up, Melissa was *that girl*—the one who, when she said each lowercase *i* must be dotted with a heart, you did dot them with hearts, even though it took you twice as long to write your short essay answer on the English test and you ended up with a B minus when you should have gotten an A.

"She works at Dr. Moody's office now, you know. You could call her." Libby clearly didn't understand how two people who were inseparable as teens could grow into adults with nothing in common. She also was not wise to the fact that things between Melissa and I had soured.

Perhaps Sarita was right about the rickety china cabinet. It was only an inanimate object, a thing. Things leave imprints in the carpet. But people only leave things. They leave half-filled closets and empty chairs. They leave frilly dishes behind for which you have no use. They leave only the savage ghosts of history that we politely refer to as memories.

The competition judges informed Starene that she would not be advancing to the next round. This was a surprise to nobody except Starene. She screamed at the judges. They didn't know anything. She was born to be a star.

Starene was a complete disaster, but she turned the act of failing into an art form. I had never seen anyone fail quite as beautifully as her. I made a conscious decision to kick the RPP to the curb and make Starene my new role model. She might not have been as pleasant to be around as the RPP, but she was so much less discerning.

"Libby, can I ask you a question? Just between us?"

"Sure," she shrugged.

"If I work at the call center for a little while but then quit because I get a different job, will it make you look bad?"

"Just promise me three weeks," she said. "Can you do that?"

"Why three weeks?"

"Most new people at the call center only last two. So if you can go three weeks, everyone will think you were there a really long time."

I looked across the room at my two ghosts, hoping they would appreciate the compromise.

"Three weeks, then," I said to Libby.

"Sweet. I'll pick you up on Wednesday at three-thirty."

✳

Chapter 6

HEAVY BREATHERS

"THANK YOU FOR CALLING Triton Software Systems' Customer Support Line, how may I assist with your software problems?"

The other end of the line held no response, except . . . panting.

I hit the mute button on the headset dock and turned to Angel. "I've got a breather."

Don't be fooled by the name—Angel Marcena-Fernandez is one of the most intimidating individuals you've ever laid eyes on. Perhaps it's his six-foot, three hundred pound frame. Perhaps it's the prison tattoos that entirely cover his hands, arms, neck and portions of his face. Perhaps it's the knife scars. It's difficult to pinpoint the exact reason.

Without blinking, Angel hung up on his caller. He pulled his headset jack out of his own dock and plugged it into mine, nodding at me.

I took the mute off. "Can I help you, sir?"

The heavy breathing grew more intense. "Just tell me what you're wearing—"

"I'm sorry, but I'm only supposed to troubleshoot computer problems. If I lose this job, I'll have to drop out of college, and if I drop out of college, I'll have to move out of the sorority house, too. Those girls have compromising pictures of me. They could put them on the Internet or something."

"Just give me a hint," he said. "I'm begging you."

At that moment, Angel flipped the switch on the dock to "Headset 2." In his best ex-con accent, he told the caller what he was wearing all right, followed by a string of profanities, followed by reading the caller's phone number off the ID and threatening to personally hunt the caller down that very evening. Somewhere in the middle of this soliloquy, the heavy breather hung up and possibly barricaded the door to his studio apartment or moved to a new town. The heavy breathers always hung up on Angel. For this reason, he had developed a very rapid delivery.

Angel's talent earned him the distinction of February Employee of the Month, even though he had only been working at the call center since January. Apparently the heavy breathers were a real drain on profit and Angel's presence had already cut such calls down by thirty percent.

I had been working at the call center for one week and three days. I was informed I had a decent shot at being March Employee of the Month.

The call center was built about twenty years ago in Sherman Valley, a rural community neighboring the somewhat rural community of Commerce. Back then, it made sense to build the call center there as land was cheap and the workforce was high-school educated and desperate for something with a short commute that didn't involve operating heavy machinery. But the passage of time saw the two towns overrun by tract housing and people from elsewhere who didn't mind trading hours of travel time each day for the opportunity to own a cheap half acre. These days, it was normal for the kids who grew up in the area to go away to college (well, except for Libby). When they went away they got a taste of elsewhere and they didn't come back (well, except for me).

As a result, the call center turned to a government-funded, parolee-hiring program to maintain a sufficient workforce in a job
that most viewed as a little degrading. This hiring practice was
immediately apparent to me upon walking into the call center that
first Wednesday; however, Libby still felt the need to pull me aside
and explain it in a way-too-loud voice in the lunchroom. Then she
assigned me the carrel right next to this guy Mike, who seemed to
be suffering from some sort of major substance withdrawal, as
evidenced by the bleeding sores on his arms, among other things.
I spent the whole day taking calls with my purse (a nice 1990
Esprit de Corps number I found in the very back of the little girl's
closet) clutched between my knees and my hand clenched in a fist,
wondering what on earth had been so difficult about sitting at a
mahogany desk all day in an office in a high rise in Seattle. On the
way home that night, I begged Libby to (1) never tell any of the
parolees that I was a lawyer, and (2) move me away from Mike.
She nodded, but I could tell she just didn't get it. Libby could be
so frustrating that way—when she didn't get something, it was
almost worse that you told her about it than if you hadn't.

The next day one of the floor managers saved me. Libby was a
"shift manager," and walked around the room the whole night,
but there were others called "floor managers" who sat in this elevated control booth of sorts in the center of the room and looked
down on their minions. About five minutes after taking my seat by
Mike, floor manager Raul came down from his ivory tower and
tapped on the back of my ergonomic office chair.

"You're Libby's cousin?" he asked.

"Yes," I nodded. Mike cackled wildly at this revelation. I made
a mental note not to tell anyone else I was Libby's cousin, which
was a little sad, because it definitely wasn't the first time in my life
I had made that same mental note, just the first time in a very long
while.

"Why don't you come with me," he said.

"Ooooh. Trooouble," Mike taunted, as if I had just been summoned to the principal's office.

I stood up, intentionally kicking my purse as far under the desk as I could, but Raul motioned to my headset. "Bring your things." This required me to get down on all fours to retrieve the purse as Raul and Mike looked on.

I followed Raul to Libby, who was busy bossing around a parolee. The parolee looked like he was employing every trick he had ever learned in anger management therapy in order to avoid bludgeoning Libby with his computer monitor. He was gripping the arms of his ergonomic chair so hard that I knew they would not be their carpal-tunnel preventing selves once he released them. I thought of Aunt Sarita's ignorant bragging about her daughter's promotion. She had no idea what danger that promotion was subjecting her daughter to every day.

Raul tapped Libby on the shoulder. "Can I talk to you for a second?"

Libby flushed. "Hi, Raul."

"Did you sit your cousin next to Mike?" The chair-gripping parolee raised his eyebrows at the C-word. Great. Now everyone would know.

"Yes."

"Those who sit next to Mike tend to have difficulty concentrating," he corrected gently. "Why don't you put her next to Angel?"

"I didn't want to show her any favoritism," she stammered.

"Don't worry about that. Besides, it's a strategic move. With her voice, she'll attract a lot of breathers and she can pass them on to Angel."

Of course, on first sight of Angel, I wanted to run back to Mike, jump in his lap, and bury my head in his scabby chest. But appearances can be deceiving, and Angel's was no exception. For a guy who had been shanked so many times, he had a certain *joie de vivre.* So what if he used to be an auto mechanic making three times the money? So what if he spent a quarter of his net pay every day taking five buses to get there? So what if his past choices had permanently barred future opportunities? He was a free man, and he never took that for granted.

The little girl loved hearing stories about Angel, especially about all the tattoos and scars. The ghosts didn't come to work, and it took me a lot of midnight pondering to figure out just why. I think it was because I was too focused at work to conjure their memories and summon them to me. I was beginning to suspect it was not places, but people, who were haunted after all.

So while the ghosts didn't bother me at the call center, they loved to hear my stories after work. While the little girl preferred Angel, the attorney enjoyed tales of the lunchroom, the break room, talking over the carrels and the like.

"Who did you lunch with?" she would ask, with feigned indifference.

"We don't 'lunch' at the call center, we 'eat lunch'."

"Who did you eat lunch with?"

"Well, everybody." Everybody who was anybody, that was: Angel, this guy Rob, their friend Lamar, Raul, Libby and another floor manager, a sixty-year-old, no-nonsense, elastic-waist pants and crafty t-shirt kind of a woman named Charlemayne. Mike and the many other call center employees with nervous tics and registered sex offender cards were not invited to join us.

It was a zoo, to say the least, and the attorney always made sure to note her disapproval of such. Yet in a way, she was jealous.

"Why do you always ask who I eat lunch with?"

She shrugged. "I'm just trying to show interest in your day."

"You never ate lunch with anyone at Wallace."

"I know. It wasn't my thing."

It wasn't my thing. She had been telling herself that for years. Truthfully, the attorney didn't have much choice when it came to lunching alone. The straight men at Wallace and Kennedy would not eat with her because they didn't want to raise suspicions of office romance or open the door to a sexual harassment claim. The other women lawyers would not eat with her because there was an unwritten pact among them to avoid appearing cliquish, passed down from the female senior partners who really had to fight for respect decades prior. The staff always ate together, but the attorney couldn't join them because it was their big chance to commiserate about all the lawyers. Thus, by process of elimination, a woman lawyer's only option for friendship at Wallace was to find a gay male attorney and woo him into best friend status. Indeed, all the gay men were paired up with straight women into little friendship couples who lunched together every day. The only problem was that there were not enough gay men to go around, and the ensuing catfight was vicious.

When the attorney first started working at Wallace, every gay man was already spoken for. At that point, she still had sufficient friends from law school and even college to satisfy her social needs after work. But associates at Wallace work long hours and quickly lose contact with the outside world, so by the time Mina Chen transferred to Palo Alto, leaving Jake Hudson unattached, the attorney was hungry for a pal and ready to pounce.

"You *did* grab lunch with Jake Hudson that one time," I reminded the ghost.

She paled at the memory, and rightfully so. The lunch was the most disastrous non-date she had ever been on. Jake, who wanted a match just as much as she did, delved straight into a rapid-fire list of questions designed to ferret out any common ground.

"So what kind of music do you like?" he asked.

"Music? Well, when I was in school, I was really into alternative music, indie bands and such. I dated this drummer for a local band for years."

Jake's eyes grew wide. "Sounds juicy," he said. "So who do you like now? What's the last show you went to?"

"Huh. I can't remember the last time I went to a concert or a club. You know—work and all."

"Yeah, it's hard, but life demands balance. C'mon, at least tell me the last album you bought or what radio station you listen to."

But there was no last album and only talk radio. Her answers to the remaining questions were similarly disastrous in their emptiness. She went to the gym after work. She ate frozen dinners— the ones from the diet section—followed by chocolate chip cookies and ice cream. She cleaned her house and went shopping on weekends she didn't work. She had no pets.

One week later, the entire office snickered when Jake Hudson and dowdy Krissy Ferriss became inseparable.

Of course, in my present state, calling Krissy Ferriss dowdy was like the kettle calling the snowball black. I had devolved into one of those people with a Monday outfit, a Tuesday outfit, and so on down the week, to be washed on Sunday and repeated verbatim. I still only had the one pair of disheveled running shoes. And yes, I sometimes wore them to work with a skirt.

But while I would have been the certifiable queen of dowd at Wallace, the call center provided me with so much competition that, by comparison, I felt as glamorous and adorable as Mina Chen. The attorney didn't require much convincing on this fact, and so she eased up on her criticism of my fashion sense. In fact, she was far more concerned with what the little girl was wearing. You see, the little girl had taken to going through the closet during the day and donning old Halloween costumes and the like. The attorney put up with it until the little girl made her way through the closet to the pink dress.

"You won't believe what that little brat put on today while you were gone," she tattled. "*The* dress. The pink one. I could have smacked her."

"If it doesn't matter to her, it shouldn't matter to us."

"What if Jack saw her in it? He'd never recover."

"He can't see her. Anyway, if the dress really bothered him, he would have thrown it out years ago."

We both knew nothing could be further from the truth. Everything bothered him and yet he held onto it for dear life. The attorney's concern over the dress was nothing more than manifestation of a habit so ingrained it was impossible to break. Together, we had spent a lifetime doing backbends, turning cartwheels, setting fires—*anything* to keep Jack from ruminating on *that* day. But the little girl didn't get it, which was frustrating, because out of the three of us, she was the only one present.

You see, everyone wore black *that* day. Except the little girl. And possibly her mommy.

As for the little girl, she wore the hot pink princess ensemble from her dress-up wardrobe that probably looked every bit as cheap and acetate as she thought it looked glamorous and sophisticated.

As for mommy, the little girl wasn't sure what she was wearing. She was in a large box at the time, or so the little girl had been told. There was a short period when people were allowed to look into the box and see her and talk to her, but the little girl was prohibited from doing so because Jack thought it would be too scary for her. Jack didn't tell her that, of course. Rather, he told her to go outside and walk around the building and look at all the pretty flowers with her eight-year-old smarty-pants of a cousin, Libby. Libby, in turn, spent the hour telling the little girl all about the box and mommy's presence therein and the supposed scariness of the whole affair. Truth be told, the little girl didn't understand just what was so frightful. It was only mommy, after all. But she knew that sometimes adults were inexplicably leery of things that just didn't faze kids, like those piles of paper called "taxes." And yet they would laugh at the mention of monsters. Go figure.

So the little girl didn't see what mommy was wearing, but she did see the box. It was big and white and had gold flowers painted on it and golden rails along the sides. Mommy had always liked things to match, so the little girl imagined that she would have worn something to match the box. Probably a big white dress with lots of gold trim and beading and golden sequined shoes and one of those princess crowns on her head. Or maybe it was like a Snow White dress, because the little girl remembered that, in the cartoon, Snow White was in a box for a while, too. Although she found mommy's box to be pretty, the little girl kinda wished she had picked a glass box like Snow White's so the little girl could have seen her and maybe mommy would have waved or blown kisses.

Mommy's sister, Aunt Julie, brought a black velvet dress with a white pilgrim collar to the little girl that morning. But the little girl had been wearing the pink princess dress for three day's time and had no intention of changing. She was prepared to throw a level-five tantrum in defense of her right to wear it but, to her surprise, all it took was a single stubborn "No!" as Aunt Julie reached for the zipper before Jack said with some resignation, "Just let her wear it, Jules."

Not only did Aunt Julie give in, but she offered to do the little girl's hair fancy to match the dress. This required her to brush out the ever-present braids and, in the process, she discovered how crooked the little girl's hair had become. The little girl begged Aunt Julie not to tell Jack. Surprisingly, Aunt Julie also agreed to this and fashioned a left-parted low bun that concealed the little girl's recent mishap.

This got the little girl thinking. Aunt Julie was her favorite aunt, but that was really by process of elimination. Aunt Julie always brought the little girl souvenirs from her trips, but she would also tattle to the little girl's parents on the many occasions when she caught the little girl doing something bad. It was out of character for Aunt Julie to let the little girl wear the outlandish dress when she had just bought another, more proper one. Then, when Aunt Julie agreed not to tell Jack about the crooked hair, it was almost the same thing as lying. The little girl figured it was the first lie of Aunt Julie's entire long life and she couldn't help but wonder "Why now?"

Why now? was the real problem, not the pink dress. The little girl had never grasped the meaning of *now*, and the attorney would never forgive her for it. This was unfair of the attorney as she hadn't known the *now* of that day, only the *then*. It's always easier to appreciate the weight of *then*.

Another issue was the fact that the ghosts and I so often used different frames of reference in comparing now and then: mine was two months ago, the attorney's was two years ago, and the little girl's was the beginning of time. My first weekly paycheck for working at the call center was $302.00. It seemed like a lot of money compared to the zero dollars I had earned during the prior year, but it seemed like pennies compared to the checks the attorney used to draw. Similarly, going to work Wednesday through Sunday seemed like progress compared to staying in one's bed the whole day and freaking out at a single bus ride to the grocery store, but viewed from the attorney's perspective, the victory was empty: it was still a step back. My *then* had a bed and some dirty jammies. Her *then* had fancy suits and an office and an assistant that she shared with two other people. All the lunching in the world could never make my *now* live up to her *then*.

Three hundred and two dollars was enough to buy lunch, but it was not enough to have extra to splurge on a pair of new shoes and it was not enough to pay the attorney's mortgage. Despite the job, Jack still had to step in and pay the majority of my bills. The more he did this, the more pitiful I felt and the more angered I became at the attorney for racking up the bills in the first place. Halfway through her tenure at Wallace, she had fixated on the idea of owning her own home, only a cheaper house in the suburbs wasn't good enough for her—she needed something where she could walk to work if she wanted (she never did), where there were plenty of local eateries to go out with friends (friends she didn't have) and where she could smell the sea (a smell to which she quickly grew accustomed and thereafter never appreciated). She toured every new and overpriced condo development in the Belltown neighborhood of Seattle before finally settling on what she felt was the absolute hippest one. Then she bought in, moved in, and filled the place to its ten-foot ceilings with designer furniture and expensive closet organization systems, only to learn that her neighbors were anything but hip, they were crazy ladies with questionable skin conditions and five hundred noisy Pomeranians.

I placed that first $302.00 check on the little girl's desk where the ghosts could see it. The attorney fingered it lightly, but said nothing.

"I have no choice," I said. "I have to sell the condo."

"No," she begged. "You sold the car and bought yourself six more months of naptime. You owe me the condo."

I laid down on the bed and looked up at the faded pink canopy. The little girl sensed the tension, and played quietly with her stuffed bunny in the corner. She was wearing the pink dress, but the attorney didn't bother pointing it out. She had too much on the line to risk annoying me with such a critique. Even the sobby ghost under the bed seemed to be holding her breath.

"It's your fault, not mine," I said, taking my time. "You bought the condo, and you quit the high-paying job."

"Please…"

"Why should I take pity on you? You're just a ghost. You're not worth bankrupting myself for."

She hung her head.

"*What happened?*" I asked her.

"You've said it yourself. Nothing happened."

"No, everything happened. Time happened. History happened. Something was happening all of the time."

She nodded. "But I was nothing."

She *had* turned into nothing and it prevented her from appreciating the everything occurring all around her. She first realized it that day she massively failed the Jake Hudson inquisition. If people are a sum of their parts, then most people are a conglomeration of music tastes, free time activities, travels, friends, humor, little taco stands, midnight phone calls, guilty pleasure teenage television shows, practical jokes, skeletons in the closet, childhood fears, sorrow and empathy. By contrast, the attorney was nothing but a strand of pearls, a navy suit and a business card.

"Why are you here?" I asked.

"Isn't it obvious? I'm haunting you."

"But why come to Commerce? You don't belong here. You hate it here. Why didn't you stay back in Belltown? You could have the whole condo to yourself."

She clenched her fists and shook them. "I'm here because you're here."

I bristled and sat up in the bed so I could see her. Even the little girl looked up, alarmed.

The attorney relaxed her fists. "I'm sorry about my temper," she mumbled. "It's just that I'm desperate."

"Desperate for what?"

"For a redo. I made a mistake, okay? I thought my life sucked, but it was me who sucked. I didn't realize how fabulous my life was until it was long gone, until I was reduced to a ghost. Now I want it back. I want a second shot at it and you're my only hope."

I shook my head. "I want to help you, but…" I tried to imagine being her, but I couldn't any more than I could imagine being Libby or Sarita or Charlemayne. *Now* had moved us too far apart. "Look at me," I sighed. "I'm working at a call center for eight dollars an hour. I only have one pair of shoes. Do you really think it's possible that I'll ever be a lawyer again?"

Her eyebrows crossed. "Do I think it's possible? Do you have any idea what phrase goes through my mind every night when you come home and tell us these horror stories of lunching with sex offenders and meth addicts and people who wear elastic-waist pants?"

"I don't know. *What happened?*"

She was offended. "No," she said, shaking her head adamantly. "Three months ago the only time you got out of bed was to use the restroom. So when I hear your work tales, no matter how insane, I'm afraid I cannot help but think:

This.

Is.

Progress."

I didn't have time to thank her; I didn't even have time to process it. Jack interrupted us by knocking on the door.

"Dad, what are you still doing up?" I scolded. My shift ended at midnight, and the ghosts and I had been chatting well past one o'clock in the morning.

Jack opened the door, bleary-eyed. "I just wanted to be sure you got this message," he said, handing me a note written on one of those free pads that realtors mail out. "He called while you were at work—said he's a friend of yours from Seattle and he wants to get in touch with you."

I looked down at the note, suspicious. "Did he say what he wants?"

"No. Sounded nice enough, though. Do you know him?"

"Yeah, I know him," I lied.

"Okay then, goodnight."

I held the note close to my chest, treasuring the millisecond before the ghosts' curiosity took over. I realized now that the $302.00 check had been empowering—for some reason the low pay had given me the upper hand in my relationship with the attorney. But the realtor's note was about to tip the seesaw.

"So who called?" she asked.

I could barely whisper the name.

"Alex Martin."

＊

Chapter 7

ONE MONDAY IN MARCH

"Corey!"

"Hi, Corey."

It was a ridiculous salutation as neither of us was named Corey. Neither of us was named Alex Martin, either, if you're curious. In fact, neither of us was male.

When two women in their thirties greet each other as Corey, it is a sure sign they were best friends decades ago yet have grown so far apart that they must revert to juvenile nicknames just to establish the bare minimum of common ground necessary to carry on a conversation. My telephone call to Melissa Matthews was no exception.

Jack delivered the Alex Martin message to me late Sunday night. On Monday morning, he returned from the garden center with a new wheelbarrow and another message—this one from Melissa, who apparently was also at the garden center and who was very excited to learn of my return to Commerce and who, at least according to Jack, was sitting by the telephone at that very minute waiting to hear from me. I didn't have the heart to tell Jack that life didn't wait for telephone calls anymore, that people just took their telephones with them. I also didn't have the heart to tell him I wouldn't be calling anybody. Having provided me with two numbers in less than twelve hours, Jack clearly expected me to dial at least one of them. So while I usually would have been loathe to have any association with Melissa Matthews, I decided she was the lesser of two evils (or at least the more predictable), and I gave her a call.

Appropriately, Melissa was Corey H. and I was Corey F. Our formative years played out like a late-eighties Coreys flick, with Melissa being the beautiful, popular one who miraculously survived every misadventure she created and ended up with the guy in the process. I, on the other hand, was the less-attractive, loyal best friend, along for the ride and willing to provide comic relief when necessary.

We all know what happened to the real-life Coreys, but as I hung up the phone, I couldn't help but wonder what fate held in store for their onscreen characters. In their thirties, would they both have Mondays off, like Melissa and I did? Would they make plans to go to the Sherman Valley Towne Center for no reason in particular, as did we? Would the cute Corey have to pick up the wisecracking Corey because the latter had no car and only one pair of shoes? If we had known that, we probably wouldn't have bothered watching their movies in the first place.

Jack watched me eagerly as I hung up the phone. I looked down at my Monday outfit—the rumpled brown skirt, a t-shirt, an old green cardigan, blue socks and the running shoes. My Monday outfit was my worst outfit because it was my day off. I now lamented this schedule as it would take far more to impress Melissa Matthews than the folks down at the call center.

"I guess I should go change," I said. Jack shrugged his shoulders at this suggestion, but if he disagreed, he would have said so.

"Where are you going?" the attorney asked when I came into the bedroom.

"Jack arranged a play date for me," I pouted.

The little girl brightened at this. "Who are we playing with? Can we go ride bikes with them?"

"No," I said. "It's with Melissa Matthews."

"*Melissa*?!" the voice under the bed shrieked.

Suddenly, the bed shook like crazy. Something burst out from under the gingham bed skirt and buzzed around the room at hummingbird speed. I jumped on the bed and gripped a pillow. The little girl shielded her eyes.

The ghost was like a cartoon character, an out-of-control whir of frizzy hair and neon colors. After several minutes, her spinning began to wobble like a child's top running out of steam.

When she finally came to a stop, I could see her for the first time: the really bad perm, the teased bangs, the scrunchie holding half her hair atop her head, the layered neon shirts with a plastic belt wrapped around them, the flouncy white skort, the two pairs of socks matching the layered shirts, the white sneakers and the gigantic earrings.

She looked around the room at the two ghosts, and then, me. Her face fell to the floor. "Noooooo!" she wailed. "No, no, no, no!" she said as she approached me. "It's soooo much worse than I thought." For someone who had been hiding for weeks, she was suddenly very assertive, sticking her face right in mine. I gripped the pillow harder and looked to the attorney and the little girl, hoping they would have my back like the time the little girl threw the attorney's shoes around the closet.

"What?" I gasped.

"There is just *no way* you can hang out with Melissa looking like *that*."

The attorney burst out laughing and thereby cut some of the tension in the room. "You're not one to talk, dear. Where'd you get your hair done? Texas? New Jersey?"

"There's nothing wrong with my hair," she said, but she flattened it out all the same.

"Oh wait, I remember now—the J.C. Penney hair salon."

The little girl howled with laughter. "J.C. Penney is a store. You're not supposed to get your hair cut there."

"*Your* hair is the crookedest thing I've ever even seen," the teenager bit back. "At least I didn't cut mine myself."

"I didn't cut my hair!"

"You're such a liar, cause we all totally know that you did. Anyways, I could care less about you because you're not the one hanging out with Melissa." She turned back to me, "But as for you—"

Again, like a lightning bolt, she flew to the dresser and opened the drawer. But the attorney was way ahead of her. "Close that drawer, young lady," she barked.

"But she just needs a little makeup," the teenager explained, holding up the dated compacts.

"There is no way on earth I am going to let you put antiquated Wet n' Wild on *that* face," the attorney said, gesturing across the room to me. "Put down that cobalt eyeliner right now!"

"Do you have a better idea? Newsflash: it's the only makeup we have."

"*Newsflash*," the attorney mimicked, "do you see that acne you've got?"

"Acne?! I don't have acne!"

"Nice try with the orange foundation, but you do. We have since learned that we have sensitive skin and we have to treat it a little kinder than you're accustomed to doing."

"But I use Noxema and Sea Breeze every day."

"Exactly. Trust me on this one, dear—Sea Breeze is the source of your problems, not the solution."

"At least I don't have crow's feet."

The attorney recoiled at this. "They're smile lines," she corrected, "and I probably wouldn't have them if you weren't so fond of the astringent. Besides, would it kill you to use some eye cream every once in a while?"

The teenager shook her head. "Moisturizer causes zits. Every-one knows that."

"She's hopeless," the attorney cried, throwing her hands in the air. She went to the dresser and pushed the teenager out of the way. "There could be a few redeemable items in here," she said, holding up a pink and green tube of Great Lash. She turned to me. "How do you feel about using fifteen-year-old mascara?"

"What's the worst that could happen?" I asked.

"You could go blind."

"Surviving the day might be easier if I were blind," I offered. "At the very least, it would be a really good reason to cancel."

"Fine then, we'll wipe off the applicator really well and hope for the best," she said. "Oh no..." she moaned as she produced an amber-colored Banana Boat spritzer from the drawer. The attorney turned to the teenager, who was inspecting every pore on her face in the dresser mirror. "Is this tanning accelerator?"

"It's hardly ever sunny around here," the teenager shrugged. "How else am I supposed to get a tan?"

The attorney fumed. "You live in Oregon, not the tropics. You have no legitimate reason to be tan."

"But guys like girls who are tan."

"But men prefer women who don't look age eighty when they're really twenty-nine. I am *begging you*," she pleaded, holding the bottle between her hands like a rosary, "from now on, don't leave the house with less than an SPF 30."

"Leave the house?" the little girl laughed. "That fraidy cat can't even come out from under the bed, except to throw a tan-trum."

It was unfortunate for the teenager that Melissa Matthews was not present for this conversation, because she certainly would have stuck up for the adolescent, at least on the tanning issue. The first thing I noticed about Melissa when she picked me up that afternoon was how tan she was for an Oregon March. The second thing I noticed was her acrylic nails. The third thing I noticed was her crushing strength.

"Sam!" Melissa screamed as she waved her hands back and forth in the air. She ran towards the stairs and gave me a hug, a very strong hug. It took me a moment to realize I should hug her back and so I tried to put my arms through the motions but I was out of practice and came off stiff, like a marionette with tangled strings.

As you've probably figured out, Melissa was the most popular girl at Commerce High School, and like most most-popular girls, she didn't earn that title without a heap of behind-the-scenes effort. Teenaged me was her second banana, and was therefore privy to a lot of the more unsightly behavior going on backstage. However, the teenager never forgot that she earned her second-banana status (and the run-off popularity that went along with it) by proving her willingness to (1) never divulge the backstage shenanigans, and (2) never compete with Melissa for anyone's attention.

I had long since gotten over Melissa and the teenager's awe for her, but I had never forgotten the backstage ugliness. And so it was with some trepidation that I stood in Jack's living room and hugged this woman; by contrast, the teenager ghost was so worked up by Melissa's mere presence that she appeared as if she might bow down and start praying at Melissa's feet.

"Sam!" Melissa repeated herself.

"For gosh sakes, say something!" the teenager instructed.

"Hi," I stammered. "It was so nice of you to come get me."

"Well, I would have called you a long time ago, but I had no idea you were in town until I ran into your dad at the nursery."

"Oh... I would have called you too, but I lost my cell phone."

"You did? That's tragic. I lost mine once for two days and felt completely out of touch with the world. I just don't bother to memorize people's numbers anymore because I have my lil' phone to do that for me. Not calling anyone for two days—it was a nightmare! How long have you been without yours?"

"About eight months," I said. The teenager hid her face in her hands.

Melissa smiled nervously. The fourth thing I noticed about her was that her teeth were unnaturally white. "Oh."

Melissa was dressed as cute as ever in little jeans, a green satin top and matching platform sandals. She was wearing makeup, and unlike mine, her mascara was probably purchased within the past decade. I was wearing my best outfit—Tuesday's—the dog-walking outfit with the designer jeans, and yet I already felt dowdy and deflated.

We went to the Sherman Valley Towne Center, which was a real eye-opener as to the types of people who had Mondays off. They were not a happy or boisterous crowd. The mall was quiet, except for the piped music that seemed too loud with so few bodies and voices to absorb it.

Melissa and I went to a hundred shops. In each one, she would take two or three items, try them on in the dressing room, and come out and model them for me. She would also pile my arms with clothes she wanted me to try on, but neither I nor my three-hundred-dollar paycheck was interested. In the first few stores, I went through the motions of going into the dressing room and shuffling hangers around so she would think I was try-ing things on. But after the fourth round, I just sat on the bench and put my head in my hands and counted to a hundred, willing Tuesday to come with my beloved routine. *This is progress, this is progress, this is progress*, I chanted. But it didn't feel like progress—it felt like that icy day in Seattle where I sat at the bus stop: one step forward, a thousand steps back.

"Sam, are you still in there?" Melissa asked, knocking on the door. I looked up, wondering how long she had been knocking.

"Yes," I said meekly.

The door opened and she came in. She sat down on the bench and flashed those white teeth at me.

"I'm sorry," I said.

"You have nothing to be sorry about."

"You were so nice to do this for my dad."

"Would you stop apologizing, Sam?"

"You've probably figured it out by now anyway. Did you hear I'm working at the *call center*? All of Commerce has probably figured it out."

"Figured what out?"

"That I'm not…" I paused, and then I laughed for the lack of words to describe it. "That I'm not 'right' right now."

"That you're coming off some sort of a nervous breakdown?"

Wow. *Nervous breakdown.* Those were definitely the words I was looking for, and it was simultaneously hurtful and relieving to hear them. Did people still have nervous breakdowns these days? It sounded like a phrase from the past, from my parents' generation. These days people had episodes, they had cycles, they had attacks. Cars had breakdowns. Computers broke down. Glass broke.

For over a year, nobody had dared to utter the N.B. words to me, and yet here was Melissa Matthews, queen of the two faces, saying them. It was shocking, like being pushed into an ice-cold pool. But sometimes you need to push a person in an icy pool in order to slap some sense into them.

"I guess that's one way of putting it…"

"So what?" she said, waving her acrylic nails in the air again, waving an entire N.B. away. "Honestly? It's a bit of a relief. Now I can relate to you again."

I looked down at her sassy platforms. "But I'm wearing old running shoes."

"I'd have worn tennies, too, if I'd known you were going to," she laughed. "I *always* wear tennis shoes these days. These sandals are absolutely killing me."

"Then why on earth did you wear them?" I asked.

"Because every time I've seen you in the past five years, you've been all gussied up in some designer outfit that costs more than my paycheck and so I've gotten into the habit of, well… dressing up for you, I guess."

"You have?" I asked. I suddenly wished the attorney hadn't physically restrained that pesky teenaged ghost to prevent her from tagging along to the mall. The attorney did it as a favor to me, of course, but if the teenager could hear Melissa say this, I might earn some respect. If the teenager had heard this, maybe she wouldn't cry herself to sleep every night on account of learning how lame she turned out.

"Yeah, pathetic, I know." Melissa laughed. "You know what's really sad? As I was walking to my car to come and get you today, I passed this in*sane* gal who lives kitty-cornered to me in the complex and when she saw what I was wearing, she asked me who my 'hot date' was with."

"But you're Melissa Matthews."

"I know!" she said, mocking indignance. "But that's just not getting me as far these days as it used to."

Given our prior confessions about the limited pay our Mondays-off jobs provided, Melissa and I opted for a food court lunch as opposed to a proper restaurant. The attorney would have scoffed at the description of Roger's Roadside Grill as a "proper restaurant," but lucky for me, she was busy playing warden to the teenager.

I bought a basket of two tacos and a soft drink. It cost me $7.59. In terms of net income, I figured I worked an hour and fifteen minutes at the call center in order to pay for those tacos.

Melissa got hamburgers, fries, and a milkshake. She dipped her fries in her milkshake, just as she always had. I found comfort in the gesture, but then she scolded herself for buying fries and a milkshake in the first place and calculated how long she would have to spend on the elliptical machine in order to burn them off.

Being a grown-up, it seemed, was all about the math.

In the car on the way home, Melissa kept beating her mani-cured fist against the dashboard. "Come on," she pleaded with the radio.

"What's the matter?"

"It's this car—everything is falling apart. Do you know how hard I work just to pay for this car and what kind of love does it give me in return? Oil stains all over the carport and a busted radio." She turned to me. "Do you have a car?"

"No." I said. "That's why you had to pick me up."

"I mean in Seattle."

"I did have a car," I admitted, cautiously at first, but then the story kept falling out of my mouth in pieces. "I went through this period where I didn't leave my house much and so I never used the car. One day this guy in my building knocked on my door and said he noticed the car never left the garage and he offered to buy it off me. So I sorta sold it to him on the spot, along with my CDs and change for parking and everything else that was in it."

Melissa laughed and waived her hands in the air again, despite the fact that she was driving. "That's kind of crazy," she said.

"I know," I said, smirking a bit. "There's a part of me that still hasn't forgiven myself for it." I said, thinking about the attorney. I wanted the light joking to last the whole way home, but it didn't. The car got quiet and I, too, prayed the radio would suddenly start working.

"What kind of car was it?" Melissa finally asked, the fun gone from her voice.

I didn't want to tell her, but I was so out of social practice that I couldn't remember how to fib my way around a question that shouldn't be answered.

"It was a Mercedes," I mumbled.

"Oh," Melissa said, her voice changed. "A silver Mercedes?"

"Yes."

"Huh. I always imagined you driving a silver Mercedes."

In bed that night, the ghosts and I agreed that the Melissa encounter was not nearly as dreadful as we assumed it would be. The
teenager couldn't stop pacing the room, wringing her hands, asking for each and every detail to be repeated a thousand times. "But
how did she say it?" she asked. "Was she, like, looking around the
room when she talked to you, or did she look all right at you and
stuff? Did you run into anyone else at the mall, like Chad or Byron?"

"I seriously doubt either Chad or Byron has Mondays off," I
said.

"I'm sure they don't live in Commerce anymore," the attorney
added.

"Who cares what Chad and Byron do? Boys are so stupid."
the little girl scoffed.

"They're not stupid! You don't even know who they are!" the
teenager scolded. The little girl shrugged, and went back to fluff-
ing her bunny's ears. "And as for you guys," the teen added,
pointing at the attorney and me with disdain, "I don't even know
why I listen to you. You were wrong about Melissa. She was really,
really nice to you today. You shouldn't have said all those nasty
things about her this afternoon."

We hung our heads at that, because we had said things about
Melissa and her ugliness and, in the process, we became the ugly
ones.

It all started earlier in the day when the ghosts were giving me
my makeover. The teenager noted the running shoes and begged
me to change out of them.

"We're lucky she has those shoes," the attorney said. "The
only reason she brought them is that she wore them out the
door."

"Melissa's going to gag when she sees them," the teenager
moaned. It was the twentieth sentence she had uttered that began

with the phrase *Melissa's going to gag* in a five-minute period. The attorney snapped.

"Listen," she said, "for the past ten-odd years we've been the ones gagging at Melissa, okay?"

The teenager's orange face turned pale. "What?!" she cried. "But she's the most popular girl in school."

"Yes, she was, and that was the high point in Melissa Matthews' life—being the most popular girl at a high school in a hick town in Oregon. It's been downhill since then."

"What do you mean?"

"Well, I'm pretty sure she dropped out of community college," I explained.

"She did," the attorney confirmed. "Libby made it through more school than she did. Melissa got a job as a receptionist for Dr. Moody and she's been working there ever since. In the meantime, we got a bachelor's degree in political science, we interned for a summer in Washington, D.C., we did study abroad in London, we went to law school…" Her voice trailed off as she pretended to focus on brushing my hair.

"We worked at one of the biggest firms in Seattle," I picked up, trying to mimic the pride in her voice. "We owned a fancy apartment with designer Italian furniture. We had a nice car."

"We did," the attorney agreed. "Regardless of how things panned out, Melissa Matthews has nothing on that."

"But she's our best friend," the teenager whined. "Why are you guys all ragging on her so much?"

"Because she's a backstabber, of course," the attorney said.

"What?"

The attorney and I exchanged glances.

"How old are you?" I asked the teenager.

"Sixteen. And a half. Well, almost a half."

The attorney raised her eyebrows and looked at me. "Then she doesn't know."

"Know what?" the teen asked.

"About Dan Polanski," I said.

At the mere mention of Dan Polanski's name, the teenager flushed. "Dan Polanski?" she stammered. "Who even cares about him?"

"You do," the attorney laughed. "You're in love with him."

"Am so not!" she protested, but her cheeks grew even pinker. "Dan Polanski is a total stoner."

A wicked smile spread across the attorney's face. "More importantly, he is a drummer. The very first drummer, as a matter of fact."

That night, the teenager begged us to spill the dirt on Dan Polanski, but we declined. Melissa had clearly moved past Dan, and I decided it was time for me to follow suit. The guys at the call center were great, but I desperately needed a stable friend like Melissa, one who had proven she could say the N.B. words and still break bread with me at the food court.

When the little girl had passed out on the window seat and the teenager returned to her cavern under the bed, the attorney crawled under the covers with me and whispered in my ear.

"Melissa was just the wind-up, you know. Tomorrow, Jack will expect you to call Alex."

"But we hate Alex Martin," I reminded her.

"We hated Melissa, too."

Chapter 8

GOLDILOCKS

"I LEFT THE FIRM," Alex gloated. "I'm hanging out the proverbial shingle."

"Good for you." I tried to sound spontaneous and supportive, but I only sounded like I was trying.

"The funny thing is, when I left, I worried I wouldn't have enough clients. Now the problem is that I have too much work."

He laughed. That was just like Alex—making too much work, too much success sound like a burden or even an accident. I rolled my eyes, grateful it was only a phone call, grateful he was a hundred and fifty miles away in Seattle and couldn't catch the fact that I was trading grimaces with the attorney ghost.

I had known yet not known Alex Martin for nine years. This was the longest conversation in which we had ever engaged, and I still wasn't sure what the whole point of it was.

"So what have you been up to since leaving Wallace?" he asked. "Gosh, I guess it's been over a year—it seems like yesterday."

The attorney put her face in her hands.

"I—"

"This is boring," the little girl pouted. "When can we go ride bikes?"

"Shut up about the bikes already!" the teenager snapped.

"Go back under your bed, fraidy cat!"

The ghosts and I were in the den. The attorney was sitting on the arm of the couch, chomping on her manicured nails. I could hear Jack puttering around in the kitchen, obviously eavesdropping on the conversation. Trying to maintain normalcy on the phone with Alex while simultaneously foiling any foolish notions Jack might have regarding the meaning of this conversation while trying to keep three ghosts in line without looking or sounding like I was doing so was, needless to say, overloading my mental and social capacity.

"Until I saw you in Seattle a few weeks ago, I always figured you moved on to bigger things," he answered for me. "Maybe at that firm in Los Angeles—"

An uneasy laugh escaped me. "No," I said, "the last thing I'm looking to do right now is take another bar exam, let alone California's."

"Well, what have you been doing?"

Again I paused. I looked at the attorney and raised my shoulders, trying to convey to her that I just couldn't put it off any longer.

"I've got to be honest, Alex. I haven't been doing anything."

"Nothing?"

"Nope. Nothing at all. I mean, I have a small, part-time job here in Oregon just to make my dad happy," I fibbed, hoping Jack wouldn't hold it against me. "But for a long time I just hung out in Seattle plotting a next move that never really materialized."

"But you're Samantha Green," he said, laughing again. He kept laughing as if anticipating that at any moment I would tell him I was joking and had really divided the past year between finding a cure for cancer, making millions on the stock market and attending art exhibitions in eastern European countries.

"Yeah, well… that's just not getting me as far as it used to."

He laughed again, but a long silence followed. Finally, he cleared his throat.

"I get it."

"What?"

"I get it, Sam. I do. I've wanted to leave Wallace for a really long time. It was difficult to look at some of the partners and realize they had committed to a life of that—it just wasn't living for me. But I didn't allow myself to leave until I had a plan in place, because I know myself and I know human nature, and I could foresee a situation where 'no plan' became the plan."

I looked at the attorney and shrugged again. So Alex "got" us? So what?

She shook her head. "It's lip service," she whispered.

"And this is actually very good news for me, Sam," he continued, momentum building. "Because I'm assuming it means you're available, or that you'll at least consider my offer."

"What offer?" I asked. The attorney stood up and bolted towards the phone so she could listen in more carefully.

"When I quit Wallace, I was hoping to live the self-employed dream by cutting my hours in half and playing a little basketball, but it just hasn't happened. Like I said, I have too much work. So I've decided to outsource."

"You're outsourcing?" I repeated, confused. "What, to like India?"

"No," he laughed. "To you, I'm hoping."

The attorney gripped my elbow. "Ask him what kind of work he's doing," she goaded.

"What kind of work are you doing?"

"Same as before—securities, IPOs, setting up corporations, partnerships, LLCs, franchises. It's just the client has changed. Instead of working for the big guys and bleeding them dry, I'm doing it for every computer science grad with a dream, quick and cheap."

The attorney began pacing the room, her fingers in her mouth. "How is he generating business?"

"How are you finding these clients?" I asked.

"That's easy. I'm advertising on the Internet." He laughed uncertainly. "I know lawyers who advertise are considered schmucks, but I'm hoping my slick website and the search engine fees I'm paying are somewhat of a step up from the picture of the personal injury lawyer on the back of the phone book."

"It's actually pretty smart," the attorney said. She was right—the Achilles heel of traditional law firms was that they were so, well, traditional. They still generated business on pricey lunches and golf course referrals.

"It's actually pretty smart," I repeated to Alex.

"Don't sound so surprised," he chided. "So what do you say, Sam? I'll pay you a hundred dollars per hour to draft documents you could write in your sleep. You can recycle all you want—I even brought a few templates with me from Wallace. Then I'll charge one seventy-five for your work and make a hefty profit."

"But they were billing three hundred for me at Wallace when I left."

"Yeah, how do you think I got these new clients? I'm not charging Wallace and Kennedy prices. But my profit margin is huge by comparison. No firm retreats. No support staff. No catered lunches. No mahogany cubicles in downtown high-rises. No lobby with original artwork—"

"I get the picture."

"Ask him if you can work from home," the attorney advised.

"Can I work from Commerce?" I asked. The attorney grew stiff at this. I realized she envisioned this playing out at a different "home," one with Italian furniture.

"Sure, you can work from wherever you want as long as you have Internet access," he said. "By the way, where on earth is Commerce?"

"The middle of nowhere, Oregon."

After nine years of knowing yet not knowing each other, Alex Martin and I finally made plans. We planned for me to work ten hours a week for starters, and then increasing my time according to business needs and my own comfort. It blew my mind that by working a quarter of the time I spent at the call center, I would be making three times the money.

We planned to get my laptop so I could start working for him. The only problem was that the laptop, like so many things belonging to the attorney, was in the Seattle condo. Alex offered to retrieve the laptop and drive it out to me so he could see where Commerce was and get me "set up" to work for him. I was hesitant, but agreed. I couldn't ask Jack to drive out there and get it for me, and the thought of going back in that condo myself made me nauseous. So I told Alex where I hid a spare key and Alex scolded me because, apparently, burying one's spare key in a potted plant outside the door is not very secure, particularly if the plant is dead. I told him that he could leave the spare with the crazy lady upstairs when he left if he wanted. He said it was a tempting offer but that the dead plant was probably a good idea after all.

The attorney was positively twitter-pated at the possibility of doing honest to goodness legal work again, but she was up in arms at the thought of Alex going through her precious condo. I felt bad because I hadn't left the place in as tidy a state as she would have preferred, and so I decided to toss her a bone.

"Alex, will you do me one more favor while you're at my place?" I asked.

"Sure."

"Will you go in my closet and grab some shoes for me?"

"Shoes?"

"Yeah. I wasn't planning on staying here as long as I have and I didn't pack very well."

"Do you want a specific pair?" His utter lack of confidence at being able to identify said specific pair in a closet of women's shoes was obvious in his voice.

"No, just bring anything that looks comfortable but isn't a running shoe."

"Okay. Laptop and shoes. Will do."

Will do. Easy for Alex to say. He didn't have to tell his awkward cousin Libby that, once again, society had dictated he was somehow too good for her line of work. He didn't have to bid farewell to Angel's antics and the lunch bunch at the call center. Luckily, I had surpassed my three-week commitment to Libby. I sat there on the couch and tried to congratulate myself on being so reasonable and prudent. Yet I found little comfort in my usual *this is progress* chant. What made it so dreadfully obvious that quitting the call center and working for Alex was the "right" thing to do?

"It's extra time and extra money," the attorney explained. "Together, that means freedom."

True, but "together" was the evasive lynchpin. I had known both ends of the spectrum before—well enough to know that they were the opposite of freedom. If you have too much extra money, it means you are locked in a job that takes all your free time. On the other hand, if you have plenty of time, but no money, you are similarly incapacitated. The latter scenario results in a year spent in your jammies. The former results in delusions that a year spent in your jammies actually sounds like a good idea. It's better to have just enough of both.

I planned on resigning to Libby before she came to pick me up that afternoon, but I didn't. I wanted to have at least two days off before Alex showed up, and given the pay increase I would soon have, eight hours at the call center for sixty-four dollars gross now seemed like a royal waste of my time. But I just couldn't call Libby, and before I knew it, I was sitting in my cubicle at the call center, going through the motions.

For all our lunches, I had to admit I would have never told any of my call center coworkers where the key to my condo was buried or asked them to rifle through my shoes. And yet that's what Alex Martin was likely doing at the very moment I was taking my last calls. I thought about Alex and the faded names of every one of his high school classmates and decided not to tell anyone at the call center it was my last day. The call center had such high turnover, everyone was used to people just disappearing. Call center employees didn't keep in touch. They certainly didn't phone their former coworkers a year later to offer them a job. Well, not unless the job was of a nefarious nature.

Of course, Libby was the exception. In the car, I told her not to pick me up the following afternoon, that I wouldn't be going back. Despite the fact that I had lasted an impressive four and a half weeks, she was visibly upset. I explained to her about Alex and my dire financial straits, but she was convinced it had something to do with the Melissa Matthews reunion the day before. I was so exhausted, I didn't even try to correct her.

"That wasn't fair," the teenager chastised me up in the bedroom. "That wasn't fair to Melissa, or to Libby."

"I'll set it straight later," I sighed as I collapsed onto the bed.

"Congratulations," the attorney said. "You're a free woman." It didn't feel that way, and she of all ghosts should have understood why.

"If you have more time now, does that mean we can go ride bikes?" the little girl asked.

"Oh gag me if I hear one more word about those bikes," the teenager moaned, twirling a lock of her frizzy hair. "Why do you want to ride them so bad anyway?"

"So she can help me figure out how to get over the gulch," the little girl snapped back.

"The gulch?" I asked.

"You know what I'm talking about," the little girl stated. "You said so earlier."

The attorney crossed her beautifully manicured eyebrows. "I always thought the reason you wanted to get over that gulch was to skip out of this deadbeat town and move onto more exciting things," she said.

"That *is* the reason."

"Let me get this straight," I said. "You dragged me all the way back to Commerce just to help you figure out how to break out of it?"

The teenager giggled at this. All the teasing was distressing the little girl, but she did her best to hide it. "That's right," she said, defiantly.

"But we already figured out how to get out of Commerce," the attorney explained.

"How's that?"

"You grow up and then you leave."

"How?"

"You drive out."

"Drive over the gulch?"

"No, you drive around the gulch, on the highway, like a normal person."

The little girl's hands clenched into fists and she stomped her right foot on the floor. "But that's cheating," she whimpered.

"How so?" I asked.

"Because that way gravity wins."

Ah, *gravity*—the little girl's arch nemesis. It had been a while since I'd cracked a physics textbook, but I still believed gravity to be the force a celestial body, such as the earth, exerts on the people and things near its surface. Thus, when you throw a ball in the air, it will fall back down. If you tip over a jar of marbles, they will spill to the floor. If you sleep with bubble gum in your mouth, it will fall out and end up on your pillow and subsequently make its way into your hair. If you climb into bed for a "break," you will have a very difficult time climbing back out.

Gravity gave the attorney wrinkles. Gravity caused Mickey's drum set to leave divots in the carpet. Gravity felled cheerleading pyramids right when Dan Polanski was looking. Gravity served as the invisible gatekeeper to all that lay beyond the gulch. Everything wrong with the world was all gravity's fault.

The little girl had never seen a physics textbook and she didn't know who Isaac Newton was, but she was once informed that the thing preventing her from jumping the gulch on her bike was gravity. As a result, the little girl spent a fair amount of time thinking about gravity and she figured it out on her own terms and in her own six-year old way. The little girl had never been taught the concept of escape velocity—that is, the speed an object needs to escape the gravitational pull of another object, but she knew it existed all the same. It worked for birds. It worked for airplanes. It worked for spaceships. Therefore, she knew that if she could figure out how to ride her bike very, very fast, she could clear the gulch and land safely on the other side. To her, escape velocity was the number of helium-filled balloons required to enable the bike to float over the gulch. To her, escape velocity was the speed at which she would need to flap her arms if, as she suspected, she finally honed her own ability to fly.

This little girl was a scientific genius in her own right. Newton was still taking credit for things apparent to a six-year-old.

"I thought you didn't believe in gravity," I reminded her.

"I just say that in case it's listening," she whispered, her eyes darting around the room.

A genius, I tell you, so smart that she tricked me into going in the garage the next day. It all started with her usual pestering about the bikes. For the millionth time, I tried to explain to her why a grown woman rumored to have experienced an N.B.

shouldn't exacerbate the situation by riding around town on a tiny Strawberry Shortcake bike.

"What's the matter with Strawberry Shortcake?" she asked, clearly offended.

"Nothing, except the fact that she is for six-year-olds, not grown-ups."

"But there's a bigger bike you can use. In the garage—I've seen it."

"No," I said, shaking my head. "I never had a bike besides the Strawberry Shortcake one. I outgrew them."

"It's a grown-up bike," she insisted. "The kind that needs a key."

"The Vespa!" I cried, remembering the little orange scooter that had gotten me everywhere in college. The little girl smiled and nodded. For once, our enthusiasm matched.

I asked the attorney if she remembered where the key was, but she refused to help. Then Jack caught me rummaging through the junk drawer downstairs and informed me the key was in the ignition.

"You can't leave the key in the ignition, Dad," I scolded. "Someone could have stolen it."

"I would have been thrilled if they had. That piece of junk has been using my garage space for years and, until now, you've shown no interest in reclaiming it."

"It wouldn't hurt to have some transportation," I said.

"Good luck getting it to start," he shrugged.

For once, I was grateful for Jack's unwillingness to throw away anything that had ever belonged to someone else. I grabbed a dish towel to dust off the scooter and headed off to the garage with the gleeful little girl in tow.

But the minute the door slammed shut behind us, I realized she had stabbed me in the back.

"You tricked me!" I yelled.

"Take it easy," the new ghost instructed.

She was wearing beat-up Levis, the kind that were already beat up when she bought them, but which she lovingly beat up some more until they were just right. Jeans are funny that way. It was a wonder Goldilocks wasted her time with the porridge and the beds when she should have been trying on the three bears' jeans to see which fit the best. Perhaps she did, only Baby Bear's were a little tight while Mama Bear's hideous yet ample reverse-fit pair felt like a dream. Afterward, when her friends asked what she did all day at the Bears' house, she threw out a fib about sampling porridge and trying out beds, not wanting to fess up to the utter comfort of Mama Bear's mom jeans.

(Then again, any sort of analytical review of Goldilocks' behavior proves shocking: (1) breaking and entering; (2) binge-eating comfort food; and (3) sleeping all day. It doesn't take a psychiatrist to conclude that Goldilocks was downright depressed.)

But the ghost on the Vespa was definitely not depressed. She was the happiest she had ever been or would ever be in her entire life, only she probably didn't appreciate the fact. She probably assumed there were even better things around the corner. She was horribly wrong.

She wore a black t-shirt bought at a concert. She lived in the age of ironic apathy or apathetic irony, take your pick. The only war she had ever known lasted about thirty seconds one January in high school. She had seen images of buildings collapse, but they were vacant Vegas hotels and the like that were legally demolished, not 100-floor towers in Manhattan with thousands of people inside them. The biggest crisis she had ever known was the dot-com bust.

For these reasons, she, and everyone with whom she associated, wore black eight-hole Doc Martens boots. They were a symbol of collective visual angst when there was little personal reason to feel it. Soon, history would provide them ample things to worry about and they could all put their Doc Martens away and begin washing their hair again.

She straddled the Vespa, but when I entered the room, she turned around on the seat to face me. Despite the mangy hair, despite the lack of makeup, despite the boyish fashion sense, she was possibly the most beautiful woman I had ever seen, a fact enhanced by her complete obliviousness to it.

"Relax," she said again, "I've been here the whole time."

"You have?"

"Yeah. Hate to admit it, but I've been eavesdropping on all your drama, too." She arched an eyebrow before asking, "Melissa Matthews? Alex Martin?"

"You don't approve, I take it."

"I couldn't care less," she said in a manner that seemed condescending. "Wouldn't be my first choice in friends, but I guess you've got to do what you've got to do."

I heard footsteps behind me, and turned around. The attorney was standing there, her arms folded across her chest.

"You would have preferred some menagerie of rockers, skaters and other miscreants, I assume?" the attorney asked.

"Something like that," the college student ghost said wryly. "But it's not my preference that matters anymore."

The attorney's interrogation continued. "If you've been here the whole time, then why didn't you come join the party?"

The student laughed. "*Way* too much drama for me." Then, more pointedly, she added, "Anyhow, I don't like to meddle."

"I just want what's best for her," the attorney claimed, more than a little defensively.

"Even if she were to adopt your old life, it wouldn't resurrect you. Surely you recognize that."

"I—"

"You're just trying to clean your conscience for so royally screwing everything up."

"Easy words for someone who's never held a real job," the attorney lashed back. "I thought I was doing the right thing by quitting, I did."

"Yeah, yeah, I've heard it all before: you were miserable."

"I was, miserable at the job *you* accepted, that you had to accept because you messed everything up by summering in the wrong place. I was just going to take a short break to rejuvenate myself. Then I was going to round up my own clients—the same thing Alex Martin is doing now."

"But what happened?" the student asked.

"Yeah, what happened?" the little girl repeated.

The attorney shook her head back and forth. "Nothing happened," she whispered. "I got into bed instead."

"And the person who got out?"

The attorney nodded toward me.

"She was someone else."

*

Chapter 9

THE DAY MAXINE'S CAT DIED

THE VESPA WOULDN'T START, but Jack offered to take a look at it. Jack was an accountant by trade and a gardener by nature. Neither position qualified him as a scooter mechanic, but he seemed fixated on fixing the thing and I didn't fight him.

Alex arrived the following day and, as promised, he brought the laptop and some shoes. He brought almost all of the shoes in fact, feeling unqualified to decide which ones I needed the most. I asked him if he had any trouble at the condo, and he said he had a run-in with the crazy lady upstairs and she supposed him to be a shoe thief. Once he explained his purpose, she asked him if I was getting sufficient fresh air in Commerce and if it was doing me good.

It wasn't as weird as I expected—seeing him, that is. To be sure, he still had those long eyelashes, but they weren't as intimidating as they once seemed. When I answered the door he was just standing there, like any guy would, holding a large plastic tub full of my footwear.

Of course, I was up to my eyeballs in ghosts by that point, and each one had an opinion of Alex.

"Are you kidding? That plastic tub could contain dismembered body parts, for all you know," the student joked. She didn't care for Alex or the attorney's taste in shoes, but while she made her feelings known, she wasn't one to force them on the rest of us. To the attorney's dismay, the student had been around for less than a day and had already secured the position of most popular ghost.

The attorney's dislike of Alex was more deep-rooted than the student's, yet she recognized that working for him was her best shot—her only shot—at saving her condo and returning to Seattle. Alex was a means to an end, and there is nothing lawyers enjoy more than relying on that phrase to justify all sorts of distasteful behavior.

The younger ghosts' regard of Alex was somewhat less discerning. The teenager just wanted to know if he was cute. The little girl kept asking if he liked to ride bikes.

"So this is Commerce, Oregon," Alex said as we drove through town in search of a cable modem. I won't go into the details of how monstrously misinformed Jack was about his own Internet connection, but suffice it to say that I was now even more worried that the Vespa's fate lay in that man's hands.

"This is Commerce," I confirmed. "Now you can cross it off your list."

"Did you grow up here?" he asked.

"Yes."

He laughed and shook his head. "I never would have guessed it."

I didn't know what that meant and I didn't want to know. After several failed shopping attempts, we ended up at a new big-box electronics store in Sherman Valley, where Alex engaged in a lengthy conversation with a golf-shirted, name-tagged adolescent until they mutually decided on a modem. At the register, I suddenly felt like a girl who couldn't figure out whether or not she was on a date. Had I anticipated paying for a modem, I probably would have worked at the call center on Wednesday to help cover the cost. At the same time, it didn't seem fair for Alex to pay for it when I had already assured him of our Internet access at the house and, as it was, the shopping trip had extended his stay in Commerce by at least an hour and a half.

I tried my best to look as if a hundred-odd dollars was no big deal to me, and went through the motions of reaching for my wallet.

"I've got it, Sam."

"But—"

"I need the write-off," he insisted, as he handed the cashier his credit card.

Kindness is always welcome, but sometimes, when certain people do repeated favors, it feels like a mounting debt that they can call due and payable at their will. Such was the case with Alex Martin: first the job, then the shoes, now the modem. It was usury. On the way back to Jack's house, I tried to find a silver lining to the situation. At least I didn't need a tax write-off; given my measly year-to-date earnings, the standard deduction would more than suffice.

I let my mind wander as the final vestiges of raw land between the neighboring towns flashed by the window. I wasn't even looking for it, but I spotted it. Just as Alex turned the car down the highway heading to Jack's house, I recognized a pattern of three trees bordering a field with a small valley and I knew that somewhere behind those trees laid the little girl's gulch.

I gasped as I recognized it and tapped on the window with my knuckle. Fortunately, Alex didn't notice my reaction—he was too entrenched in a conversation I didn't realize we were having.

"Besides, it was meant to be," he said.

"What?" I asked.

"Our working together. We keep crossing paths."

"But you hunted down my dad's number and called me," I reminded him. "It's not like that was by chance."

"No, but chance caused me to hunt down your dad's number and call you. On my last day at Wallace, the boys were taking me out to lunch, I was having a great time with everyone and thinking about how much I'd miss the place, and right when I'm wondering if I've made the worst decision of my life, I look up and see a couple of scary little dogs and who is with them? You."

Oh yeah, *chance.* "Two Pomeranians," I told Alex, lacking both the heart and the nerve to tell him the rest of the story, namely that our chance meeting had resulted in my running away to Commerce with two cents and one pair of sneakers. I didn't tell him that chance caused me to take a nearly minimum-wage job at a call center with a slew of parolees despite my overdone education. I didn't point out the irony that chance turned around and brought Alex to Commerce along with his money and the rest of my shoes. I didn't raise the issue that chance was a sadist, that chance was in likely violation of several provisions of the Geneva Conventions. Instead, all I offered was a vapid explanation. "They belong to my crazy neighbor, the one you met."

Alex smiled. "That figures."

When we got back to the house, Libby and Sarita were there. Libby had called in sick to work, her apparent illness being that she was still overcome by pouting about my hasty departure from her employ. She glared at Alex, but that wasn't half as bad as the obvious once-over that Sarita gave him, only to ignore him entirely and announce, "I brought lasagna."

"Great," I sang, plastering a smile across my face. "Um, Alex, this is my aunt, Sarita, and my cousin Libby," I murmured, doing my best to inject some civility into the situation.

Alex extended his hand, but nobody shook it. Placing it back in his pocket, he offered, "I'm Alex Mar—"

"The new boss," Sarita nodded. She looked him up and down again. "I can see why Melissa Matthews wanted you around."

"Melissa who?" Alex asked, confused. I shot visual darts across the room to Jack, but he just threw his hands up in the air, signaling that there was nothing he could do.

"Alex has never met Melissa," I explained, more curtly this time. At that point, Libby put her head on the table like a five-year old.

"Well, Alex," Sarita said with slightly more warmth. "Maxine, the gal who does my hair, one of her cats died this week, tragically even, got hit by a car, so I had no choice but to bake her a lasagna. And if I'm going to go to the trouble to make one lasagna, I figured I might as well make two, so I brought one over to Jack and Sam because unless Libby and I keep them fed, it's nothing but fast food and T.V. dinners."

"She's exaggerating," Jack said.

"Oh, but I'm not. I'll tell you, back when Sam's mother died, they ate at McDonald's every single night."

The room grew cold for a second. Jack stiffened at the mere mention of my mother, her death and the zombie-like period that followed. Libby raised her head, knowing that speaking of my mother in Jack's presence was generally taboo. Poor Alex, who was just trying to "set up" my computer, who had known but not known me for nine years and yet had never heard that my mother had died, just stood there in the middle, still holding the box with the cable modem, suddenly at the center of a Green family drama twenty-five years in the making.

Even the ghosts were quiet. Since Alex's arrival, the attorney and the student were doing their best to entertain the others so that I could focus on the task at hand—that is, faking normal so Alex would not rescind his offer.

"Can you imagine?" Sarita asked. "A child eating McDonald's every single night?"

"I'm probably not the best person to answer that question," Alex said. "Cheeseburgers are an entire food group for me."

Jack chuckled at this. Sarita smiled and pretended to jab Alex in the cheek. "Then you, sir, are going to have a double serving of my lasagna tonight."

"I wouldn't miss it," Alex said, all the while increasing my indebtedness to him.

Alex installed the cable modem while Sarita fixed some garlic bread. At one point Alex got stuck and, surprisingly, Libby of all people was able to figure out how to make the darn modem work. Apparently she had absorbed a few things from the canned computer advice she had been doling out at the call center for over a decade. Alex did the right thing by big-dealing her expertise and I could tell she was beginning to forgive him for stealing me away from the call center—that is, until the five of us sat down to dinner and the doorbell rang.

It was Melissa.

She had two guys with her, one named either Derek or Jared and the other named Joe. Aunt Sarita looked at them like they were hooligans; as the corners of her mouth turned downward, I knew she was trying to remember where she had set her purse. Of course, they weren't hooligans. They were probably realtors or car salesmen or the like, although Joe did look a little rough around the edges. Sarita, on the other hand, was the one with the faux-Goth daughter who hung out with ex-cons. Still, I'm sure she was scheming how to prevent either of them from eating any of her precious lasagna. She was funny about her food that way.

The teenager ghost saw Melissa first. "Oh my goodness," she gasped. "Libby's here. This is going to be a five-star disaster."

Sure enough, when Libby walked in the room, her eyes got so big I thought they might pop or at least stretch out to the point of blinding her.

"She's going to pee her pants," the teenager declared.

"For heaven's sakes, she's a grown woman," the student said, albeit unconvincingly. As for me, I stood there in the entry, grip-

ping the banister post as hard as I could in an effort to will Libby
to simply survive the moment.

Melissa was Libby's gravity. Although Libby was always one
grade ahead of us in school, the fact that she repeated so many
classes put her squarely within Melissa's social jurisdiction. Needless to say, the two had never been very friendly. However cliché,
Melissa was the captain of the cheerleading team, while Libby
never even made the drill squad—you know, the girls who spin
flags for the marching band wearing those unflattering calf-length
skirts—until her senior year, and at that point everyone knew it
was a pity appointment by the school's administration. Had they
known the humiliation Libby would suffer at her very first football game when that gust of wind blew her calf-length skirt up
over her head, impairing her vision and causing her to catch that
flying flag with her face, sidelining her for the rest of the year and
forcing her to wear a pirate's patch over her eye to school, they
never would have done it.

Melissa had gotten a lot of mileage out of that pirate patch. Although it seemed like ancient history, Libby's stunned reaction in
the entryway led me to believe that, despite the fact that they had
both remained in Commerce, the two women had not had much
contact since Libby graduated high school.

As it turned out, it was the Happy Meal's fault that Melissa
and Libby were now face-to-face without prior warning. Okay, so
it was Jack's fault, too, but I was willing to cut him some slack under the circumstances. Apparently Melissa had called for me while
Alex and I were at the electronics store. Jack, still eager to act as
my social secretary, informed her that while I was not home, he
was just sure I would be available to hang out later that evening.
He both reasonably and prudently expected that Alex would have
left by then. Melissa told Jack that maybe she and some friends
might stop by to visit, and Jack promised to pass on the message.
But then Maxine's cat died and the extra lasagna was made and

Sarita brought up McDonald's and, as usual, Jack had forgotten everything except the woman who used to own the china now piled on the floor in the dining room. Upon realizing the mix-up, Melissa apologized profusely for something that wasn't her fault and Jack invited the whole gang in for lasagna while Sarita frowned some more.

Then a funny thing happened: Melissa locked eyes with Libby and pretended to have noticed her for the first time. She waved her acrylic nails back and forth in the air with excitement, called out Libby's name, and went and gave the would-be Goth a huge hug.

Again, Libby looked stunned.

"Great, now she's going to pee her pants and end up peeing all over Melissa," the teenager predicted.

"Enough about the peeing," the attorney barked.

And then a funnier thing happened: Melissa introduced herself to Alex and all but forgot that Derek (or Jared) and Joe were there, even though it sort of seemed like she and Joe were there together.

The whole mismatched gang sat down to dinner, although I'm sure the three most recent arrivals had originally anticipated eating out. But Melissa was too enraptured by the notion of a tall, dark and professional newcomer, and the guys were apparently too polite to back out themselves. The only upsides of the situation were (1) Melissa's talent at keeping the conversation going and (2) Sarita's excellent lasagna. Melissa deftly brought Alex and the other two up to speed on how everyone in the room knew each other. She also confirmed that she was there with Joe and that the other guy was supposed to be there with me, although I never really caught his name. Once that was finally accomplished, she moved on to entertaining the group with stories of all our shenanigans in high school, giving me far more credit than I was due.

Of course, the best way to tell a story about when one was in high school is to paint one's high school self as kind of lame and misguided. This fact was not lost on Melissa, whose social skills were as polished as ever. Every tale seemed like the foolhardy adventures of Natalie and Tootie rather than the back-stage scheming of the captain and co-captain of the cheerleading squad. Everyone was choking on their lasagna, they were laughing so hard.

The only problem was, the ghost of *my* high school self was actually sitting in the room, at the feet of her idol.

"Can you even believe what we used to wear back then?" Melissa asked. "Gosh, you could sure tell we were small town girls without a clue. My favorite outfit was a pair of short-shorts that had an overall bib on them, and then I would wear anklets and flat dress shoes with them."

"Short-short overalls?" the Derek-ish guy asked. "I can't even picture them."

"Oh, but it was the height of *Saved by the Bell* chic," she promised him. "What's worse, they were bright yellow and had some sort of print on them."

"It was a Hawaiian print," the teenager murmured.

"It was a Hawaiian print," Libby said.

"That's right!" Melissa cried. "Gosh Libby, you should be telling these stories—you have such a better memory than I do."

"How could she forget?" the teenager asked, growing less enchanted with her hero every minute.

"And you—" Melissa exclaimed, touching me on the shoulder. "You always wore a flouncy skort—do you remember those? Thank goodness they stopped making them."

"What's a skort?" Alex asked, looking at me curiously.

Melissa explained, "It's this gosh-awful thing made out of jersey that is ruffled at the absolute worst part—right around your hips—and it looks like a skirt when you're standing but it's got legs. It's almost like a cropped pair of culottes."

"Oh, Libby had one of those, too," Sarita cried, clutching her chest fondly at the memory of her pre-faux Goth daughter.

But the teenager wasn't quite as amused. She looked down at the skort she was wearing and pulled at it until it just looked like an ugly skirt.

"Do you remember our prom dresses, Sam?" Melissa asked. "Don't even get me started on those."

"I remember mine—magenta sequins, head to toe, with a matching scarf," I said. "It looked like something an aging television actress would wear to the Emmys."

"Mine had sleeves the size of Manhattan," Melissa said. Then she turned to Libby.

"Don't!" the teenager whispered.

"What did you wear to prom again, Libby?"

Libby looked down at her plate. "Uh, I didn't go to prom," she mumbled.

"You didn't go junior *or* senior year?"

"Nope."

At that point, the teenager smacked me hard on my shoulder. "You've got to stop her," she yelled in my ear.

"That's funny," Melissa said. "I totally thought you were prom queen one year."

"Say something!" the teenager instructed. But what could I say? The conversation was rolling like that boulder in the *Indiana Jones* movie—it had already built too much momentum to stop it. There was nothing I could do but run for my own life.

"Um," Libby said, "That was for Homecoming. I was the Homecoming queen my senior year."

"*What?!*" Sarita gasped, nearly spewing lasagna across the room. "How come this is the first I've heard of this?"

But Libby was already crying into her garlic bread at that point. "I don't want to talk about it, Mom," she said, as she pushed her chair away from the table and stormed off upstairs.

Then everyone looked into their lasagna in silence. For a really long time.

Joe was the first one to speak. He asked the other guy if the real estate market was still booming in the Commerce-Sherman Valley area, but unfortunately he didn't use his name. Then Alex jumped in, asking questions about the history of the market in the area and if people really live here and commute to Portland every day and what kind of farms were sacrificed in the process. Soon Jack was talking, too. The conversation was dominated by the men and awash in statistics. They didn't joke about what they used to wear in high school— although, I'm sure Alex's wardrobe would come as no surprise—but they joked about knowing people who bought only five years ago for under $200,000 and can you believe their luck?

At one point, Jack stood up and started clearing the dishes. When he passed by me, he discreetly whispered into my ear, "Why don't you go check on your cousin?" It was embarrassing to have to be told to do it.

I excused myself from the table and walked through the entry and towards the stairs. I didn't see the teenager ghost creep up behind me until she had already grabbed me by the neck and pushed me through the door leading to the garage.

The door slammed behind me and I looked around the room. All the ghosts were in there.

"What's your deal?" the teenager asked, pulling at her permed hair. "Why didn't you stick up for her?"

"For Libby?" I yelled. "That's funny—I was just going to ask you the same thing."

"What do you mean?"

The student explained: "She means that if you hadn't allowed Melissa to walk all over Libby in high school, she wouldn't be in this jam now."

"You don't remember how bad it is in high school. You have to totally get with the program or else. But now you're old. You're not supposed to care about those things."

She was tearing up now, and her five coats of Great Lash were beginning to run down her cheeks.

"Do you know what your problem is?" the attorney asked the teenager. "You didn't have a mother to tell you not to wear that much makeup. You had to figure all of these things out for yourself."

"Lay off her," the student said. "The only one of us who had a mom was the little one."

"You're wrong," the little girl corrected. "We all have a mommy."

"She died," the teenager said.

"I know that!" the little girl said. "She had cancer. But now she's up in Heaven, watching us, and if she saw you guys fighting, you'd all be in really big trouble."

The teenager opened her mouth but the attorney cut her off. "Leave it alone," she instructed.

The teenager turned to the attorney, enraged. "Do you know what *your* problem is?" she asked. "Your problem is that you're totally not as smart as you think you are. You've made some really lame decisions for such an old person."

"I know that now," the attorney said, the fight gone from her voice. "But on the same line, you don't give yourself credit for being as smart as you really are."

The teenager opened her mouth but stopped short of saying anything as she repeated the attorney's words in her head.

"I agree," the student said. "You let that ridiculous Melissa call all the shots when you're twice as smart as she is."

"I don't get it," the little girl said, furrowing her brow.

"You're six, dear," the attorney said. It was the first time I heard a note of kindness in one of her *dears*, as opposed to insult.

"Confusion comes with the territory." She turned to the student and the teenager. "I feel bad for Libby, I do. But she wasn't supposed to be here today and neither was Melissa. Our only goal is to survive the meeting with Alex, to get that job and, eventually, to move back to Seattle. Picking a fight with Melissa at the dinner table does nothing towards that goal."

Our goal. It was the first time I heard her state her understanding of things so unequivocally. I had been laboring under the misconception that *our goal* was just to look normal, that *our goal* was just to make a little more money. It was time to set the record straight.

"I hate to tell you this," I said, shaking my head, "but if I *were* to go back to Seattle, it wouldn't be exactly the same."

"What do you mean?" she asked.

"It wouldn't be nearly as excessive."

"Amen to that," the student said.

"What—are you talking about the car . . . and the suits?" the attorney asked, nervously fingering her pearls.

"And the couch," I added.

"And those stupid shoes," the little girl offered.

The attorney backed down. "I can deal with that," she said, nodding. "Really, I can. That stuff doesn't mean as much to me as you all think it does anyway."

The student turned to me. "I hate to point out the obvious, but you have a house full of people waiting on you," she said.

"I know."

"So what are you doing in the garage with a bunch of ghosts working out their mother issues?"

I nodded and turned towards the door.

"Wait!" the little girl cried.

I turned back around. "What?"

"Just so you know, it's true," she said solemnly.

"What's true?"

"We did eat at McDonald's all the time."

The attorney reached out her hand and stroked the little girl's crooked hair. "We all know that, dear," she whispered.

When I walked back into the house, Melissa's guy Joe was standing there, looking confused. "Is that the bathroom?" he asked, pointing to the door I had come through.

"It's the garage," I said, opening the door to prove my point. I had no explanation for why I had been hanging out in the garage in the middle of an impromptu and eventful dinner party, but I didn't know this guy from Adam and felt no need to explain. "If you keep walking past the stairs and turn right, there's a bathroom."

But Joe's attention was diverted to the garage. "Is that an old Vespa in there?" he asked, reaching over me to push the door open again.

"Yeah," I said, propping the door open so he could see it.

"Is it yours?"

"It used to be. I guess it still is. It doesn't run anymore, though."

"Mind if I take a look at it?"

"Be my guest," I said, as I rushed up the stairs, ghosts in tow.

We found Libby pacing my bedroom. Her tears had turned to anger. "I need you to be honest with me," she said. "Did Melissa tell you to quit the call center?"

"Libby, *no*, she had nothing to do with it. I did it because I need the money," I stated, my voice unwavering, unapologetic for once. "Desperately. You know that. He's paying me a hundred an hour. I had no choice."

Libby's jaw dropped to the floor. "A *hundred* bucks an hour?!" She pulled the chair out from under the desk and collapsed into it. "I didn't know there were jobs where people got paid a hundred bucks an hour."

"It's ridiculous, I know."

She looked me up and down, a little disgusted. "Ew, Sam. What exactly are you doing for him?"

"For goodness sakes, not anything bad, Libby! It's legal work. Drafting contracts and letters."

"Writing letters? I could write letters. It's not like you're saving anyone's life."

The attorney shook her head, fuming, while the teenager let out an exasperated sigh. "She can't even spell," the teenager muttered.

"A hundred bucks an hour," Libby repeated. "You'll make as much as I do for the year in only—"

"Don't," I begged her. "Forget the math. It won't do any good. Just know that I had to take this job and it had nothing to do with you and it certainly had nothing to do with Melissa."

Libby's shoulders sagged. "Why did she have to bring up the Homecoming thing, Sam? Everyone knows they just voted me in as a joke."

"No, Libby, only three people downstairs knew that and so, theoretically, you could have played it off. Even your own mother was oblivious."

Indeed, when Libby and I descended the stairs, Sarita was in the entry with the others, putting on her coat while balancing an empty Pyrex dish. "Libby!" she scolded. "You should have told me. A mother has a Constitutional right to take pictures any time her daughter wears a tiara."

Jack shushed his sister and pushed her out the door.

"I guess you still have to work," Melissa said to me, "but we'll catch you another night. We're going to hear Joe's band play. He's a drummer, you know," she said, her raised eyebrows ripe with insinuation.

"He's actually a mechanic who happens to be in a band," the Derek/Jared figure corrected her in a voice as bland as his name. "And I think he's got his eye on your scooter."

Finally, everyone left but Jack and Alex. Four hours after our field trip to the electronics store, Alex finally finished setting up my computer. I slowed him down a bit by repeatedly apologizing for all the interruptions and drama, but he just laughed me off.

"Can I ask you one thing, Samantha?" he said as he was finally getting into his car. The attorney had followed us out there to make sure I didn't screw things up at the end, but I begged her to keep her distance.

"Of course."

"Why are you keeping your apartment in Seattle?"

"It's a condo. I own it."

"Why haven't you sold it?"

I looked down the driveway towards the attorney. Her padded shoulders were hunched together, her arms were folded and she paced the small spot to which she had been banished.

"There's a part of me that is hoping I'll just get over myself, move back there and pick up where I left off."

"Do you think that's possible?" he asked.

"I don't know," I shrugged. "But I think I owe it to that part of me to at least try."

✳

Chapter 10

RIDING BIKES

THE THING ABOUT DRUMMERS IS that they have amazing biceps but an otherwise nonchalant build. Drummers come by their biceps without spending the whole day at the gym or in front of the mirror.

The other thing about drummers is that they are cool enough to be in a band, but are not attention hogs like lead singers or lead guitarists or, worst of all, lead singers who are also lead guitarists. If you look through the annals of rock history, you will find that there are only a few exceptions to this—and that those exceptions generally left the band they drummed for in order to be the lead singer and/or lead guitarist of a new band.

The final thing about drummers is that they can count Dan Polanski, Mickey and Melissa's boyfriend Joe among their numbers, and that is very important.

As you've probably figured out, Joe was a drummer by night but a mechanic by day. He usually worked on cars but was interested in learning how to restore old Italian scooters. He undertook a rebuild of the Vespa as a study in how they were put together, doing the work for free in exchange for my agreement not to sue him if he royally screwed the thing up in the process. The only problem was that he couldn't do it at work because, if his boss found out, he would surely have to charge me. As a result, Joe had been hanging out in Jack's garage quite a bit.

The little girl liked Joe because, in her six-year-old way, she understood the Vespa project was one step closer to fulfillment of her bike-riding fantasy. In addition, she was fascinated by watching him disassemble the machine. The teenager was wary of my spending too much time with Joe, given his intimate connection to Melissa, but was otherwise happy to see me interact with members of the male gender that weren't named Jack or recently released from prison. The student was very fond of the grungy music Joe's band played and the grungy appearance of his drummer's hair and mechanic's hands. She said the reason drummers were so great was that they brought a certain rhythm to life, but I knew she was really talking about the biceps. Regardless, it was nice to see her admit the existence of a guy other than Mickey, even if it was in a hair-of-the-dog-that-bit-her sort of a way.

As for the attorney, she just thought Joe was okay. In the spirit of getting along with the other, well, spirits, she tolerated his presence so long as he didn't overly distract me from the work I was doing for Alex. This was a difficult balance to strike, as the work was just as plentiful as the time Joe spent in Jack's garage.

Speaking of Alex, we were getting to know him now—or at least we had learned more about him in the past month than we had in the preceding nine years combined. As the job required us to communicate by phone or email several times a day, we had become privy to each other's routines. He woke up early and went running. During the run, he would draft a mental list of the day's priorities. Upon returning home, he would call me to discuss said priorities while loudly chomping on a bowl of sweetened cereal. I did not wake up early and would therefore take the calls from bed on my new cell phone. I also did not see the point of running three miles in Seattle rain only to down an entire box of Apple Jacks in one sitting. Alex didn't mind my working from bed so long as I didn't mind his early calls and incessant chomping. We agreed that a work meeting held over cereal and down pillows was a definite improvement on the mile-long conference room table at Wallace and Kennedy. We further agreed to disagree on the Apple Jacks issue.

April brought big changes yet they had been surprisingly easy to slip into. For one, I bought the cell phone. It only had seven numbers programmed into it: Jack's, Alex's, Melissa's, Joe's, Sarita's, Libby's and 911. The last three were added at Sarita's insistence upon seeing the gadget and conjuring up all sorts of emergency situations in which a woman with a cell phone might find herself, but I didn't mind because they nearly doubled my contacts list.

Another change was that I was a lawyer again and yet I didn't have a single suit in my closet. Working for Alex didn't feel like a job so much as it felt like working with a friend on a group project for school. This was odd considering that, prior to my present employment, Alex and I had been neither friends nor group project partners, but it was such a relief compared to the type of high-stress and competitive lawyering the attorney ghost had done. The paychecks weren't as good as hers had been, but they were far better than the ones the call center was doling out, and for that I was very grateful. The only bill Jack had to help out with these days was to top off the mortgage payment on the condo, and he swore up and down that he was happy to do it.

"Your dad is paying for a condo that nobody lives in?" Joe asked when I let the detail slip one evening over the Vespa's crankcase.

"He's only helping to pay at this point," I said, perhaps too defensively.

"So *you're* paying for a condo that nobody lives in. Why don't you rent it out?"

The attorney stiffened at this. "'Nobody lives there' is not an accurate statement," she said. "I still live there."

"Then why are you here?" the student asked her.

"I'm just visiting," she said in all seriousness as the other ghosts giggled. "All my things are still there."

"That stuff is meaningless now," the student said, and she was right. The thought of going back to the condo to pack up things I had forgotten I owned felt like an anvil chained around my neck. But I couldn't explain that to Joe because he didn't know enough of the back story and I couldn't explain it to the attorney because she knew far too much. So I simply shrugged and said:

"I've got a lot of stuff there that I'd have to pack up."

"I'll help you pack it up," he shrugged. "Then you can sell the place, pay your dad back and clear your conscience." He looked up and smiled slightly at the end to let me know he was kidding— sort of.

"That's the thing about drummers," the student observed later that night, laying down in the soggy field and looking at the stars. "They don't beat around the bush. They're very direct and to the point."

"Oh yes," the attorney agreed, but she was rolling her eyes. "Mickey was nothing if not an expert in the economy of speech."

"Oh gag me. Who even cares about drummers anyway?" the teenager yawned.

The student, the attorney and I all looked at her with incredulity. "*You* do," we said in unison.

"Does the name Dan Polanski ring a bell?" the student asked.

"Why are you always teasing me about Dan Polanski?" the teenager asked defensively. "He's a total stoner and I don't like him. I like Jason Bernard."

"Jason Bernard," the attorney repeated, laughing. "I had forgotten about him."

"At least her story's consistent," the student replied, smiling.

As usual, the little girl was the only one not in on the joke, but she didn't seem to mind. She paced the edge of the crevice deep in thought. When I told her I had finally located the infamous gulch, she had temporarily traded in all whining about riding bikes for a new mantra: "When are we going to go to the gulch?" Lucky for her, I couldn't sleep after Joe's offhand suggestion that I just pack my things and sell the condo. In fact, I couldn't sit still. So I left a note for Jack and went for a midnight walk with my four ghosts following close behind. Somehow the whole gang had ended up right there, at the gulch's edge.

The gulch had been carved by a ribbon of stream and was about twenty feet deep. Jack once told the little girl that it was originally dug by settlers trying to divert water to their land, but it looked far too wild and craggy for that story to be true. It was smaller than I had remembered, but still too wide to jump across. As an adult, it looked possible (albeit difficult) to simply climb down the rocks, splash through the water, and climb back up the other side, but the little girl would have nothing to do with this suggestion.

"We can't go *down* there," she cried as she tossed a rock into the water.

"Why not?" I asked.

She grunted in exasperation. "Because that's where the gravity is."

"That's right," the attorney said, turning to me. "You see, it's not back in Seattle after all."

I didn't respond. She looked away.

"You're not going back, are you?" she finally asked.

"I'll be the first to admit it's not what we had in mind," I said. "But I think I could make a life out of this."

The corners of her mouth turned down, but she nodded. "I suppose you could."

The little girl interrupted us with rabid scratching at her head.

"What's the matter?" the attorney asked her.

"These braids are itching me," she said.

"That's because you never let anyone take them out and brush them," the attorney explained. "Come here. I know how to do it the way you like."

The little girl reluctantly sat down and let the attorney rebraid her hair. The attorney was right; the reason they were so mangy was because the little girl refused to take them out and wash her hair and let Jack yank his way through the resulting tangles with his black comb. Initially, the little girl had refused to bathe altogether, and she got away with it for awhile. But then Jack gave her some fancy bubble bath that used to belong to her mommy and which she was normally not allowed to use, so she made a concession on the condition that she didn't have to take the braids out. The bubble bath came in a bottle that looked like champagne, but it wasn't champagne, it was only pretend. The little girl knew this for a fact, because she drank a little just to make sure and it tasted like dishwashing soap, which, for reasons I don't entirely understand, she had also sampled on a prior occasion.

And then there was the McDonald's issue, which Sarita had thoughtlessly mentioned to Alex. On their way home from the hospital that one night, Jack asked the little girl what she wanted for dinner and, being six years old, she naturally chose McDonald's. Jack stopped at the drive-thru and bought her a Happy Meal. The next night, Jack asked her what she wanted to eat and, again, she said McDonald's because, being six years old, it was really the only restaurant she knew. Jack bought her another Happy Meal and even went back in the restaurant and asked to switch out the prizes because the little girl had gotten the exact same one as the night before. Mommy had never allowed the little girl to eat at McDonald's on two different occasions so close together that she risked getting the same prize. Yet from that night on, the little girl and Jack ate dinner at McDonald's until she was no longer a little girl. The prizes piled up so high, she didn't care about them anymore. She gave them to friends, strangers, the school bus driver and even her bossy cousin Libby. The only one she kept was the one she got on that first night, back when going to McDonald's was a treat rather than a chore. It was a plastic figurine of Grimace, the McDonaldsland character who's a big purple blob.

In retrospect, "Grimace" was an unfortunate name for a prize given to a child only hours after losing her mother.

"What's gotten into you?" I asked the attorney after the younger ghosts had fallen asleep that night. "You're mothering the little girl and you haven't yelled at the teenager for days."

She shrugged her shoulders as if she had no idea what I was talking about. "Not everyone needs to be melodramatic all of the time."

The student rolled her eyes. "Seriously, what gives?"

"Fine," the attorney sighed. "A few weeks ago, when the tyke was talking about her mommy and how she's up in Heaven, it kind of got to me. So I decided to make an effort to be more sympathetic. So sue me."

"Do you believe in Heaven?" I asked her.

The attorney raised her eyebrows. "Are you asking me or asking yourself?"

"I don't know," I said. "I suppose it's the same thing, right?"

"Well, the way I see it, some people have the luxury of choosing whether or not to believe in a heaven." She took a deep breath as she watched the little girl sleeping on the window seat. "Those of us who lost parents as children do not."

I nodded in agreement. It is the same reason the lower class plays the lottery when, of all people, they are the ones who can afford to gamble the least.

"I have a favor to ask you," I said.

"What's that?" she asked.

"Will you go on a scooter ride with me?"

"That's her thing," the attorney said dismissively, waving her hand towards the student. "Ask her."

"Oh, I'm coming," the student assured her. "I have to remind her how to drive the beast."

"But we need you there, too," I said.

"Why?"

"For moral support."

"Since when do you need *my* support?" she asked.

"Since I first changed out of my jammies," I reminded her. "I haven't done a thing without you since then."

"Those contraptions barely fit two people. It's illegal to drive them with three."

"Good thing two of us are ghosts," I shrugged. "I'm sure you can make it work."

For all her huffing and puffing, the attorney seemed genuinely flattered.

She made good on her promise two days later when we all heard Joe revving the Vespa's engine in the driveway. I put the student's old black helmet on and headed out the garage with the attorney and the student in tow. The helmet smelled like patchouli oil. The little girl saw us and immediately ran for the old, rusted Strawberry Shortcake bike.

"Well, I took it around the block a few times and everything seemed to work," Joe said. "Are you sure you don't want me to ride with you the first time, just in case anything happens?"

"No," I said. "But keep your cell phone on unless I have to call you to come pick me up or take me to the emergency room."

Joe laughed. "I thought you used to ride this thing all the time."

"I did, but it was a million years ago."

"It will all come back when you're on it."

I hopped on the seat and positioned myself. With the scooter on the center stand, my feet wouldn't reach the ground.

"Remember, you have to take it off the stand before you hop onto the seat," the student instructed. I nodded, stepped down and pushed forward to roll the scooter off of the stand. It took me a few tries and I felt like a dork. When it finally worked, I almost dropped the thing as I forgot how heavy 200-odd pounds could feel. Joe had to reach out and grab one of the handles until I steadied myself.

All my fumbling made Joe look a little worried. Then Jack came outside to watch the show too, making me feel like a child whose training wheels had just been removed from her bicycle.

"Are you ready?" Joe asked.

I nodded, and hopped back on the seat, leaning the scooter far to the right so that the tip of my right foot could touch the ground.

"I think so."

The two ghosts hopped on the back. The student sat directly behind me, her arms wrapped around my waist. Due to the constraints of her pencil skirt, the attorney sat side-saddle behind the student, holding onto the student's waist with one hand and maintaining a firm grip on the rear rack with the other.

Jack stood back and folded his arms.

"Have fun, kiddo," he said.

I gave a twist on the gas and the engine revved, but we didn't go anywhere.

"You have to let go of the brake," the student said. I followed her instructions, but let up on the brake too fast, and the scooter shot down the driveway like a bat out of hell. Instinctively, I let go of the gas, but then we quickly slowed to the point that I had to swerve side to side so as not to go down. I put my right foot on the driveway again and could see Joe walking towards me in the side mirror.

I held up a hand to stop him. "Don't worry, I've got it," I said. Then I started again.

This time it was smoother, and I headed down the long driveway to the end of Jack's property and took a quick right turn onto the street. The rushing air pulled my cheeks back and caused the hair out the back of my helmet to fly all over the place.

The student spat some of my hair out of her mouth. "Next time, wear a pony tail," she yelled over the roar of the wind and the buzzing of the little two-stroke engine.

I reached up with my left hand and tucked my hair in the back of my shirt. It took a very long time as I was loathe to move too quickly and lose my balance, like when a gymnast does a handstand on the balance beam.

In my left mirror I could see a car approaching that seemed to be moving faster than the speed of sound. I edged to the very right of the road and again, carefully, waved it past me. When it did, it must have been going ninety miles an hour as I was sure I was at least going seventy. Then I looked down at my speedometer, which registered at a measly thirty-five. It just felt like seventy.

Soon, the little girl had caught up with us on her bicycle. The teenager was riding on the handlebars. Despite all the extra weight, the little girl didn't seem to have any trouble managing the speed even though such would have been impossible were she not a ghost. The forceful wind only exaggerated her gigantic smile and made the red and pink streamers on her handlebars flutter like crazy.

We approached some curves in the road and I grew tense. "Remember," the student yelled, "it's better to think of it as pushing down on the handlebars, rather than steering them like a car." I followed her advice and pushed the handlebar and my bodyweight down to the left, and then to the right. We clung to the curves with ease. "Woo-hoo!" the student shouted, holding her arms up in the air like a mischievous juvenile on a roller coaster. She fluttered her fingers in the wind. In my right mirror, I could see the attorney lift her hand off the rear rack for a split second and do the same thing.

We got to the stop sign at the end of the road. "Where should we go?" I asked the ghosts.

"Anywhere," the little girl said. "Just don't turn back yet."

None of the ghosts had worn a helmet, which I suppose was okay given their phantasmic nature. The student's slightly greasy hair looked like a lion's mane, and wisps of the attorney's hair had come undone from her bun.

The attorney smoothed out her hair but said, "We've come this far. We might as well go through downtown."

Downtown Commerce was a single street, Commerce Avenue, that housed a series of narrow storefronts in old buildings. There had been a bit of an effort to restore the area, and so it was filled with coffee shops and boutique clothing stores that didn't require a mall to survive. The traffic and stop signs on the Avenue permitted us to slow down a bit. I had forgotten how much riding the scooter was a full assault on all five senses.

A car is a cocoon, but you're really outside on a scooter. You have no choice but to listen to the jackhammering of the construction workers, the kids talking in the crosswalk while you are stuck at a light and, most of all, your own obnoxiously loud motor sputtering away the whole time. You feel the wind and you have to adjust your balance to accommodate every bump in the road. If it is hot, you feel the heat. If it is cold, you feel the chill in the air. You taste the exhaust from the car in front of you whether you want to or not.

But the most noticeable difference is the smells. We drove past the bakery and could tell a batch of sourdough had just come out of the oven. We could smell the deep fryer before we even saw the diner. As it was spring, we could smell the blossoms on all the trees as they wafted down all around us. I looked in my mirrors and saw the ghosts both had blossoms stuck in their hair.

When we got to the end of the Avenue, I cut through the narrow streets of old homes surrounding it. When I was a kid, they were always in a state of disrepair, but the commuter crowd had begun snatching them up and renovating them. We made our way back to the highway, and this time I didn't have to move over for the other cars; this time, I held my own at a higher speed.

I pulled into Jack's driveway and raced the little girl through the trees towards the house. Jack and Joe were still standing there, waiting for me. I wondered what they had talked about, then figured they hadn't talked at all. Men tolerate silence far better than women.

I came to a stop and planted my right foot firmly on the ground, demonstrating the improved balance I had gained in only twenty minutes. The ghosts dismounted first, after which I tried to put the scooter back on its center stand. Despite Joe's oiling attempts, it was still pretty stubborn, and he finally had to come over and help me.

I took off the smelly helmet and tussled my matted hair.

The ghosts were out of breath.

"Admit it," the little girl said, beaming. "That was fun!"

"It was fun," I said, nodding.

"Glad to hear it," Joe said.

The attorney had a huge smile on her face. "It was," she agreed. "For a minute I thought I was Audrey Hepburn, cruising through the streets of Rome." Commerce was most undeserving of her comparison, but the student certainly got it.

"That's the ultimate Vespa high," the student said, "when you lapse into the *Roman Holiday* fantasy."

The attorney took a step forward, but she was shaky from the ride and almost lost her footing in her heels. Still smiling, she reached up behind her head and began plucking bobby pins out, one by one. The student and I watched the transformation, mesmerized. Once all the pins were removed, the attorney shook out a luxurious mane of hair. She smiled again, and looked straight into the sun.

"You're in a trance," Jack said, breaking my fixation on the attorney and her long hair.

"It was fun," I said again. "Joe, thanks so much for fixing it."

"It was worth all the work just to see that smile," Joe said.

I didn't even realize how hard I had been smiling until he said that, until I purposely relaxed my cheeks and they ached.

"You look ten years younger," Jack said. "Maybe I should take a ride on that scooter."

I smiled again and looked back at the ghosts to gauge their reaction to all the compliments.

The student, with her wild, wind-blown hair, was still beaming. The teenager's skort was all twisted up, but she looked thrilled regardless. As for the little girl, she appeared as though her tiny body would burst at its seams with joy.

But the attorney was gone.

And I mean *gone.*

※

Chapter 11

MARCO & THE CLAY THROWERS

APPARENTLY I WASN'T THE ONLY PERSON who admired the magnificently tragic singing of one straw-haired, muffin-topped woman named Starene. A television producer who shared my particular sense of fameworthiness decided to give Starene a regular segment on a third-rate entertainment news show. I spent the latter part of the spring eagerly awaiting the lifetime achievement accolades this particular producer would no doubt receive at the next awards ceremony.

Starene's new job consisted of chasing down lesser celebrities at well-known West Hollywood eateries with a camera crew in tow. Starene would then, in her marvelously unrefined manner, confront the surprised starlet with any of the following embarrassing personal tidbits, as applicable: (a) the poor box-office returns of the starlet's latest film; (b) tales published by the starlet's roommate at a certain rehabilitation facility; or (c) compromising videotapes of the starlet that had made their way into the hands of nefarious DVD "distributors" operating out of the San Fernando Valley. In the beginning, the stunned expressions and bewildered responses of Starene's victims were voyeuristic gems. After a few weeks, however, Starene became so recognizable in her own right that everyone just smirked a little when they saw her coming and delivered a canned response. The interesting thing was that they never ran away. The Starene blitz had become a Hollywood badge of honor.

For all our differences, the student, the teenager, the little girl and I each got a big kick out of Starene's successful rise to stardom in light of the many forces working against her. But if the attorney had been there, she would have hated it.

"What happened to her anyway?" the little girl asked.

"She let her hair down and disappeared," I said.

"How?"

"I don't know."

"Maybe it was the bobby pins that were holding her together all along," the student suggested.

Indeed, there were no more bobby pins, pearl earrings, patent heels or top-stitched suits. Nobody asked about Seattle anymore. Nobody harped about how thirty-one year-olds aren't supposed to live in their father's house in a deadbeat town. Nobody went by "esquire" here. Rather, the fun factor of our life had significantly increased in her absence. We stayed out late with Melissa and went to watch Joe's band play. We buzzed around town on the Vespa if we had the slightest craving for a popsicle or a cupcake or just the wind in our face. We combined her designer clothes into crazy mismatched outfits in which she wouldn't have been caught dead, despite her ghostly nature.

And yet we missed her. We were funny like that.

As it turned out, we missed Joe, too. With the Vespa in working order, neither he nor his drummer's biceps had reason to spend long afternoons in Jack's garage anymore. The only time we saw him was if I was invited to accompany Melissa to watch his band play and possibly to hang out afterwards.

The student was the first one to come right out and say it:

"That Joe is kind of cute."

The ghosts and I were sleeping out on the old trampoline in Jack's backyard. It was only May and therefore a bit cold still, but we had taken to doing that lately.

The teenager and I exchanged uneasy glances at the student's statement. "But Joe is Melissa's boyfriend," the teenager ventured.

The student shook her head. "I'm not so sure they're exclusive."

"You're not?" I asked.

"No. Melissa still flirts with tons of guys even when Joe is around. Remember the night Alex was here?"

"But that's just Melissa," the teenager explained.

"It's not high school anymore," the student said. "She can't call dibs on *everybody*. Besides, they're a complete mismatch of a couple."

"But she's our friend."

The student laughed out loud and I smiled. "Oh, she's not *my* friend," the student said, "and she shouldn't be yours either, especially when it comes to drummers."

"Beggars can't be choosers," the teenager warned. "If it weren't for Melissa, who else would she hang out with?"

The student flicked a strand of grass in the air before turning to me. "You can hang out with whomever you want, but if it were up to me, I would pick just Joe."

I smiled. "I'll file that one under easier said than done for now."

"Thank goodness," the teenager sighed.

The student shrugged. "Whatever."

But the unspoken irony was that it was the teenager's fault we all liked Joe in the first place. She could have saved us a lifetime of Mickeys if she had just resisted the urge to take art as an elective in the tenth grade. Everyone knew that "art" was simply the study hall of choice for stoners—everyone except, it seemed, the teenager. By the time she realized the bulk of the class consisted of people throwing clay or breaking colored pencils while Mrs.

Lankershim pretended not to notice, it was too late to transfer into choir. So the teenager made an effort to draw still-lifes and self-portraits and otherwise fulfill the assignments which, as time wore on, it appeared were only given to her. Mrs. Lankershim was quick to pick up on the fact that the teenager had a hunger for rules and regulation and she did what she could to appease it amidst the art class anarchy.

The infamous Dan Polanksi was affiliated with the clay-throwers, yet for Dan, clay-throwing was a spectator sport. Dan never did a single assignment and didn't seem to care a whit about his grade. He just sat there watching his friends throw clay while he absent-mindedly drummed his hands on the table. Every once in a while, he would bring actual drum sticks and beat them on the table until Mrs. Lankershim said "Mr. Polanski?" and he would stop. Dan and Mrs. Lankershim seemed to have some sort of understanding: he didn't have to do anything so long as he did absolutely nothing. Art was the only class Dan Polanski wasn't failing. Dan was a junior and had somehow gotten away with taking art all three years.

Dan's brown hair extended down to his chin and, if he were a girl, it would have been called a bob. Sometimes Dan wore his hair in a small ponytail fastened by an elastic band bummed off a girl in another class, but most of the time it was down and a little stringy. Dan's friend Marco had the same haircut and the same schedule. On the first day of class, Marco quickly identified the teenager as an easy target. One of Marco's favorite pastimes was fashioning primitive, anatomically-correct objects out of the clay. He would make a big to-do out of wrapping his work in notebook paper and comic strips and he would give it to the teenager as a present and the whole clay-throwing, pencil-breaking gang would explode in laughter when she unwrapped a new set of clay boobs or the like. The experience was the closest the teenager would ever come to truly identifying with Libby. Her cheeks would turn red, but she would set her mouth in a pout and return her focus to the assignment at hand. As Melissa Matthews' best friend, she took comfort in the fact that there was little they could do to harm her outside of class.

"What's your name?" Marco finally asked her one day.

"What do you care?" the teenager asked, never removing her eyes from her sketch pad.

"I'm getting a new tattoo. It's a heart and some angels and I'm going to have your name put on it, but I need to know it first."

This produced howls of laughter from the clay-throwing galley.

"Why would you get a tattoo devoted to someone whose name you don't even know?"

"Because I'm madly in love with you. I wanna have forty babies—"

"I think her name's Samantha," Dan piped up.

The teenager couldn't help it: she looked up from her work at Dan Polanski. It was the first time she could remember him saying anything in class.

"It's Sam," she corrected him.

"My mistake," Dan said. He wasn't wearing a hat, but he made a motion that was halfway between a tip of his hat and a lazy salute. For some reason, that unidentifiable gesture made him seem slightly more civilized than his comrades.

The moment passed. For one glorious minute, Marco found himself on the other end of the teasing stick as the clay-throwers ruminated on the implications of a guy walking around with an "I love Sam" tattoo.

A few weeks later, Marco approached the teenager and informed her that he had penned her portrait during class. It was a crudely-drawn picture of a woman that bore little resemblance to the teenager on account of the latter being nearly flat-chested and so fully clothed. Yet to eradicate any doubt as to his subject,

Marco had also drawn an arrow pointing to the woman with a bubble that said "Samm."

As ridiculous as the picture was, and as ridiculous as it was for the teenager to expect anything more, she was seriously hurt and ashamed.

"Knock it off, Marco," Dan chastised.

"Dude, I was just—"

"I said knock it off. What are you, twelve or something? The joke is old, okay?"

Marco slinked away. The teenager sat there for a long time, frozen, wondering if she should thank Dan, wondering if it was the kind of thing for which thanks are due. But then the bell rang and she just walked out without saying anything.

The next day, Dan sat in the seat right next to hers, and he stayed there for the rest of the semester. Marco never bothered her again.

But the ghost of the teenager was loathe to remember such details as we all huddled under the blankets and looked up at the Oregon sky.

"Why are we sleeping out here again?" she asked.

"Cause it's fun," the little girl said.

"Go back inside if you want to," the student offered. But we all knew that would never happen because the teenager, more than anything, hated to be alone. It is why she hid under the bed of the pink room rather than under someone else's bed in China. "But you'll miss so much in that plain old bed," the student continued. "Here, we can experience the world at the same time we're sleeping."

"Like multitasking," I said.

"I hate that phrase," the student shuddered. "But yeah, something like that."

The ghosts and I slept outside because it smelled of spring, because it made some of us young again, because inside wasn't big enough to hold us anymore and because sleeping outside wasn't really sleeping at all. Jack, on the other hand, preferred to sleep inside. He just rolled his eyes at me these days due to my ghost-inspired antics. I had taken up jogging in the rain and playing the student's old CDs really loud in the pink bedroom with the door shut while I drafted documents for Alex. At times, it seemed said antics made Jack a little worried. But he was less worried than he had been six months prior, and so he just accepted it and rolled his eyes now and again. At least he didn't put his face in his hands anymore.

Of course, it was Alex who paid the real price of our sleep deprivation. Although Alex was technically my boss, I had the hardest time viewing him as anything more than a peer or co-worker. I took his morning calls outside in a heap of wet blankets and ghosts and fully disclosed the details of an evening spent on the trampoline, something I would have never confided in one of the partners at Wallace. For his part, Alex didn't seem to mind my unconventional schedule so long as I got the work done and provided a listening ear for the personality differences he sometimes had with clients. As for the work, drafting the same type of contracts again and again seemed criminally easy in light of my recent stint at the call center, but Alex reminded me that it was only easy due to my fluency in legalese. As for the clients, I was just very grateful I didn't have to deal with them myself. My experience at Wallace and Kennedy had taught me that most clients are determined to shoot themselves in the foot, at least from a legal standpoint, and then they huff, puff, whine and shout when you try to talk them out of it.

Alex feigned jealousy of my ability to sleep outdoors on the trampoline. He was a Seattle native and claimed to have never lived in anything other than an apartment his entire life. As a kid, he always wanted a big trampoline, but the largest piece of outdoor space he had ever owned was the balcony of his current place, which was too small to house a big trampoline. Still, I got a big kick out of the mental image of Alex in his cargo shorts jumping up and down on a high-rise trampoline in the middle of the Seattle sky.

If the little girl had followed my thought process, it might have occurred to her that if we chained the old trampoline to the Vespa and towed it to the edge of the gulch, we might figure out a way to successfully catapult ourselves over it. But she was off in her own six-year-old world, thinking her six-year-old thoughts.

"I wish you could remember what happened to her," she said without explanation, "cause the thing is, I sorta need her help."

"Whose help?" I asked.

"I think she's talking about the lawyer again," the teenager said.

The attorney—she had only been gone for three crazy weeks and I was already starting to forget she had ever existed.

"Why do you need *her*?" the student asked, the disgust apparent in her tone.

"Well, I know she was a meanie most of the time," the little girl said sheepishly, "but she was pretty smart and I need someone to figure out how to get over that gulch."

"What are you talking about?" I asked.

"*We're* smart," the student offered.

"We're totally smart," the teenager agreed.

"But I need someone who's *really* smart," the little girl sighed, "and who's not busy talking about boys all the time. And the mean lady didn't care about boys, except for that one boy Alex, but only because she wanted to get some more money so she could go back to her house and buy some more shoes."

We didn't fight her on this. The other ghosts and I realized the little girl would only acknowledge our collective intelligence once she accepted the fact that the attorney was gone. And the other ghosts and I knew that the true meaning of "gone" always managed to elude the little girl. Exhibit A: that one time that little Libby and the little girl had a sleepover and watched *Old Yeller.*

"The dog died," Libby observed at the end of it, as if it wasn't obvious.

"I know," the little girl said, rolling her eyes.

"Like your mom."

The little girl hadn't made that connection before. She was always a little sad when the dog died, but secretly fantasized that now the boy could get a new dog, and maybe a white one with curly hair and pink bows, which, in her humble opinion, would be a slight improvement on the yellow one. But the little girl wasn't looking to upgrade her mommy—there was no such thing as a better version unless maybe it was the exact same mommy only not so sick.

As she worked these thoughts through her head, the little girl nodded pensively. By force of habit, and with nothing else to say, she recited her catch phrase: "Yeah, Mommy died. She had cancer."

Libby's eyes grew wide, crazy with the kind of horrified curiosity with which one drives by the scene of a gruesome car accident. "I know," she whispered, as if she were launching into a ghost story. "And she's never coming back."

"Nope," the little girl agreed, reveling in her cousin's pity, "probably not for a really long time."

Libby's eyebrows darted toward one another at hearing this. The voice of reverence was replaced with her usual, obnoxiously authoritative tone. "No, Sam—not ever! Once people die, they don't come back."

"Well..." the little girl thought again about how her mommy was lying in a box somewhere and how Snow White was also in a box for awhile but then later she got out of it and married the prince. "I think sometimes they do come back."

"No! They don't!"

The little girl didn't know where Libby was getting her information from, but she was pretty sure they were questionable sources at best. Snow White, Sleeping Beauty—pretty much all of history's finest princesses had come back from the dead to be with people they loved. Surely then mommy would come back to be with her. It occurred to the little girl that perhaps Aunt Sarita had told Libby that dead people don't return because she herself had no intention of returning for Libby but didn't want to hurt her daughter's feelings. Feeling a little sorry for her soon-to-be-abandoned-yet-bossy cousin, the little girl just rolled her eyes and said, with both confidence and condescension, "I'm pretty sure my mommy is going to come back for me."

"You're wrong, Sammy. How many dead people do you know?"

"Don't be a smarty-pants, Libby."

"Just tell me how many dead people you know."

"None."

"That's not true, you know one—your mom. But I know more, because my Grandpa Billingsley died and my Great-Grammy died and a girl in my class at school is gone and nobody knows where she is and these policemen named Officer Ron and the other one came and they talked to us and they said that maybe she died, too. And trust me, none of them ever came back."

"Maybe they did only you don't know that because they didn't come to see you."

"What?!"

"I'm just saying, maybe you were too bossy around them."

"That's crass! Mom!" Libby stood up, still half-wearing her Garfield sleeping bag. "Mom—"

Aunt Sarita rounded the corner, dishrag in hand. "Stop shouting, Libby—I'm just in the next room."

"Mom, tell Sammy that once people die they don't come back anymore. She thinks that her mom is going to come back—"

"Libby!" Aunt Sarita shrieked as she swatted the girl across the mouth with her dishrag.

Libby stumbled backward at the impact, however soft.

It took Aunt Sarita a moment to catch her breath. "Libby," she finally said, "How dare you! What did we talk about?"

Libby looked bewildered. "But I was just explaining—"

"You go to your room. Now. For the rest of the night."

"But the peach cobbler—"

"Samantha can have your share."

Sarita tactfully tucked the dishrag in her back pocket before turning to the little girl. "How would you like a double helping, sweetie?"

The little girl licked her lips. She probably wasn't capable of eating a double helping, but she sure liked the idea of it and the whole deal was made sweeter because she knew it would make Libby mad. "Yes please, Auntie."

Her syrupy good manners were the last straw for Libby. Libby's lip quivered. "It's not fair," she whimpered, "I was just telling the truth."

At that point, Libby started to tear up and, in a misguided effort to avoid further embarrassment, she awkwardly ran up the stairs, tripped twice on her sleeping bag in the process, stumbled into her bedroom and slammed her door so hard that it popped wide open, revealing her small frame sobbing face down into a pillow on her bed with her nightgown hitched up just enough that, through the spindles of the banister, the little girl could see the training pants underwear which, at age eight, Libby still had to wear at night. The little girl mentally congratulated herself on her understanding of death (as confirmed by Sarita's reaction to Libby's theory) as well as her superior bladder control. The cousins didn't speak to each other for the rest of the night, but they made up in the morning over reheated peach cobbler and cartoons.

No matter the insult or nature of our differences, Libby and I always made up. This was largely due to the fact that I was usually the one in the wrong and Libby had the loyal and forgiving nature of a golden retriever. It only took a few days after that last disastrous dinner for Libby to completely forget that I had ever quit my job at the call center with a mere sixteen hours' notice or that Melissa had attempted to resurrect the humiliation that only Libby could find in being elected Homecoming Queen.

Although I was undeserving of Libby's generously short memory, I paid for it by extending the same to Melissa. By and large, the Melissa of now was more mature and less conniving than the high-school version the teenager had known—with the occasional, minor slip-up. Although the student was willing to hold a grudge against her for misdeeds past, I generally sided with the teenager, who was not. I was grateful for a friend who commiserated with my third-life crisis despite the fact that hers didn't seem to have knocked her out of her green platform shoes and into an ergonomic chair at the call center the way mine had. For this reason, I was inclined to turn a blind eye to any attractiveness Joe might hold given Melissa's involvement with him.

"But it's quid pro quo," the student argued. "Joe for Dan."

When the teenager and Dan Polanski first started talking in art class, it was forced conversation about the teenager's artwork. After a few weeks, the discussion extended to school, friends and even dead parents. Dan told the teenager all about his band, in which he was the drummer. He asked her if she had ever listened to the Cure. She hadn't, so he made her a mix tape full of songs sung by Englishmen in eyeliner. At first she didn't like it because it was so different than the Top 40 music she danced to with Melissa and the rest of the junior varsity cheer squad, but she forced herself to listen to it anyway because it sounded the way Dan looked. By the one hundredth playback, it was her absolute favorite tape on the planet.

But although the teenager and Dan were good friends in art class, it was as if they didn't know each other beyond the door to Mrs. Lankershim's room. Commerce High was a small school and they would frequently cross paths in the hallways, the locker bays, the center solarium and the cafeteria, but they would do so without making eye contact or exchanging a word, each person traveling in the bubble of his or her own social circle.

Until the spring basketball game against Sherman Valley High, that is. By then, the teenager had been elected junior class president for the coming year and had made the varsity cheer squad and therefore had a double duty to attend the game. More importantly, it was also a big night for Melissa, who was named the sophomore class "princess" on the prom court and had to participate in the prom-themed halftime ceremonies. Melissa and the teenager stood under the bleachers and fixed Melissa's hair and makeup while her "prince," Jason Bernard, impatiently tapped his foot several yards away. Also nearby was a group of hooligans, greasers, punks, what have you, which were commonly referred to as "stoners" at the time. The stoners looked towards the two cheerleaders and snickered at their primping.

Melissa turned toward the group and shot them a dirty look. "We can hear you," she said.

This only resulted in high-pitched taunts of "We can hear you" from the huddled mass of black t-shirts and Vans sneakers.

The teenager rolled her eyes at the group, but in the process she locked on a familiar head of bobbed brown hair and smiling eyes. A certain boy without a hat nonetheless made a gesture halfway between tipping his hat and a lazy salute.

"Hey, Sam," he said.

"Hi, Dan," the teenager nervously responded as she tugged Melissa's arm and pulled her away.

"Who was that?" Melissa demanded once they were back in the benign company of his royal highness Jason.

"Just the guy I sit next to in fifth period," the teenager shrugged.

"Are you friends with him or something?"

"Not really—I mean, we talk and stuff," the teenager responded, just as surprised at her answer as Melissa was. "So, I don't know . . . I guess we kind of are."

I guess we kind of are. Those words, however ill-phrased, were ammunition stored in Melissa's mental armory. It was the only thing the teenager would ever say to Melissa regarding Dan Polanski, but it proved to be more than enough.

The ghosts and I were shaking the leaves off the blankets when my cell phone dropped to the ground. As I bent to pick it up, the student grabbed my shoulder.

"At least give him a call," she dared.

"What on earth would I say?"

"That's easy. Say there's a problem with the Vespa. The scooter has always been boy bait."

"What makes you think he'd rather hang out with me than Melissa anyway?"

"Also easy—you're the kind of girl who traded her Mercedes in for a Vespa."

"He probably won't like you," the teenager warned, "but you shouldn't risk it anyway."

"Dan Polanski," the student urged. "Quid pro quo."

As I pushed the "talk" button, my heart fluttered and I couldn't help but feel a bit like Starene: a veritable cave woman on the prowl, ready to pounce on her beautiful yet unwitting prey. But Joe actually bought the story about the "funny noise" the Vespa was making and asked me to swing by the shop during his lunch break so we could ride around awhile and determine what the problem was and then grab a bite to eat. As the student was quick to notice, he didn't invoke Melissa the way a good boyfriend would, as in ". . . and

I'll call Melissa and see if she wants to join us." In fact, he never mentioned her once.

By the time the call was over, I still felt like Starene, only in an entirely different way: I felt like a straw-haired nobody whom fate had just hammered into the big time, if only to play a practical joke on the universe.

✳

Chapter 12

SECOND VERSE, SAME AS...

By virtue of her position in life, the student was constantly surrounded by people: roommates, classmates, fellow customers at the student union, her coworkers at the library, the regulars at the bars she frequented, etc. This fact distinguished her experience from that of the rest of the ghosts, who were either only children or single women living alone. The odd thing is that it made her a bit of a loner. What you already have you don't think you need so much. As a result, the student was never content with the rather rich and frothy cup she had been handed in life. She was always looking to top it off with that something more or something else that she was convinced was out there waiting for her, although she would have been hard-pressed to define it.

So it was that day as she walked up University Way towards the bookstore. If it hadn't been such an exceptionally sunny afternoon, she probably wouldn't have done it. But it was sunny and the sun caused the chrome trim on the old orange scooter to positively gleam, blinding her to the tear in the vinyl seat and the rust on the rims of the wheels. It was illegally parked on the sidewalk and clumsily chained to a tree with the words "for sale" grease-penned on the skirt of the rear wheel, but as it stood there, it whispered promises of romance and adventure, promises a mere object could never keep. The student should have realized this, but it was love at first sight, so she blocked any initial doubts by bolting a mental door shut.

Mind you, if you are going to go to the trouble of falling in love with a vehicle, you should probably avoid doing so when it is parked. If the student had only seen it in action, she might have realized a classic Italian scooter is as loud as a riding lawnmower and has about the same amount of get-up-and-go on a hill. If she had only taken it for a test drive, she might have recognized its wheels were no bigger than those on Jack's wheelbarrow and were therefore destined to lose any battle waged against a Seattle pot-hole. If she had only observed its owner taking the bus on rainy days, it might have occurred to her that a scooter is not a practical form of transportation in a city known for its wet weather.

Within a five-minute period, the student went from someone who had never considered owning a scooter to a rabid Vespa fan. She skipped her sociology class and sat on a brick retaining wall eating yogurt, waiting for the owner to come out. When he finally did, she should have asked him about the history of the scooter and why he was selling it, but she didn't. No, the student asked only one question that day: "How much?" He wanted $1200 but she talked him down to $950 and patted herself on the back for doing so without wondering why he didn't put up more of a fight. They walked together to the on-campus bank where she withdrew money that was supposed to cover her expenses for the rest of the semester and he signed the title over to her in front of a notary public. Afterwards, they made their way back to the scooter where he showed her how to kick start the darn thing, gave her the key to the bicycle chain, told her to buy a helmet and walked away.

She didn't immediately go home. Rather, she went to a pay phone and enrolled with the first insurance company she located in the phone book. It was the only smart thing she did that day aside from accepting the advice of a biker gang. Next, she walked to the financial aid office and applied for an emergency short-term student loan. She continued on to the library where she signed up for some extra shifts, after which she remained in the library to meet with a study group. During the study session, she forced the keys to the scooter and the bicycle lock onto the small ring that held the key to her apartment as well as one to Jack's house. She looked down at the now overcrowded set of keys and felt like a bit like a janitor. If complications could be measured in keys, then in only two and a half hours, her life had grown twice as complicated The second thoughts settled in before she even had a chance to drive the thing for the first time which, by the way, was well after dark.

The student had never needed a car because her apartment was only four blocks from campus. Yet an hour and a half passed between the moment she removed the bicycle chain and when she finally parked the darn Vespa at her building. The first block was the most touch and go—it finally occurred to her that her very life depended on her successfully driving the scooter home and she was ill-prepared in experience and accoutrement. She was wearing dark clothing. She had only acrylic mittens for gloves. She had no helmet.

Five miles per hour felt like five million, and the wind was blowing at her from the right side which made her feel as though she would topple dead left if she didn't overcorrect. The first stop she came to was on an incline and no sooner had she planted the tip of her toe on the asphalt than the whole 250-odd pounds of metal and motor began to roll backwards against her. She had to lay it down on its side, still running, to prevent it from rolling right through her. She stood there just staring at the mess for several minutes before two bikers rolled up on their hogs. They helped her pick the Vespa back up and made her drive it about 400 feet out of her way into the parking lot of a convenience store. She was devastated at the momentous back-tracking this would cause, but didn't feel she was in a position to argue with the bikers given her present status as a damsel in distress, which she absolutely abhorred.

The bikers made her turn figure eights in the parking lot until she was more comfortable handling the scooter. They also taught her how to release the rear brake *after* twisting the gas a bit in order to avoid rolling back on the hill. In the interim, a handful of convenience store customers congregated to monitor her progress. When she successfully executed a particularly tight turn, they applauded. Then the bikers followed her to her apartment complex, scouted the best parking spot and laughed when she pulled out the bicycle chain. They told her it wasn't worth it to bother with the chain: if someone really wanted to steal it, they could and they would.

After the bikers roared off, she sat on the curb and stared at the Vespa for a long time, as if it would cease to be hers the minute she took her eyes off it. She couldn't sleep that night despite the fact that she was exhausted—it was just one of those days where she felt like a different person going to bed than she was when she woke up that morning. Despite her second thoughts about the financial burden and the unexpected driving lesson, the Vespa had, indeed, brought adventure to her life in the half day she had owned it: she was nearly bursting with adrenaline, she had hung out with bikers and her rapid progress had earned her a standing ovation at the convenience store.

Over the next few weeks, the student discovered there were other perks to using such a frivolous form of transportation. She could park it just about anywhere and it used very little gasoline. It was also a real attention-grabber, especially when it came to the type of boys who wore black concert t-shirts or dark-rimmed Buddy Holly glasses before they really came back in style. They would pull up alongside her, roll down their windows, and ask where she got it. She would come out to the parking lot to find a group of them gathered around it, guessing its year and arguing over whether it was actually manufactured in Italy or India. She got to know a few of these boys better and she would take them for rides on the Vespa, but only two did she ever let drive it.

One was named Mickey.

The other was named Joe.

I sat on the back of the scooter, arms locked tightly around Joe's waist as he rode the Vespa at the highest speeds it had ever known, trying to get to the bottom of the "funny noise" I had complained about. It was a fine illustration of what the student had always referred to as the "Matterhorn Effect"—namely, the fact that carpooling on a Vespa or in a Disneyland bobsled naturally involves more full-body contact than sharing the front seat of a sedan.

"Is that it?" Joe yelled over the roaring buzz of the engine.

"No—that's just the way it usually sounds."

We approached the one stop light marking the entrance to downtown. I noticed that a Department of Transportation crew was installing a left-turn light, Commerce's first.

"I don't know what to tell you," Joe said once we came to a stop.

"It was doing it this morning," I said.

"You probably picked up a rock or something that chinked around in the wheel well before getting spit out."

"So it fixed itself?"

"More like it was never broken in the first place."

I assumed Joe was calling me on the carpet for my lame attempt at five minutes of Matterhorn Effect. I've always been a firm believer that you shouldn't play crazy relationship games unless you're looking for a relationship with someone who's clueless, stupid or crazy himself. But I've also always believed that if you insist on playing, as many women do, you must play at an Olympic level—and needless to say, I was sorely out of practice that day I threw out the idiotic and has-been "funny noise" excuse. As far as the sport of dating of dating was concerned, I had been on the injured list for some time.

"But don't worry," Joe continued, patting the place where my hands were clenched together around him. "It's always better to check out a weird noise than to ignore it."

I found myself nodding as best as I could while wearing a helmet. Joe was right—I had acted both reasonably and prudently in reporting the noise.

"The RPP himself would approve," the student said when I recounted the conversation later that night.

"Duh, except the noise didn't even exist," the teenager scolded.

The teenager was sulking because the scooter ride had culminated in a long lunch at Roger's Roadside during which many topics were discussed but none of them were Melissa Matthews. That wasn't my fault—talking to the guy you would never guess he had a green platform-wearing, acrylic nail-flashing girlfriend. Joe spent half an hour ranking the french fries at every diner in town, but he never got around to Melissa.

"I thought they were dating, but now I'm not so sure," I said in my defense. "He never so much as said her name."

"Then *you* should have brought her up," the teenager said.

"Why?"

"Because by not doing it, you're just letting yourself get away without feeling guilty about sneaking behind your best friend's back."

"Oh grow up," the student sighed. "It was just lunch. Adults go to lunch together all the time and it doesn't mean they're going steady the way it did in high school. Nothing happened."

"Something did happen," the teenager argued. "Just going to lunch without at least inviting Melissa is something."

The student turned to me and threw her hands up in the air. "It's time to tell her about Dan Polanski," she insisted.

"We can't," I said, shaking my head. While the teenager's puritanical opinion was growing annoying, I knew her intentions were good and I saw no need to hurt her when the same was so easily avoided. "She'll never get over it."

"But *we* had to," the student bit back.

"And she'll never stop crying," the little girl offered.

I looked at her, surprised she was paying attention as she was so often in her own little world. "You don't even know the Dan Polanski story," I said.

"So what? I just know she's a big cry-baby," the little girl explained.

Sure enough, the teenager started tearing up at the mere accusation. "Forget about the lunch," she said, her lip quivering. "It was dinner that was the problem."

She was absolutely right. When I got back to Jack's house after lunch with Joe, he was in the backyard with Alex Martin pulling weeds.

"Alex!" I said, my voice a mix of surprise and confusion and a wee bit of embarrassment that I wasn't hard at work.

Alex waved a gloved hand at me. He was wearing gardener's gloves—Jack's gardener's gloves. "I'm so sorry to drop in on you like this, Sam. I had to meet a client this morning in Olympia, and I figured that as long as I was halfway here, I might as well swing by so we could knock out the Hutchinson articles of incorporation together."

"Oh, great idea," I said.

"I tried to call you, I swear."

"I was running an errand on my scooter. The thing is so loud, it drowns out the sound of my cell phone."

"You shouldn't talk on the phone while you're driving anyway," Jack said, shaking his head. The man didn't harbor many strong feelings or grudges, but those that he did ran deep. Unfortunately, people talking while driving was one of them due to a parking lot fender bender he once had with Sandy Michaels' seventeen-year-old daughter.

"I don't talk on the cell phone while riding the scooter, Dad," I said. "It's not even possible—it takes two hands to drive and my helmet covers my ears. I'm just saying, I still like to know when I've missed a call." I realized the last sentence created a misconception that I actually received a lot of calls outside of the work-related ones from Alex, which I did not. I left it out there anyway.

Alex and I spread our laptops and files across Jack's dining room table. "Welcome to my office," I said.

Alex had to bend over the stacks of china to plug in his computer. "It sure beats the setup in my apartment," he said. "I have a card table for a desk and I have to wear earplugs the whole time to drown out the sound of my roommate's stereo."

"You still have a roommate?"

Alex winced as he sat down at the table. "Yeah," he said sheepishly. "I know, I know… I need to grow up."

I couldn't help but giggle at the thought of this grown man, who had been pulling six figures for several years, shacking up with his college pal and using a card table for a desk. Alex covered his brow with his hand. "Is it really *that* bad?" he asked.

"How should I know?" I asked. "I'm living with my dad. I drive a scooter. You should see my room—it's decked out in pink gingham and has child-sized furniture and *Tiger Beat* centerfolds on the walls."

Alex smiled.

I couldn't help but think of all the desks and condos he had never purchased. "You must be loaded," I sighed.

"I am," he said as if he were confessing a sin. "I'm a loaded tightwad who just can't shake the feeling that he'll always be the nice but poor kid from the only part of Seattle that has more free clinics than coffee shops."

"It's better to be frugal. I learned that the hard way."

Alex shrugged. "To a point it is. But honestly, Sam … it's so bad that my resolution this past New Year was to cut Ramen noodles out of my diet."

I giggled again and he smiled, but he shook his head.

"Do you want to know what mine was?" I asked, my voice growing smaller as I realized what I was about to say.

"What?"

"To get out of bed."

It's a good thing the attorney ghost was long gone as she would have bit my head off for spilling all to one Alex Martin right there in front of the homeless china. But although Alex's eyes grew a little sad at the revelation, his smile never wavered. "We're pathetic," he said, laughing again.

Over the next several hours we tried to focus on Norm Hutchinson and the needs of his closely-held corporation, we did. But the mood was more high school study session than corporate attorney power meeting: about fifty percent work and fifty percent gossip. After every tangential conversation, Alex would stop and ask how long we had been off topic so he could adjust our bill accordingly. Regardless, he insisted on paying me for my full time. I had never been paid to chew the fat with someone in my Jack's dining room before. For a self-professed tightwad, Alex was certainly generous. I briefly regretted the many years wasted in knowing but not knowing each other.

"You Commerce women certainly have a type," he said.

"What do you mean?"

"Well, your friend's boyfriend—he's a dead ringer for that guy you were dating in law school."

"I can't believe you remember Mickey," I said. "You only met him that one time—"

"Well, that 'one time' was pretty memorable. It was the closest I've ever come to getting in a bar fight that didn't involve a major sports championship."

"Mickey could be a jerk," I conceded.

"And you were dating that jerk because...?"

Now it was my turn to wince. "Because he was a drummer."

Alex rolled his eyes. "Don't tell me you're one of those—"

"I'm over it now, I am," I said defensively, thinking back to my Matterhorn moment with Joe earlier in the day. "But yeah, for a while my drummer fetish was, shall we say, well-known. Even my cousin Libby—I think you've met her..."

"I certainly have," he nodded.

"One year in college I was home for the summer and Libby calls me up and tells me she's got this guy she wants to set me up with and she makes a big to-do over the fact that he's a drummer."

"Well, your preference must be legendary if even cousin Libby picked up on it."

"Exactly. The only problem was that this guy wasn't a drummer in a band, *per se*. He was a performance artist who went by the stage name 'The Human Metronome.'"

Alex burst out laughing. "*The Human Metronome?* That can't be real."

"Longest date of my life," I said, thinking of the poor student who had suffered through it.

"Is there a big market for performance art in Commerce?"

"No, there's absolutely no market for it. Commerce is still getting used to stadium seating at the movie theater. I don't think he made any money off his act—he did it free in the park or something until the cops chased him away."

"How did he survive?"

"Oh, he worked the graveyard shift at the call center."

"The call center?" Alex asked with a sour face. "Is that as dreadful as it sounds?"

I looked down at the papers, unsure how to answer. On the one hand, I was grateful that Alex had rescued me from a call cen-

ter career. On the other hand, the snobbishness towards such
work so characteristic of those in the legal profession might have
driven me there in the first place.

In the end, I didn't have to answer. "Then again, what do I
know?" Alex asked, backtracking in the face of my silence. "Before Wallace and Kennedy, I never worked a single job that didn't
require a rake."

As with all high school study sessions, ours eventually recessed
while we sought out fried foods. Because their french fries came
highly recommended, I suggested Roger's Roadside for dinner.
Alex insisted we take the scooter, and I insisted on driving it, and,
unlike a Mickey, he didn't argue the point. However, like most tall
guys who have legs long enough to do it, Alex kept putting his
feet down on the ground at stops, which was irritating. Apparently
he doubted my ability to balance the both of us as well as the
scooter on my very tippy toe. After the third time, I spanked his
knee and warned that if he was fond of his feet, he would keep
them on the passenger pegs at all times. I was still scolding him
about it after we parked the Vespa and walked into the Roadside
and nearly crashed into Melissa and Joe.

It's funny how, in an emergency, you can instantaneously de-
velop telepathic communication with a person you barely know.
Such was the case with Joe and me that night: we said worlds
more to each other in stolen glances than we had ever said out
loud before.

*Why on earth did you go to the same place for dinner as where you ate
lunch?* I asked him across the table while Melissa read her menu.
At Melissa's acrylic-nail-waving insistence, the four of us decided
to share a booth. I had never been on a double date/work meeting before, and it was a little awkward.

That's funny, Joe said with his eyebrows, *I was just about to ask
you the same thing.*

My boss wanted a hamburger and it was the first place I thought of.

Your "boss"? Do you take all your bosses for rides on the back of the Vespa that I worked so hard to rebuild?

That depends. Do you take all the women in your life to the same greasy diner?

And then he kicked me—playfully, in the leg, under the table—but it made a noise and caused me to scowl all the same. It was just a little kick and Melissa barely paused in her diatribe on the magnificently salty-sweet combination formed by milkshakes and french fries, but for some reason, the evening just wasn't the same after that kick. For one, Alex started blinking. Maybe he had something in his eyes or maybe he was tired, but he just wouldn't stop blinking those embarrassingly long lashes. For another, that kick had kick-started a heartbeat somewhere in the background. I could have sworn it was the student's as Joe was primarily her crush after all. But the student hadn't come along and I could hear the heartbeat in my own ears. I finally realized that, present or not, the student didn't have her own heartbeat anymore seeing as she was a ghost and all. That hussy was using mine.

The thing about drummers is that they are rhythmic in every aspect, and Joe was no exception. They talk in low staccato. They walk in a steady, even pace. If you are a person like me that feels a need to be grounded, a kite that needs someone to pull her string, then drummers are a very comforting bunch to be around, especially when they are wearing nice t-shirts. And after he kicked me, I happened to realize that Joe had donned a very nice t-shirt for the Roadside that evening.

"Sam knows exactly what I'm talking about," Melissa said.

I looked up from my menu, dizzy from my overactive heartbeat. "What?"

"About malt versus milkshake?" She turned back to Alex. "We always fought about that one in high school. Have you had their malts here, Sam?"

I scratched the back of my neck, thinking of the malt I had downed earlier in the afternoon but not necessarily wanting to open the doors to an admission that the only Roadside malt I had ever had was earlier in the afternoon. "Nope," I said. "Can't say that I have."

Melissa shrugged and resumed her one-woman show.

I looked across the table at Joe. *Does she know that we had lunch together?*

I sure didn't tell her. Did you?

No.

But the more Joe and I communicated through facial expressions, the harder Alex blinked. It's as if those gargantuan eyelashes were some sort of telekinetic meter. For all his afternoon blabbering, Alex didn't say much that night. Oh, he answered Melissa's many questions about his food preferences and business and life's goals—questions that, in several years of circling him, I had never bothered to ask. He responded with the requisite "Oh, that's interesting," to Melissa's tales of the embarrassing maladies she's been privy to at Dr. Moody's office. So, yes, Alex went through the motions, in fact, he was a veritable study in going through the motions, but other than that, he didn't have anything to say. He didn't have to. The sound of all that blinking was deafening, and it would have drowned his voice right out.

But the more Alex blinked, the harder my chest thumped. After a while, it almost seemed as if my heartbeat and those long lashes fell into the same *pat-pat-pat* rhythm, backed by the staccato softness of Joe's low drawl as he rejoined the conversation by regaling Melissa with his theories on french fries. All the while, he was reaching for my knee under the table. I don't know how he pulled the two actions off simultaneously, but maybe it was a drummer's secret. To me, it seemed as difficult as patting your head while rubbing your belly. My confusion over Joe's actions and my own surprisingly strong reaction thereto was causing my head to spin. So by the time Melissa blurted this out:

"Alex, you've simply got to come with me and Sam sometime to hear Joe's band play. He's a drummer, you know."

I thought my heart would downright explode.

For a split second after she said it, Alex gave the blinking a rest. He looked up from his menu at the space between Joe and Melissa and smiled wanly. But then the eyelashes went at it again, only this time even harder.

I shook Joe's hand off my knee and jumped to my feet.

"I just realized I drove the scooter over here and never washed my hands afterwards," I explained, as Alex also stood up to let me out of the booth. "They're black from the handlebars. I better clean up before the food comes."

In the bathroom, I scrubbed at my hands and attempted to catch my breath. I felt the omen of a bad decision hanging over me and wondered why I was doomed to live certain scenarios on repeat. I liked to consider myself a smart woman, but for all my schooling—and I'd had more than my fair share—I'd never figured out the psychological phenomenon that converts particular wants into needs with seeming randomness but definite cruelty. How was it possible for a college girl to wake up one morning and walk to campus as usual but drive back home on a Vespa? And how was it now possible for me to splurge my one-on-one lunch with Joe but suffer every second of dinner that his attention was turned to anyone but me? Joe was a man with whom I had little in common and even less in potential, and yet I was suddenly powerless to prevent a kaleidoscope of thoughts involving wedding flowers and first children and two old people on a porch swing watching a sunset without exchanging words, all of them thoughts I had thought a million times before, but none of them starring Joe until that very minute.

When I exited the bathroom, Joe was standing there. It was a small and noisy hallway behind the kitchen. There was a payphone on one wall and Joe grabbed my shoulders and pushed me up against it in one short motion before he kissed me.

It was a brilliant kiss, but after a few blissful seconds, I pushed him away from me.

"What are you doing?!" I asked. "We're here with other people."

"I thought he was just your boss," he taunted as he brushed my cheek with his thumb.

"What about Melissa?"

"What about her? We're not dating."

"Would she say the same thing?"

He paused, which was all the answer I needed. The jerk paused long enough that it was uncomfortable and I had to kiss him again just to shut the silence up.

It's embarrassing to admit, but it had been a long time since I had kissed anyone—so long, in fact, that I sometimes wondered if I would remember how to do it. Fortunately, kissing Joe was the kind of kissing that required no forethought whatsoever, just pure instinct. His hand gripped my lower back and pulled me close to him and the whole thing was just a hot mess of lips and arms and hair in hands and gasping for air. I wondered if kissing was ever this good for Melissa and Dan Polanski. Just knowing the possibility existed forced me to finally forgive her a bit.

"It was beyond me," I told the ghosts later that night, "a momentum I couldn't stop. There weren't any decisions involved. I couldn't decide not to do it anymore than I could decide to fly."

"So you're saying…" the little girl started.

"Gravity," the teenager finished, rolling her eyes. "You're saying gravity made you kiss him?"

The little girl gasped at the mention of her enemy. It was cruel and admittedly misleading for me to invoke its hated name here, but I was desperate to make ghosts of all ages understand why I did what I did.

You see, during the six months after her mother died, the little girl grew justifiably weary of McDonald's' dinners and stolen cheese slices. It was around that time that she began to fantasize about riding her bike out of Commerce and starting a new life for herself. Because she was only six and didn't have a whole lot of other stuff on her mind, the fantasy soon graduated to an obsession. She made mental lists of the things she would take with her when she left: her Strawberry Shortcake sleeping bag, Jack's tent and some hot dogs because she knew that you could roast hot dogs over a campfire and they tasted delicious but she also knew that you could eat them cold out of the refrigerator if your daddy forgot to fix you lunch.

The only thing standing in her way, of course, was the gulch. No matter how many times she attempted to take a practice ride out of Commerce, she was stopped dead in her tracks once she reached it. In her short life, she had thought of a million and one ways to get over the gulch: building a bridge out of twigs she found on the ground; waiting until snow and building an ice path across it; taking some string and drawing a tight wire over it like at the circus; tying a bed sheet to a tree and swinging across it like a monkey; and convincing some doggies to all line up tail to mouth and permit her to drive over them in exchange for doggie treats. But every time the little girl went to put her plan in action, something foiled her. The twigs were scratchy. There was no tree close enough for the bed sheet or tight wire plans to work. It didn't snow enough in winter time. She only knew two dogs and neither was very gullible.

It got to the point where she was thinking about that darn gulch so much she was dreaming about it. In her dreams, she would ride her bike really fast and pop the front wheel up at the very last moment, and she would sail right over the gulch and land softly and safely on the other side. But the dream evolved. Soon, she didn't even need the bike. She would just spread her arms like an airplane's wings and fly straight across. In a lot of the dreams, her mommy was flying right there beside her in the Snow White dress she wore in the box. She had the dreams so often and preferred thinking about them to the realities of her crooked-hair life that she began to believe that maybe she really was special, that just maybe, if she tried really, really hard, she could fly.

Then Jack made her mad one day—*very mad*. He had to stay late at work, so he arranged for her to spend the night at Libby's house, *again*. Sometimes she liked going there because Aunt Sarita always made good dinners, but then again, there was a price to be paid—hanging out with her bossy cousin. Also, Aunt Sarita always tried to trick the little girl into taking a bath, and it took a hefty and exhausting tantrum to get out of it. Even though she was a good cook, the little girl couldn't trust Aunt Sarita to keep her mouth shut and the last thing on earth the little girl wanted was Aunt Sarita combing through her crooked hair and tattling to Jack.

And so as soon as she learned of this latest arrangement (through Libby, on the playground, naturally), the little girl took off after school on her bike and headed for the gulch. Her irritation at the forced sleepover had fueled her faith in her flying capabilities. She rode her bike so fast through the wilderness that she felt like she was flying already.

But when she got there, she simply lost her nerve.

She laid her bike down and sat on the edge of the gulch for what seemed like an eternity. She kept calling on herself and her dead mommy to give her the will to do it, but the will never came. It began to get dark. Finally, she heard Jack's voice calling her name through the trees.

"Sammy!" he cried when he saw her. "Sammy, we've been looking *everywhere* for you!"

He rushed towards her and sat on the dirty ground even though he was wearing his nice work pants. He pulled her head to his chest. She opened her mouth to speak. She had every intention of telling him she was just fine and he shouldn't worry but that she had forgotten to pack hot dogs for her trip and so would he mind going back to the house and getting some for her? But when she went to speak her throat was dry and her lips were wet and she realized she was crying. She brushed a tidal wave of tears from her cheek with the back of her dirty hand and figured she must have been crying for a very long time.

"What are you doing out here Sammy?" Jack asked as he patted her braids.

"I'm leaving."

"Where are you going?"

"I don't know," she sniffled as she shrugged her shoulders. "Someplace else."

"So you're running away?"

"No. I'll come back and visit."

"That's very considerate of you," he said, rubbing her back. "Tell me, what are your plans for getting over this gulch?"

"I'm going to fly over it."

"You are? How are you going to do that?"

"I'm going to run really fast and then jump and flap my arms."

"Huh. Well that works fine for birds, but I'm afraid it just doesn't work for human beings like you." He picked up a small rock from the dirt. "Do you see this rock?"

She sniffled again as she nodded her head.

"Watch this," he said. He held the rock up high and released it. It dropped to the ground. "Do you see the way the rock falls when I'm not holding it up?"

"Yes."

"I'm afraid that's exactly what will happen to you once you jump off the side of this gulch."

She hadn't thought about it in that exact way, but she already sensed that something just like that was holding her back, making her hesitate in the first place.

"Why do rocks fall like that, Daddy?" she asked.

"Because of gravity," he said.

She nodded. So that was its name. She had heard it once before. She vowed to never forget it again.

✳

Chapter 13

SKORT REVIVAL

IN THE LAW, there are three kinds of contracts: (1) written contracts, (2) oral contracts and (3) implied-in-fact contracts. The agreement between Joe and me to play kissing games behind Melissa's back definitely fell into the third category. Although we never discussed it, our mutual assent to certain kinds of conduct constituted the requisite meeting of the minds. I'm ashamed to say examples of said conduct included meeting up while Melissa was at work, very late night phone calls, parking the Vespa behind the dumpster at Joe's apartment and pretending we hadn't seen each other for days when it had only been minutes and Joe had snuck out the back door of Jack's house only to come back around to the front door and knock on it again.

Admittedly, it was all wrong. For one thing, it was wrong to go behind Melissa's back when she, of all people, had been willing to break bread with me in the Sherman Valley Towne Center food court when I only had the one pair of shoes and no hairbrush. For another, it was wrong for a supposedly grown woman to so willingly play second banana.

But despite my status as the other woman, and despite our conspiratorial agreement, Joe still wouldn't acknowledge he was even dating Melissa. I couldn't figure out who, exactly, he was trying to fool: Melissa, me or himself. It seemed downright idiotic except for the fact that it was brilliant. Since Joe refused to admit he was dating Melissa, I never really had the opportunity to suggest that he stop dating her.

"He's totally using you," the teenager said with a roll of her eyes.

"Don't listen to her," the student instructed. "You're using him."

"How am I using him?" I asked.

"Because it's just a fling or entertainment—something to keep you occupied while you're here in Commerce."

"Whatever," the teenager huffed. "Even when they're just flings, I always demand one-on-one status."

The student burst out laughing. "What are you talking about? You haven't had any flings."

"Sure I have."

"Name one."

"There was my summer fling with Marcus Weathersby."

The student laughed again.

"I'm going to have to agree with her," I said. Going to one movie and holding hands a few times is not a fling."

The teenager's lip quivered, but she held her chin up. "Maybe not in your world, but at least I'm not a slut."

Still laughing, the student shrugged her shoulders. "Are you calling us sluts? Because, first off, we're so not. And second, we wouldn't argue the point anyway."

"So are you saying I should insist on exclusivity with Joe?" I asked the pouting teen.

"Of course not!" she gasped. "You can't do that to Melissa."

This is how all conversations regarding Joe went with the ghosts: in complete circles. It was all Melissa's fault.

As I'm sure you've figured out, Melissa Matthews was the most popular girl in the sixth grade at Commerce Elementary

School—at least I think it started in the sixth grade. She was also the most popular person at Commerce Junior High, at Commerce High School and, to this day, I am sure she remains the most popular person at the office of James Moody, M.D.

Of course, Melissa was no Starene in that nobody outside of Commerce, Oregon even knew who she was. This was probably why Melissa chose to live her entire life in Commerce—it was her universe, and by remaining therein, she maintained her position as most popular person in the universe. Melissa was smart that way. She always had been.

The relationship between teenaged Melissa and the teenager ghost was always crystal clear: Melissa liked to be the center of everything, and the teenager was there to ensure that happened. The teenager was her assistant, her sidekick, the Ethel to her Lucy. Her primary purpose was to help Melissa in every way—help her get the guy she liked, help her pick out the perfect prom dress, help her pass the English quiz even though she hadn't bothered to read a word of the assignment. In exchange for all this assistance, the teenager received a reserved spot next to Melissa in the cafeteria and was officially known by the coveted title "Melissa Matthews' best friend."

Some friend, I thought as I hung up my cell phone. I had just finished a call with Joe wherein I had casually inquired as to whether he wanted to "hang out"—that is, make out—that evening. "Not tonight," he had said uneasily. *Not tonight* was code for "I've got plans with Melissa." I didn't ask him to break them, but I was angry. The only problem was, I couldn't figure out where to place that anger. I was angry at Joe for getting away with phrases like *not tonight*. I was angry at Melissa for spending time with Joe. But mostly I was angry at myself for feeling angry in the first place. After all, Joe was just a fling.

Since it was a draw, I decided to direct my anger at the completely innocent and uninvolved Enid Thompson. I mean, Enid was sort of the unwitting source of this whole mess with Melissa and Joe. Mind you, I hadn't seen Enid Thompson in over twelve years, but the mere thought of her still filled me with immense guilt and a sense of inadequacy. Enid Thompson had all the posture and consideration of the RPP with a congenial twist.

Melissa was popular. Enid, on the other hand, was well-liked. In fact, Enid was so well-liked that Melissa, being the shrewd social engineer that she was, felt compelled to associate with Enid on a regular basis. Consequently, Enid ate lunch with the teenager and Melissa every now and then. The trio studied together at times. She spent the night at their houses and vice versa.

The only problem was that Enid didn't fit the Melissa mold the same way the teenager so willingly did. First and foremost, her name was Enid. It was a family name, but still. Second, Enid was a smart kid and a sportswoman, not a bubblegum-smacking cheerleader. She was involved with many clubs and had served as class president for as long as anyone could remember. Finally, Enid was far from ugly but she wasn't "cute" or "hot" either. Her clothes weren't dated or unfashionable, but they definitely weren't trendy.

The only other problem was that Enid was a little too well-liked, especially for someone who could care less about being hot or trendy. Melissa was completely confounded by Enid's laissez-faire attitude regarding her own image and, as a result, was always leery of the poor girl even as she passed her notes in biology class.

The backstabbing began by paper cuts. At first, it was as simple as Melissa and the teenager heading to the mall and "forgetting" to invite Enid. The teenager felt guilty, of course, but she rationalized her acquiescence with the fact that Enid was so terribly busy with her extracurricular extravaganza. However, things escalated quickly, and soon it seemed that Melissa and the teenager were always talking behind Enid's back.

The whole thing culminated one Friday night. Chad Latham was throwing a party. To be sure, the high school parties in

Commerce did not ascend to the level of those in a John Hughes movie. The houses were smaller. The school was smaller. Nobody was particularly wealthy. But to high schoolers in Commerce, such parties were everything. Melissa claimed that showing up at Chad's party with Enid would be social suicide. The teenager doubted this as Melissa was bulletproof—she could show up with anyone she wanted and nobody would question her. By the same token, the teenager didn't question Melissa on anything, including this. So despite her reservations, she went along with Plan Ditch Enid.

Like most teenage plans, this one was needlessly complicated. That Friday night, the teenager drove Enid and Melissa to the football game in Jack's truck. After the game, Melissa and the teenager were going to "call it a night." The strategy was to drive Enid back to her house and continue on to Chad's party without her. The problem was, Enid lived closer to the teenager than Melissa did; therefore, in order to avoid raising suspicion, the teenager had to first drop Melissa off, then take Enid home, then drive all the way back to Melissa's and pick her up. Conveniently, this also gave Melissa plenty of time to change out of her cheerleading outfit and into a party dress. By contrast, the teenager had to dress in the front seat of the truck. Melissa was able to kiss her parents goodnight and pretend to go to bed. The teenager had to call Jack from the party and pretend she was at Melissa's for a sleepover, while drunken Adam Pfizinger whooped and hollered in the background.

Melissa was shrewd. Enid, on the other hand, was smart. Once the three of them were piled in the truck's bench seat, it was clear to the teenager that Enid's suspicions were not quelled by her taking Melissa home first.

"Boy, am I tired," Melissa yawned unconvincingly.

"Really? It's only ten thirty," Enid noted, "on a Friday night. Are you sure you guys don't want to catch a movie?"

"No," Melissa said, nudging the teenager in the ribs the whole time. "I think I'll just go home and do some reading for English."

"Suit yourself."

The teenager dropped Melissa off as planned, then continued on to Enid's house. In silence. In awkward silence. Finally, the teenager pulled into her driveway. Enid didn't get out.

"Samantha, can I ask you something?"

"Sure."

"Are you guys going to Chad Latham's party?"

Of course she knew about it. She was well-liked. People wanted her at their parties. She was good company. She had a way of making you feel like you could tell her anything and she wouldn't judge you. She could ask if you were planning on backstabbing her and phrase it like pleasant small talk.

It was the teenager's big chance to come clean. But she was a bit spineless and felt she was in too deep. She couldn't figure out how to explain it to Enid even if she did tell the truth. She wasn't really sure of the reasons why they were doing it, other than the fact that they could get away with it. So she simply said:

"No. I didn't even know Chad was having a party."

Enid feigned a smile and got out of the car.

Melissa and the teenager walked into the party an hour later. Getting Melissa out of her bedroom window was more difficult than they had anticipated, even though it was on the ground floor. The tightness of her party dress made it near impossible. She finally had to pull the skirt portion up around her waist and jump out in her underwear, one leg at a time. It was awkward and unflattering. Sneaking out was never so ugly in John Hughes movies. They felt misled and rightfully so.

These escape mishaps gave Enid plenty of time to beat the schemers to the party. She was sitting there when they walked into the room. She just looked at the teenager and gave her the same knowing smile she did in the truck.

After that, Enid never sat by Melissa or the teenager in school. She avoided them, but not in a spiteful way. Like everything she did, Enid even managed to dump her friends with grace. But Melissa couldn't handle being dumped. She wanted the world—and by "world," I mean the student body of Commerce High School, of course—to know that *she* had rid herself of Enid first. Melissa waged a holy war against this poor girl who never did anything wrong except be well-liked despite being neither hot nor trendy. She waged a war and, as usual, the teenager was her foot soldier.

Sixteen years later, I let myself dwell on this ancient feud with Enid because I thought it would make me feel better about the Joe and Melissa situation, but it only made me feel worse. Usually, such thoughts conjured up the necessary spite towards Melissa for me to continue seeing her boyfriend, but not this time. All I could think about was me telling Enid that I didn't know Chad Latham was having a party. All of a sudden, it sounded an awful lot like the phrase *not tonight*.

These thoughts raced through my head at Jack's dining room table. The dining room had become a conference room of sorts for Alex's work visits, which were growing more regular and always ended with him helping Jack with something in the garden. Jack did not seem to mind that we had commandeered the only nice room in the house, and not once did Alex ask about the stacks of china on the floor. But despite such consideration, I was having a hard time focusing on the work at hand that particular afternoon—

That is, until I heard a light clicking sound that brought me back to reality.

The clicking was very faint, but it echoed. Instinctively, I put my hand up to my ear, sure I had lost an earring. It was an odd gesture, given the fact that I hadn't worn earrings for over a year and a half and that I would probably have to have the old lobes repierced if I ever wanted to make use of the ample jewelry collection rotting away in a cedar closet in Seattle.

But while some ghost's habit had me reaching for my lobe, Alex was inspecting his shirt. "My button!" he exclaimed. Like everything about that afternoon, the sentence just seemed strange.

"What?" I asked. Alex was already crouched down and feeling around on the floor. He stood up triumphantly, holding a small white button in his long fingers.

"The button came off my shirt," he said.

Indeed, the blue checked shirt was gaping in the middle, flashing his white t-shirt underneath. I must admit, I've always had a soft spot for guys who have the decency to wear an undershirt, and I always assumed Alex was one of those guys.

"I have some white thread upstairs somewhere. We can sew it back on if you want."

Alex looked embarrassed. After everything he had done for me, he still couldn't bear the thought of imposing on me to fix his shirt. "I wouldn't even bother," he stammered, "It's just . . . the meeting."

I nodded as I headed upstairs. "You can't meet a client with your shirt looking like that," I said. "Don't worry about it."

By that point, Alex had been to Jack's house so many times that I assumed there were no surprises left. It didn't occur to me that he had never been in my room until I saw him sitting on that pink canopied bed, looking quite out of place. In the closet, back behind the magenta princess dress, I found the old sewing basket. It was wooden and had several hinged layers that opened up like a toolbox. It was old and smelled of oldness and, I suspect, a bit like its prior owner.

"I never knew you were a seamstress," Alex said.

"I'm not. It's my mom's old sewing kit," I explained. "But I had to learn how to fix a button along the way."

I located the old paper pack of Dritz needles that I had used my entire life, and a bobbin wound with white thread. After threading the needle, I turned to Alex sitting on the bed, looking more out of place than ever. The room belonged to the little girl and the teenager. Alex belonged to the student and the dearly departed attorney. His disjunctive presence produced such confusion that I found myself fumbling over how to ask him to remove his shirt. It was ridiculous, I know—we were both adults and the man was wearing an undershirt for crying in the night. It just seemed inappropriate given our purported working relationship, so I decided I could just reattach the button while he was still wearing the shirt.

Needle in hand, I knelt on the floor in front of Alex and reached across his endless knees. I grabbed the placket of his shirt and pulled it toward me.

"Uh, would this be easier if I just took the shirt off?"

Yes, it would have been *much* easier—only by that point I felt like an idiot for being too shy to suggest it in the first place and was therefore wed to my decision to sew the button while it was still on. I blushed at my sudden bout of girlish prudishness and blamed it on the fact that I was in my childhood bedroom with a boy, which, technically, was against the rules.

"No, I can do it this way," I said, needle in mouth as I smoothed out the placket. "It will just take a second."

But Alex's broad shoulders were blocking my light from the window, and I had to squint so that I could see the holes from where the button had been sewn on before. For some reason, I felt a desperate need to succeed at the button repair, as if, by doing a good job, I could begin to pay down my gargantuan debt to Alex.

However, Alex was fidgety, like a kid when his mom is holding his face still and about to wipe a wet washcloth all over it. I placed a hand on his shoulder. "Hold still," I instructed, "unless you want to get stuck with the needle."

"Sorry, okay." Alex straightened up, only now his breathing was uneasy, as if he was concentrating too hard on staying put. I secured a knot in the thread and began my work on the button.

"So this is your room?" he asked.

"It was growing up," I said. "I mean, I guess it is now, too."

"It's very pink."

"My mom decorated it when I was little and, like anything in this house that she ever did, any mention of changing it was strictly forbidden."

"Well, you've clearly added your own touch along the way," he said, looking to the dated *Tiger Beat* posters. He was speaking low. I don't know if it was because he was trying to avoid yelling in my ear as I sewed or if, like me, he sensed some sort of adolescent inappropriateness to the situation and was afraid that, if he talked too loud, Jack would walk in and find him and throw him out of the house and call his dad.

I finished the button and snipped the thread. I buttoned the button, smoothed out the fabric, and leaned back to admire my handiwork. I didn't realize that I had rested one elbow on Alex's knee until he very gently reached down and lifted it up.

"I'm sorry, Sam," he said as he stood up.

"For what?"

"I just can't sit this close to you."

And with that he swiftly walked out of the room. I heard him go down the old stairs and out the front door, but I didn't get up to stop him. Instead, I sat there on my knees, staring at the checked pink bed skirt for a very long time, wondering how the Alex Martins and the Enid Thompsons and the RPPs of the world always managed to get under my skin.

After being dumped by Enid, Melissa forced the teenager to run for junior class president. By doing so, she robbed Enid of the perfect record the girl had been working towards since she was elected their class representative for the first time back in first grade. With Melissa's support, which included much blackmailing, the teenager easily won the election. But being junior class president was one of the most trying experiences in her short life.

Although you'd never know it from her crazy hair and dated fashion sense, the teenager was a bit of a perfectionist, and perfectionists are ill-suited to managerial positions because they are incapable of delegating to nonperfectionists. Most high school students are nonperfectionists. No two of them will twist a paper streamer the same way. The inconsistency is maddening—some are tightly wound, while others barely twist at all. Roughly eighty percent of a class president's responsibilities involve overseeing the twisting and hanging of paper streamers; the remaining twenty percent is a combination of balloons, shouting, clapping and metal cash boxes. Consistently dissatisfied with the work of others, the teenager had to re-twist each streamer herself. She twisted thousands of streamers that year. She never slept. Her grades suffered. And to top it all off, halfway through the year Melissa cut her from the cheer squad because her presidential duties were consuming too much of her time and attention.

The teenager was run ragged. Jack put his foot down and told her she couldn't run for student body president at the end of junior year. She never loved him more.

But if only it stopped there. When it came time to submit her petition to run for student body president, Enid approached the teenager in the hallway and casually asked if she was planning on running as well. As if the teenager hadn't ruined her life. As if Chad Latham had never thrown a lame party. She was just so nice about it.

And so the teenager told her, "No, my dad says I've got too much going on. But you should totally run, Enid. You'll win for sure."

Nice enough, right? The only problem was that Melissa was standing right next to her when she said it. Melissa was infuriated, not only that the teenager was not running in accordance with her wishes, but that she would be so kind to Enid.

The price to pay for those words was steep. Melissa immediately hooked up with Dan Polanski. Despite the fact that he was a nonchalant drummer with a reputed drug problem who tipped a hat he didn't wear, even *he* couldn't believe his sudden good fortune at becoming the object of affection of the most popular girl in the universe. The Melissa-Dan hookup was the topic du jour of junior year. It was the only part of their high school experience that was, indeed, like a John Hughes movie—lowly rocker boy gets hot cheerleader. Too bad for the teenager that she was cast in the role of the jealous and deeply hurt best friend. Too bad she spent her junior year days with a fake smile plastered on her face and her nights weeping Great Lash residue into a pink gingham pillow. Too bad she went to junior prom with Dan's friend Marco, he of the clay boobs fame, so Melissa and Dan could have another couple to share the cost of the limo and take pictures of them all night.

It was horrible, like putting a shock collar on a dog. One seizure-inducing jolt of pain was all it took and the teenager never broke rank again, not until she went off to college and Melissa stayed in Commerce, a.k.a. the universe. The teenager—by then a college student—never looked back.

But I looked back—I looked back a lot as I sat across the booth from Joe and Melissa at Roger's Roadside, sitting next to Jared, whose name I had written on the inside of my palm so I would remember it. It was like prom all over again, with Melissa sitting by *my* drummer, except maybe this time she had first dibs. Also, we ate at a much nicer restaurant for prom, but that's beside the point.

Jared, who was an accountant or an engineer or something other than a drummer, was figuring out how much everyone owed on the check when Melissa nudged Joe in the ribs and asked if he was coming back to her place to hang out.

"Not tonight," he said.

Not tonight, said to Melissa in my presence, was code for Joe's invitation for me to come to his place after Melissa dropped him off. It was my understanding of this code that found me, forty-five minutes later, sitting on the Vespa behind the dumpsters at his apartment complex, waiting for Melissa's car to leave. I had beat them there by taking a side street. The dumpster smelled disgusting and I was beginning to wonder what chain of decisions had specifically led to my voluntary association with garbage when my phone rang.

It was Alex. He apologized for calling late. Then he talked about how his client meeting had played out the day before. Then he apologized for droning on about the client meeting when I probably had better things to do. By this point, the malodorous dumpsters had forced me to pinch my nose shut as I talked to him, so everything came out a bit on the nasal side. Then Alex apologized for leaving so suddenly the day before after I was nice enough to sew the button on his shirt, but he didn't say why he did it. Then he abruptly changed the subject.

"I know it's none of my business," he blustered. "But are you dating that guy?"

"What guy?"

"Your friend's boyfriend."

It felt awful to hear it put that way.

"Yeah. I guess I am."

Alex's voice got a little high and I swear I could hear him blinking through the receiver. "Okay then."

"I know it makes me sound like a jerk—" I began.

"Like I said, Sam, it's none of my business."

"Wait!" I plead. "There's an explanation, a backstory, from when we were in high school—"

"*High school?*"

The blinking stopped. *High school?* I was thirty-one years old. I had a professional degree, and yet I was holding on to a grudge from *high school?* I thought of the names of all of the people in Alex's graduating class and wondered if any of the girls ever broke his heart or if he ever got in a fight with one of the guys and, if so, if he still thought about it. But then I remembered that this was Alex Martin I was speaking to. Alex Martin was only slightly left of the almighty RPP himself. He would never let his ghosts get the best of him.

"Never mind," I said as I hung up the phone.

"Psst," a voice called out from the other side of the dumpster. The teenager ghost stepped out from behind the cinderblock enclosure. As she walked by the trash, she waved her hand in front of her face and looked nauseated. "Oh gag me," she said through dry heaves. For once, the phrase applied.

"What are you doing here?" I asked. It had been a long time since any of the ghosts had followed me outside Jack's house without an express invitation.

"Duh, I snuck out," she said dismissively, "like I always do. But what are *you* doing here, hiding behind garbage cans? It's pathetic."

"I'm just waiting…." I began, but didn't finish.

"Just leave, okay?" she asked. "You're embarrassing yourself and sooner or later you're going to get caught by Melissa."

"If you knew the whole story you'd understand," I explained, wishing the student was there to back me up.

"Why are you so secretive about this Dan Polanski thing?" the teenager asked.

"It has to do with Enid Thompson," I said, "if that tells you anything."

At the mere mention of Enid's name, the teenager's cheeks turned bright red and she looked to the asphalt. "Melissa made me do it," she said.

"I know."

Melissa made me do it had always been her mantra and the older ghosts and I had looked down on her for it. Yet I realized that I was invoking *Melissa made me do it* as my reasoning for the whole Joe debacle. Truth be told, Melissa didn't make us do anything to Enid or with Joe. I had a gut feeling that the old eye for an eye approach had only ever resulted in two half-blind men instead of one.

"Forget it," I said, as I powered up the Vespa. I patted on the back of the seat and she hopped on, smiling.

As we drove back to Jack's house in the dark, I appreciated the skort for the first time in decades. It was a skirt one could safely wear on a scooter without having to clutch the middle of it between one's knees—an engineering marvel.

*

Chapter 14

SPARKLERS IN THE CAKE

THE STUDENT WAS FURIOUS with the teenager for sneaking out of the house and talking me out of a tryst with Joe. I woke up the next morning to find her pouting as she flipped through the many missed calls from Joe on my cell phone. It was surprising. For one, she was not inclined to pout. For another, I hadn't realized she knew how to use a modern cell phone.

"Tell her you made your own decision," the teenager begged me. "Tell her it wasn't my fault."

I could sympathize with her anxiety: nothing feels worse than to have a seemingly easy-going person go crazy on you. It's easy to take crazy from the obsessive-compulsive, but a mellow person gone mad makes you feel as if you really screwed up.

"Not your fault?" the student mocked. "For crying in the night, the entire drummer obsession is your fault."

"Stop talking about that stupid stoner Dan Polanski!" the teenager cried. "Okay—so I have a crush on him, but as far as you're concerned, that was a million years ago. Who cares? I also have a huge crush on Luke Perry, but I don't hear you freaking out about that. Chill already."

The little girl held her hands to her ears and shut her eyes at the arguing.

"You promised me we could go to the gulch today," she said.

"I haven't forgotten," I assured her.

Only I had. It was Saturday morning, but it's sometimes hard to keep track of the days when you work from home and have a fairly fluid schedule.

"Do *they* have to come?" the little girl asked, motioning with her elbow at the other ghosts.

I didn't know the answer. Although I thought I had figured out how to keep the ghosts from following me around in public (a delusion disproven by the teenager's appearance in the parking lot the night before), I didn't really know how to separate one from the other. It seemed where one ghost went, the others naturally followed. Or so I thought. Again, the teenager's appearance the night before made me question my assumptions as to how the whole haunting worked.

Sure enough, when the little girl and I left for the gulch, the others headed out, too. The student and the teenager kept their distance from each other on the way. When we got there, the little girl began counting steps and taking other nonsensical measurements that she failed to write down. The rest of us sat under the shade of some neighboring trees.

The student lay back in the wild grass and rubbed her eyes. "Man, I hate being so worked up." She said it to me, but loud enough that the teenager, who was sitting under a tree a few feet to my right, could hear. "It's not my scene. It's just that I get so frustrated with her." Despite her professed frustration, she sounded a lot more relaxed than she had been that morning.

The teenager rested on her palms and set her jaw square. "Why?" she asked, quietly.

"Because you don't realize how important you are. The power, the choice for that first love—that was entirely within your control. It was a life-defining decision and you got to make it and determine the fate for the rest of us. And I'm jealous and a little mad, I guess."

The teenager shrugged and twirled a blade of grass in her fingers.

"You had so many of those things," the student continued. "Those 'firsts,' the ability to make choices that the rest of us would have live with for eternity. It seems so strange and unfair given your age and your maturity, but that's the way it came down."

"If I would have known you guys would end up such gosh-awful messes, I never would have done it," the teenager said. She truly seemed sorry about it, but the student and I couldn't help but laugh.

"It may be too little too late," I said.

"Not if you can manage to get a clue already," she said.

"What do you mean?"

"I don't like Dan because he's a drummer. I like him because he's kind of cute and because he's nice to me in art class and because he likes to talk about different things than all those guys that Jason Bernard hangs out with. Mostly, that he doesn't want to spend the whole time talking about Melissa, I guess."

The student ghost and I traded nervous glances on that one.

"What?" the teenager asked.

"It's just—" the student ghost started.

"It's nothing," I said.

"Anyways, it's not like you guys ever listen to me or anything, but before you blame this drummer obsession on me, you should know that I just like nice guys—"

"Who are also cute," the student corrected.

"Yes," she agreed. "And I happen to think that, for an old guy, Alex Martin is kinda nice and kinda cute."

"*Alex Martin?!*" the student asked, grimacing.

"*What?!*" I added.

"Sure, why not?" the teenager replied defensively. "I mean, where would you even be if he didn't help you by giving you that job? You'd be working at the call center with Libby," she said, disgusted at the thought, "and you'd still only have one pair of shoes."

The little girl giggled from across the field. "She's right, you'd just have those one yucky pair of tennies." It was always anybody's guess as to when she was listening.

"The point is, if it were up to me, I would totally pick Alex instead of this Joe guy. I don't even know what you see in him. He's a loser and he has no money and his hands are always dirty and he's disgusting."

"And he's Melissa Matthews' boyfriend," the student snarked.

"That too," the teenager agreed.

Way across the field, the little girl jumped up and down and shrieked "I've got it!"

I was still thinking about this conversation three days later, sitting across the dining room table from Alex. He was engrossed by something he was penning on his laptop, which gave me the opportunity to sneak multiple glances at him in an attempt to figure out why the teenager thought he was so great. Don't get me wrong—his generosity and my enormous indebtedness thereto was obvious. As were the eyelashes. And maybe the freckles. And the dark curly hair. But he didn't have drummer's arms—he had weekend basketball player's arms. They were far better than theater major's arms, mind you, but they were completely void of tattoos or popping veins.

"Are you okay, Sam?" he asked, suddenly.

It was rather embarrassing. I was still looking at his arms while he, apparently, had been looking at me.

Moreover, his question was an interesting one given that he provided no frame of reference. Compared to the RPP, I was not okay—after all, I was a thirty-one year old woman haunted by ghosts, living with her father, driving a scooter, dating her best friend's boyfriend who she liked less every day and essentially working a part-time job to pay the mortgage on an empty condo in Seattle. But compared to the pajama-clad, sleepy-headed person I was seven months prior, I suppose I was pretty okay. And compared to someone starving in a refugee camp in a third world country, even she was very, very okay.

"Sam?"

"I've got a problem, Alex. A silly one."

"Try me."

"How are your carpentry skills?"

Alex winced at this. "Had to be carpentry, didn't it? Couldn't be sports or heavy lifting or analytical problem solving—you went straight for the power tools."

"A little rusty, then?"

"To say the least."

"Do you think you could at least help me figure out how to build a decent ramp?"

Ten minutes later and we were both standing at the edge of the gulch, peering over the rim. Alex's arms were folded tight across his chest and his brow was furrowed. The little girl ghost peeked out from behind a distant tree trunk, eyes wide and fingers in her mouth. Again, I was confounded. I hadn't invited her, but I suppose it was a given that the gulch was her territory.

"You know, Sam," Alex said as he took measured paces back from the edge of the gulch, "next time you ask for help in building a ramp, you might want to mention that, if built improperly, you could die before you get the guy to sign up."

"Thanks for the tip," I said. Despite his whining, Alex continued with the paces, the arm-crossing, the brow-furrowing. More importantly, he resisted the urge to ask the obvious question—*Why?*—and he deserved loads of credit for that. For all his free t-shirt quirks, Alex was one of the few people I knew that understood a person will offer the *why?* upfront if she feels like offering it at all.

When we got back to the house, neither of us explained the nature of our field trip to Jack. Jack had Alex go out to the garden and pick some Early Girl tomatoes to take home, which had matured even earlier than usual. Then he invited the poor guy to drive all the way back to Commerce the following weekend to attend Aunt Sarita's infamous Fourth of July barbecue and to watch the fireworks at Sherman Valley Park.

And what an Independence Day it was. Aunt Sarita had pulled out all the stops with the menu: your choice of a freshly grilled hamburger or bratwurst, the triumvirate of summer salads (three-bean, potato and coleslaw), grilled corn on the cob and a large cake decorated to look like the American flag with white nondairy topping for frosting, a blueberry corner, strawberry stripes and sparklers for candles. The Billingsleys' entire neighborhood smelled of seared meat, sunscreen and sugar.

Libby had invited call center manager Raul to the gathering and she was acting more awkward that usual—an awkwardness of the gooey-eyed variety. To my surprise, Raul didn't seem to mind. He also seemed very at home behind the grill with Uncle Stanley, the two of them silently focusing on the meat at hand while the old biddies of Commerce did their biddying around them. With Libby and Raul apparently paired up, and with Joe officially coupled with Melissa for the fireworks in the park, I was glad Alex was coming just so I had someone to hang out with aside from Jack.

But then Alex showed up with Mina Chen. She looked as tiny and poised as ever in a pair of plaid Bermudas and an expensive white polo shirt.

"Sam, you remember Mina," he stated as I hurriedly smoothed out my denim skirt and hair. At least I had pulled it back into some loose semblance of a bun; hopefully that helped her to recognize me.

"Hi!" Mina and I said to each other simultaneously as we ex-changed a limp handshake.

Of course I remembered Mina, she of Wallace and Kennedy super-associate fame and, to the extent allowable by big firm poli-tics, I suppose we had actually been work friends. Still, I wasn't expecting her to show up in my cousin's backyard three years after she left the Seattle office for the patent fields of Palo Alto.

Vegetarian Mina quickly filled her plate with the three-bean salad, some coleslaw and a cob of corn that was thicker than her ankle. She sat down across from Jack at one of the picnic tables covered in a disposable plastic tablecloth. That left me standing in line behind Alex with a Chinet plate full of open hamburger bun, waiting for Stanley to finish grilling the meat and generally feeling like an unkempt cow.

"I hope it's okay that I brought Mina," Alex said.

Aunt Sarita caught his comment in passing. "Of course it's okay, Alex," she said, patting him on the back, and then "She's *so* darling," before making her way to the buffet table to replenish the sherbet punch.

"Yeah, it's fine," I said unconvincingly. "I mean, I wish I would have had a little warning so I could have bought a whole new Fourth of July outfit and all and maybe got my hair done."

"It's *Mina*," Alex laughed. "She doesn't care about that stuff."

"I know," I whined. I wished she did care about it, because then all the negative feelings I had against her would have had a justifiable basis. Alas.

"So..." I began. "So... like, are you guys seeing each other?"

"We hang out sometimes," was the evasive answer. "But I wasn't about to come alone. I figured you'd be with your guy all night."

"No, he's uh..." I stammered, kicking the grass with the toe of my flip-flop.

"With his girlfriend?" Alex asked with more than a hint of distaste in his voice.

"Yeah."

Alex clenched his jaw and shook his head. He didn't say anything else, he just shook his head.

After the barbecue, we all caravanned to Sherman Valley Park, our arms loaded to the hilt with blankets and lawn chairs and coolers full of soda and ice cream sandwiches. Libby and Raul were walking way ahead of everyone, followed by Alex and Mina, followed by Aunt Sarita and Uncle Stanley, followed by me and, of course, Jack. Because they were in the lead, Libby and Raul were the first to run into Melissa and Joe.

"Hi!" Melissa exclaimed as she waived her fingernails back and forth. She reached her hands out and wrapped them around Libby in a huge hug. Libby stiffened and stood there, mystified. She couldn't hug back because, like the rest of us, she was too busy working as a pack mule.

Don't do it, Melissa, I couldn't help but think. *Don't pick on her. Not in front of Raul.*

But to my surprise, Melissa cordially greeted Raul and introduced the couple to Joe. Libby did not mention that she had already met Joe back when I met him, over Aunt Sarita's lasagna. Joe didn't seem to remember. That was Joe.

Melissa and Joe continued down the line, approaching Alex and Mina. Alex was curt towards Joe, but the drummer didn't seem to pick up on it. He was too busy admiring Mina's adorable plaid Bermudas. Some people just don't have a type, I guess.

But things didn't get really weird until Melissa proceeded to greet Aunt Sarita as if she were her own Aunt. Sarita, who usually didn't trust Melissa further than she could spit, was either flustered or flattered. With her, it was so hard to tell the difference.

"Melissa dear, you and your sweetheart should have come to our barbeque," Sarita said.

"Don't worry," Melissa cooed, "we had our own picnic. But I'm sure the cake wasn't nearly as good as the one at yours."

Sarita blushed as Melissa and Joe continued toward Jack and me.

"Hi, Mr. Green," Melissa said, while Joe simply nodded his head in recognition of us. And then to me, she said...

Nothing.

Nothing at all.

She did not waive her fingernails. She did not offer to take one of my lawn chairs. She did not even acknowledge my presence.

Everyone laid out their blankets and waited, seemingly forever, for the summer sun to go down. Joe and Melissa were within eyeshot. There appeared to be less canoodling on Melissa's part than usual. I tried not to stare at them, but it was hard, because I was bored and, as the seventh wheel to our party, had nobody to chat with. Uncle Stanley brought his portable chess set and Jack was more than happy to play with him in silence for the duration of the evening. Raul was busy explaining to Libby and Sarita all the precautions that had to be taken when dealing with fireworks; I'm not sure how Raul got to be such an authority on the topic, but he neglected to mention that the first precaution to be taken is to make sure Libby is nowhere in the vicinity. Alex and Mina passed the time by gossiping about our former coworkers at Wallace and Kennedy. I recognized most of the names, but had a hard time putting faces to them. Then Mina told Alex she was transferring to the Portland office. He was super excited at this news, almost to the point that it concerned me. Even more concerning was the fact that he, too, had a difficult time tearing his eyes away from Joe and Melissa.

The fireworks display finally happened, and when it did, it was about as lackluster as a bright, shiny and noisy controlled explosion can get. The show was accompanied by the Commerce and Sherman Valley combined Junior High Summer Marching Band, which experienced some difficulty in keeping time with the fireworks. Apparently it had never occurred to anyone on the Sherman Valley City Council that a CD player with a Neil Diamond and Bruce Springsteen mix was the better way to go.

After the show, I volunteered to dump the now-melted ice out of one of Sarita's coolers. In turn, Alex volunteered to help me, but he was cut off by Joe, who insisted. Things got tense, and for a second, I almost thought Alex and Joe were going to fight over it—a cooler of all things. Melissa pouted a few feet away, while Mina just looked like it was the most entertaining thing she had seen all night and, no doubt, it was.

Finally Joe won, and he towed the cooler (and me, at the other end of it) several yards away from the rest of our party. He berated me for not returning his calls as of late, but then changed the topic before I even got a chance to defend myself.

It was then that Joe, in a rare emotional and frantic display, laid out his Master Plan for me. The Master Plan involved a questionable combination of Greyhound buses, bartending, crossing borders and opening a scooter rental shop in Jaco, Costa Rica. It sounded absolutely ridiculous, yet I felt as though I hadn't accumulated sufficient sanity points since walking Two Pomeranians through downtown Seattle to deserve to call another person ridiculous.

"So are you in?" he asked, breathless.

"What?"

"Come with me, Sam. We can run the shop together—you at the counter and me in the garage. What do you say?"

"I—I don't know. What about Melissa?"

"I already told her I'm going."

"Did you ask her to go with you?"

"Are you kidding me? There's nowhere for her to get her nails done in Jaco. I already told her I was going to ask you."

"You told her *what*?! So she knows we've been . . . you know, hanging out?"

"Well, I didn't spell it out for her . . . ."

The puzzle pieces of the day flew into place as I thought about Melissa's uncharacteristic desire to befriend Libby and eschew me. I felt like the world's biggest idiot while simultaneously feeling like the world's biggest jerk. Even the name Dan Polanski offered no consolation.

"How about it, Sam?"

"Just one question, Joe," I said. I tried to stop myself, I did, but I just didn't have the willpower of Alex. "*Why?*"

His shoulders—the same shoulders that had the strength to carry around his beautifully massive drummer's arms—sank a bit at the question. "It's just really important to me," he said.

Of course it was. That's always the answer to *why?*

When we finally did dump out the cooler, I got water all over my shirt, freezing water. I walked back towards our group, now headed by the picture perfect Mina Chen. Well, almost picture perfect: she had a blade of grass in her dark silky hair, which Alex tenderly removed just as I walked up. He did it so softly that she didn't seem to notice.

I pouted as I sped-walked my way through the parking lot towards Jack's truck. Alex briefly broke with Mina and caught up with me.

"Sam, what's wrong?" he asked. "Did he—"

"Relax, Alex," I snapped. "The only thing he did is ask me to spend the rest of my life with him."

Alex stopped dead in his tracks and let me continue on.

Back at the house, Jack dragged Alex into the garden to take some more produce off his hands. Alex was kind as ever to Jack, but he made a point of avoiding me. I couldn't believe it. I hadn't been subjected to the silent treatment since third grade, and now I was getting it for the second time in one night.

"So what are you up to these days, Sam?" Mina asked innocently enough, her tiny frame nearly buried by the worn cushions on Jack's old couch.

"Well," I began. And I don't know why it all came spilling out at that moment of all moments to that person of all persons, but sometimes life is just like that. "Did you see that guy earlier—the one with the drummer's arms?"

"I might have," she said, wriggling her eyebrows suggestively.

"I'm dating him. On the sly. Well, it used to the on the sly. The blonde girl that was with him—"

"The fingernail waver?"

"Yeah, her—she's my best friend from high school and one of my only friends right now. Uh, no offense."

"None taken."

"Thanks. So I had this heavy crush on another drummer in high school and she stole him from me. I thought I had gotten over it and maybe I had, but I used it as an excuse to go out with her boyfriend, the current drummer. It was just a fling, or so I thought. But tonight he pulled me aside and told me that (a) he already told her about us, which explains a lot of her behavior toward me, and (b) that he wants me to move to Costa Rica with him to open up a scooter shop and, what's more, he thinks we can get there by taking a bus. Crazy, huh?"

"Not really. I know a friend who drove from Vancouver to Chile, so you probably can take a series of buses to get there."

"No, I mean the plan as a whole—isn't it absolutely nuts?"

"Oh yes, it does sound nuts," she agreed, shaking her head. "So are you going to do it?"

"What?" I asked her, barely whispering, still running through the prior second to assure myself that she had even asked it.

"Are you going to do it? I suppose it depends on the guy... But at least tell me you're going to think about it."

"Would *you* consider doing it?" I asked her.

"Maybe," she shrugged, sinking even further into the cushion. "It sounds romantic and adventurous. Sometimes I get bored with the daily grind. Again, it depends on the guy."

Mina Chen did me a huge favor right then, one for which I would never be able to repay her. Like most things lately, the unexpected offer from Joe had left my head reeling and I was totally incapable of weighing the pros and cons, doing a cost-benefit analysis, or any of the other level-headed things the RPP would do before making a big decision. But it's easy when you're viewing it as *someone else's* decision—it's always clear what *someone else* should do. It's why the world is full of single women shilling out dating advice. We would never counsel *someone else* to spend a year in bed "thinking about things," but when it comes to ourselves, that's somehow where we always end up.

Mina's suggestion that *she* would move to Costa Rica to start a scooter shop made me envision her doing that very thing, in her plaid Bermudas as a matter of fact. And when I did so, the answer was crystal clear:

Don't do it, Mina.

I tried to explain. "This guy commented to me that the other girl—you know, the high school best friend—was ill-suited for the venture because there would be nowhere to get her nails done in Jaco."

Mina's face scrunched up at this information. "What—does he think it's all mud huts and taco stands down there? It's a resort town that caters to Western tourists. Of course there will be a nail salon."

"Exactly."

"He clearly hasn't thought this through well enough."

"I know."

"You shouldn't go unless you've done your own research and formulated your own plan."

"No. I won't."

I kept this turn of events to myself later that night as I sat on Jack's rooftop with the ghosts, scanning the skyline for Commerce residents illicitly setting off their own fireworks. We could hear them better than we could see them, but the twirly whistle-boom seemed to satisfy the little girl, who clapped and giggled for almost an hour.

I had real problems weighing on me, but I couldn't confide even in these nonexistent friends without the risk of starting a fresh debate. If I did, surely each one of them would be highly opinionated as to what I should do. With all due respect to the ghosts, their advice simply wasn't as reliable as that of, say, Mina Chen.

After it was clear that no further fireworks were to be expected, the ghosts and I huddled under the pink gingham covers telling ghost stories. I have to admit that I instigated it—I wasn't sure where the day had left things with Melissa or Joe or Alex. Perhaps I would have to go to Costa Rica after all, having lost my job and two of my three friends. Due to the uncertainty of tomorrow, I forced the ghosts to hold onto today for as long as they possibly could.

The teenager told the story that begins with two lovebirds in a convertible, which has an extensive midsection where a particular scratching noise is described ad nauseum and which ends with the young man hanging from a tree branch. The student's story was simply a lazy retelling of the plot of *Scream*, but the younger ones didn't recognize it. When it was my turn, I told a lesser-known tale about a boarding school student who spent the whole night listening to her roommate rock in a rocking chair counting to ten, only to discover in the morning that it was a woman who escaped from an insane asylum counting the hairs on her roommate's severed head. Unfortunately, it had been so long since I told it that I messed up on the ending and kept having to repeat it until I got it sort of right.

Finally, the teenager butted in. "Your turn," she said to the little girl.

"For what?"

"To tell us a story."

"A ghost story?"

"No. I'm not in the mood for a ghost story, and you don't know any that could scare me anyway."

"You want a fairy tale, then?"

"Tell us a story about Mom."

"Okay," the little girl said, obviously confused by the request. Still, she settled into the pillows. "Once upon a time there was a mommy—"

"Our mommy?"

"Yes."

"Was she pretty?" the student asked, playing along.

"Yes, she was pretty as a princess."

"What did she look like?"

"She was smiling, and she had brown hair."

"What color were her eyes?" the teenager pressed.

"Ummm . . . I think they were blue."

"You don't remember?"

"I said I think they were blue."

"How can you not remember?"

The little girl yanked on my sleeve. "She's not letting me tell my story," she whined.

"Let her tell it her way," I said.

"Once upon a time there was a mommy," the little girl began again. "And she lived in a big white castle and she slept in a big silver bed and wore a white nightgown. And she even had a TV in her room. And she had a magic tray she could eat off while she watched TV with a place to hold the cup so you don't spill. And she ate a lot of Jello—"

"No, we don't care about that stuff," the teenager said, clearly annoyed. "Tell us what she was like before all of that."

"I was getting to that part," the little girl said defensively.

"Forget the story, just tell us what she was like."

"She was really nice."

"How? What did she do? What things was she good at? Think!"

The little girl pressed her fingers to her temples, as if it could make her remember that of which she hadn't bothered to note. I felt sorry for the little girl, but I empathized with the teenager's exasperation. How was it the little girl had memorized the plot of every movie she had ever seen, that she could look at a coloring book outline of Snow White and color in her dress by memory, yet she couldn't recall even the simplest details of her own mother, guardian and primary caretaker?

"I've got it," the little girl said, raising one finger in the air. "She was very good at making dinner. She made the yummiest dinners, even though you had to eat all your veggies or she would get mad and Daddy never gets mad and Daddy never cooks veggies."

The teenager was hanging on to every word at this point, her soreness dissipated. "What would she make?" she asked.

"Umm . . . macaroni and cheese . . . soup . . . something red with noodles and hot dogs . . . grilled cheese sandwiches . . . little pizzas on toast—"

"I remember the little pizzas," the teenager said solemnly.

"I do too," the student said. "With sliced black olives on them, right?"

"That's right—"

The teenager piped up, "And sometimes she would make them on English Muffins instead of toast—"

"The circle toasts?" the little girl asked. "Oh yeah. And she never, ever forgot about dinner. We had dinner every single night."

The exasperation floated out the window at this last line, which the little girl delivered with the same sense of luxury as if she were saying "We had caviar for breakfast," or "We drank out of bejeweled goblets and then tossed them in the trash compacter because we didn't want to bother with washing them." I thought of the little girl sneaking cheese slices up to her bedroom to eat because her forlorn father had forgotten about dinner—again.

"Oh, and you know what else she was good at?" the little girl asked.

"What?"

"She was very good at brushing all the tangles out after bath time. Very good. She knew the soft way to do it."

"And she would do your hair and put ribbons in it," the teenager offered.

"Yes," the little girl said, wrinkling her nose. "But I don't like the ribbons."

"Good for you," the student laughed.

The teenager rolled over on her back and looked at the ceiling. "I would have loved them."

The corners of the student's mouth turned up. "Me too," she whispered.

✱

Chapter 15

LOCATING COSTA RICA ON A MAP

THAT NIGHT, I tossed and turned in bed, unable to sleep, and when I did actually sleep, I dreamt with such detail that I awoke more tired than I was when I went to bed. The dreams were like a video loop playing over and over: me, running through the streets of what I assume was Costa Rica, chasing behind Joe until I caught up with him. Only the end of the dream changed. Sometimes Joe turned around and extended a greasy mechanic's hand towards me. I never really saw his face, just his grimy fingernails.

Other times, when Joe turned around he was holding drumsticks and my dead grandmother's blender. Except in those instances, I realized it wasn't Joe after all.

It was Mickey.

The ghosts' reactions to Joe's Costa Rica idea were mixed. The student thought it was the offer of a lifetime, and she immediately buzzed around the bedroom, talking to herself about what I would need to pack. The teenager, on the other hand, was less than thrilled. She didn't like the idea of leaving Oregon for a foreign country far away from family and friends, she didn't like the idea of a career as the cashier at a scooter rental shop and, most of all, she didn't like the idea of my going with Joe. Finally, the little girl didn't know what to think. I told her Costa Rica was "the beach," and she seemed to approve of that. But she grabbed my hand and pleaded with me not to go until we had resolved the gulch-crossing issue. After all, she pointed out, she had only recently "figured it out," and we had just barely enlisted Alex to help build a ramp out of who-knows-what. I didn't have the heart to tell her that, after the previous night, I wasn't so sure Alex was keen on helping us with our crazy schemes anymore.

But despite their varied opinions on the topic, the ghosts seemed to unanimously assume one thing: that I was going.

"You'll need sunscreen," the student said. "You'll be spending a lot more time outside than you do now."

"Oh, but not *too* much sunscreen," the teenager said. "It wouldn't hurt you to get a little tan."

"And not the smelly kind of sunscreen, either," the little girl added.

"What kind is the smelly kind?" the student asked.

"The pink kind," she said as I put my fingers to my temples, feeling a massive headache coming on. "The pink flavor smells yucky."

I was still sitting in bed as they raced around, ranking the qualities of various brands of sunscreens, none of the names of which any of them could remember. Perhaps it was the stress caused by a major life decision for someone who was probably very ill-equipped to make one, or perhaps it was just a nondairy topping hangover from the cake the night before, but I reached my breaking point. "Shut up already about the sunscreen!" I yelled at all of them. "You can buy sunscreen in Costa Rica. There are bigger issues here."

"Like what?" the student asked.

"Like, how am I going to finance this? How am I going to tell Jack? How much notice am I going to give Alex? And why on earth would I be willing to bank everything on a guy with no education, seemingly little business sense or foresight, and who hasn't been faithful to me since the day I met him?"

The ghosts stood silence for a minute. But then the teenager couldn't help but remind me that, "He was Melissa's boyfriend first. What did you expect?"

I slid under the covers and pulled a pillow over my head.

"What do you want?" the student asked, her voice a little more sympathetic. "Do you want a plan?"

"Yes!" I cried from under the pillow.

"A plan's no problem. We can make a plan," she said as she sat down at the foot of the bed.

"I'm listening."

"Sell the condo and everything in it. There's your nest-egg money. Plus, you won't need nearly as much to live once you're not paying a mortgage or HOA fees anymore. The process will give you time to provide more than enough notice to Alex and, as for Dad, you just sit him down and tell him. When has he ever questioned something that you really wanted to do?"

She was right. That was the problem with the student—underneath her easygoing, slacker veneer, she was a very smart girl. Still, I whimpered from under the pillow. "So what—I'm just never going to be a lawyer again?"

The weight at the end of the bed shifted and I imagined the student had put her head in her hands. "You've got to be kidding me that we're still going through this," she mumbled. "So you have a law degree, so what? It's not a life sentence."

"No, but it was the plan."

"Plans are only good so long as you realize they are always changing," she lectured. "For crying in the night," she mumbled again. "I should have gotten that tattoo while I still had the nerve."

The good thing about having a conversation with the ghost of a former version of yourself is that either of you can throw out lines like that without any explanation. It sounded random, I know, but I knew exactly what she meant. Back in the day, the student read a fanzine article about a guitarist in an alternative rock band whose hands were covered in tattoos. When asked about the tattoos, the guitarist said she got them to prevent herself from ever having the kind of workaday office job where tattoos all over one's hands were frowned upon. It struck a chord with the student, and she seriously considered getting them. There were only two problems. The first was that she didn't want to just out-and-out copy the life philosophy of this particular guitarist because, by so doing, she would actually contradict said philosophy, which promoted individuality and originality and the premise that the terms "got the idea from" and "selling out" were synonymous. In retrospect, her theory was a bit misguided, as there is a lot to be learned from people who have weathered life before you, but people are entitled to their beliefs, I guess.

The second problem was that the student was deathly afraid of needles.

And so the life-saving tattoos had never happened. I could tell the student was seriously regretting it now. She was thinking that if only she had taken some valium or whatever would have enabled her to endure the sheer terror of someone needling her arm for several hours, it would have been easier than dealing with me now.

I went through the motions of the day, or at least the semi-motions of a day after a holiday, but I just couldn't shake the feeling of running and running and running in my dream, only to catch up to Mickey, the most memorable features of whom were apparently (1) that he was a drummer, and (2) that he stole my blender. Of course, the similarities of Joe's Costa Rica offer and Mickey's yesteryear press for the student to run away to New York with him days before she took the bar exam were not lost on me. New York was a lot closer than Costa Rica; the student wouldn't have needed a passport or visa or whatever it was that I would need to reside and work in Costa Rica. Mickey had been to New York before and some of his former bandmates had already moved there. The student had never asked him, but I'm pretty sure Mickey was at least generally aware that, if she wanted to, Melissa Matthews could find a nail salon in the greater New York area.

I also couldn't shake the sense of uneasiness caused by the fact that Joe hadn't called me. Surely he recognized that I was a bit shell-shocked by his initial offer the night before. Surely he would want to go over the details—of our travel, the business, the whole thing. But there was no call.

"Maybe he's at Melissa's," was the teenager's surly suggestion when she saw me check my cell phone for missed calls for the millionth time that morning.

"I told you, it's over between him and Melissa," I said a little too defensively.

"Sounds like it's over between you and Melissa, too."

I ignored the comment and turned to the student.

"He'll call," she assured me.

"Maybe Mina was right," I said. "Maybe he's too unreliable a person for such a drastic decision."

"He might be," she shrugged. "That's why you're going to take Mina's advice and do your own research and plan things out yourself. Didn't she say she would have done it if it were her?"

"Yeah, she did."

"And didn't you say she's super smart and sensible?"

"She is," I nodded. In fact, I had always hated her for it. I told Alex as much when he called uncharacteristically late that day to touch post-holiday base on our various projects. To his credit, he pretended that things between us hadn't ended on sore words the night before. Yet for some reason I picked a fight with him about Mina anyway. I was mad at him for having the audacity to call about work before Joe called about the rest of my life.

"Mina?" he asked, incredulously. "I thought you were friends at Wallace."

"We were," I admitted, while whining. "At least so far as girls were allowed to be friends."

"What does that mean?"

I suppose I was mad at Mina, too. I had a feeling she had told Alex about Joe's offer and the promise of all things Costa Rica, and my conviction of this fact was as strong as my anger at her for it. Mina and Alex had a long drive back to Seattle after the fireworks, and surely it had come up in the conversation. But Mina should have known better. It was personal and therefore my story to tell, even if I wasn't wearing perfect plaid Bermudas.

"You brought Mina to my house and my town and to meet my family even though you knew she would make me feel uncomfortable," I said to Alex. They were gut-wrenching words to force out of my mouth to this man to whom I already owed an unpayable debt, but in that moment they were somehow far easier to utter than the word *Costa* followed shortly thereafter by *Rica.*

"Sam—"Alex stuttered, obviously dumfounded.

"It's not fair," I continued, all control lost to verbal momentum, "because as my boss and one of my very few friends, you have so much ability to hurt me and I have no ability to hurt you."

There was an extensive silence on the other end of the line.

"I always thought you were the smartest woman I had ever met, Samantha Green," he finally said. "But if that's your perception of things, then I was dead wrong." With that, he hung up the phone.

Eventually, I hung up my phone, too. That's the problem with cell phones—no dial tone to snap you back to reality and make you take note of the fact that you are sitting in an upright fetal position, knees tucked under chin, squished between your childhood nightstand and the window seat.

Alex's reaction made me realize, albeit belatedly, that maybe Mina hadn't told him about Joe and the southern hemisphere after all. This made me just as mad at her as I previously was back when I thought she *had* squealed. If, as Alex contended, she was my friend, she would have explained everything to Alex so I wouldn't have to do it. It was like that one time when I needed to give Libby notice that I was quitting the call center, only I didn't have the guts and so I ended up working another eight-dollar-an-hour night anyway. Only the thought of telling Alex was for some inexplicable reason a thousand times worse.

"I need a plan," I said to the student the next day.

"We went over this yesterday," she said. "We have a plan."

I nodded. "Yeah, but I need a firmer one."

"You sound like the attorney," she scowled.

I nodded again, even shaking a bit.

"You don't need *everything* planned out," she said, both con-cerned and annoyed. "That kills the spontaneity of it. Look at you. Did you plan any of this?" With this last question, she waved her arm around the room in as grandiose of a manner as she would permit her slacker-self to display.

"No," I snapped. "And quite frankly, it's been an uphill battle of a year."

When would she learn what I had learned—that it is harder to recover from the lack of a plan than to take the effort to make one in the first place? That it was harder to rebound from the lack of a plan than from the disappointment of a failed plan? That was the problem inherent in dealing with the ghosts—both time and memory only moved in one direction. Having never spent a year in her jammies, the student couldn't truly appreciate the pitfalls of failing to adequately plan.

Sell the furniture. Sell the condo. Tell Jack. Tell Alex. I chanted the tenets of our alleged plan over and over, but it didn't help me shake the feeling that there were obvious and dangerous conse-quences to be had for the Costa Rica move. The student preferred not to consider the cost of such actions, but had she gone through

with the hand tattoos, I would have paid the price by being relegated to a life working in a coffee house or a body shop or even
the call center. I wanted to point this out to her and more, but I
didn't. She, and the rest of the ghosts for that matter, were simply
too set in their ways. And so I didn't tell her. But thank goodness
for needles.

It was three o'clock in the afternoon on the *day after* the day after Fourth of July when Joe finally called to see if I was in or out.

"I think I'm in," I said unconvincingly.

"Sam! That's *awesome!*"

"Yeah. I think I'm going to sell my condo in Seattle so we'll
have some seed money for the scooter shop."

"What?"

"Well, I don't want to use all the equity on the shop, just a
little. I need to put some in savings just in case."

"That's great, Sam, but can you get a realtor or your dad or
someone to sell it for you?"

"I'd certainly need a realtor's assistance," I said, a little confused.

"It's just, I was sorta counting on leaving Monday."

Monday. The problem with Monday was that Monday didn't allow for any plans. In fact, Joe hadn't seemed to do any planning
on his own beyond buying a bus ticket to San Diego with a departure date of, you guessed it, Monday.

The student was fine with Monday. In fact, it became a sort of
mantra for her. "We won't have to worry about that after Monday," she'd say. "That won't even be an issue come Monday."
"Wait until Monday and you'll forget all about it." To her, the
world began on Monday. As for me, I couldn't help but suspect
that, in a way, it would end.

Tell Jack. Tell Alex. Pack Bags. Ask Alex to take or sell the furniture.
Ask Jack to sell the condo. Buy Spanish Dictionary. Look at a map of the
world and make sure you know where Costa Rica actually is. If, as you sus-

pect, it is in Central America, research political and socioeconomic stability of Central America. The list was getting longer yet I had so much less time in which to complete it. I wasn't sure how I was going to ask Jack to sell the condo for me when I had implicitly refused to sell it myself for so long. I also wasn't sure how to tell Alex I was leaving as of Monday when I wasn't even certain we were still on speaking terms.

"And what about Melissa?" the teenager asked.

"What about her?"

"Duh—shouldn't you call her and at least say you're sorry for stealing her boyfriend and moving out of the country with him before you go?"

"I—"

"Forget it," the student instructed. "You'll never have to see Melissa again after Monday."

"And how 'bout the gulch?" the little girl asked. "Can we jump the gulch before Monday?"

"If we have time," the student promised.

I shook my head at the lie. When would the student learn what I had learned—that when you've always got your eyes on the door, you never remember what the room looked like? The student lived life with her shoelaces tied and her finger on the trigger, jumping from thing to thing and dream to dream as if the unknown and "out there" were the only things that could possibly bring happiness.

But the more I tried to teach her by pointing out the uncertainties and loose ends, the more she ignored me and pressed forward with the situation. In a day, she had researched everything there is to know about Costa Rica, including the geography, climate, history, culture and ability for foreigners to work and own property. In another day, she had my measly life completely crammed into an old camping backpack of Jack's that I could barely put on without the weight of it pulling me backwards to floor like a belly-up turtle. I wondered how long it would be until I would be able to unpack it.

By then, there was only one day left and far fewer things on the to-do list. *Tell Jack. Tell Alex. Let the bank have the condo and everything inside.* Of course, that day was Sunday and I didn't have reason to talk to Alex. We didn't talk anymore anyway, we just emailed, but even the personal disconnect provided by electronic communication didn't make it easier to do.

Joe called on Sunday. He said to meet him at the bus terminal at eight-thirty in the morning. It was pretty early for Joe who, like most drummers, preferred a later start time to the day. I figured if he could manage to get somewhere by eight-thirty in the morning, I could manage to tell my own father I was leaving.

I was wrong. Jack had to ask me.

"Are you planning a trip somewhere, Sam?" he asked that evening, during the commercial break to a *Law & Order* rerun.

"How did you know?"

"I couldn't help but overhear you on the phone. And I saw you dragging that old pack upstairs."

"I haven't decided yet whether or not to go," I said, surprised at the express admission. The student's eyes grew wide at this.

"Why wouldn't you go?"

"It's a really long trip."

He was quiet for a minute as he took this in. "I see. Have you told Alex about it?"

"Not yet," I said, ashamed.

"I see."

"Do you think I should go, Dad?" I asked.

He shook his head. "I think you're more than old enough to decide for yourself," he said. "I would do almost anything for you, Sam, I think you know that. But I won't make decisions for you and I also won't tell Alex you're gone. After everything he's done, he deserves to hear it from you."

I had never, ever felt like a bigger flake in my life. This was disconcerting as, after all, I had once flaked out on an entire year. Jack's words made me doubt the Costa Rica plan all the more; at the same time, they made me yearn to go there, as if I could somehow escape my own flakiness by leaving the country in which it was sown.

Tell Alex. I wholeheartedly agreed with Jack about what Alex deserved. But the phone call simply refused to be made.

At eight-thirty the next morning, I was waiting in the bus terminal with three ghosts and one giant backpack. Joe was nowhere to be found.

"He's probably not coming," I said, as I headed toward the exit.

"Figures," the teenager said.

The student grabbed my hand and stopped me. She grabbed it hard.

"Are you okay?" a woman asked, her face clouded with concern. "You look a little distraught."

"I'm fine," I nodded, wondering if she had caught me talking to ghosts she could not see. "My backpack is a little heavy."

"You should take it off," she said. "And maybe drink some water."

"Thanks, I'll do that," I said, as she grabbed her rolling suitcase by the handle and walked away.

"I'm crazy," I said once she was out of earshot, "and other people can see it. And this whole idea is too crazy. Crazy people and crazy ideas are a bad mix."

"Shh!" the student barked. "Here comes Mickey."

"Mickey?" I asked, confused.

"I mean Joe," she stammered.

Sure enough, Joe was approaching us from the other end of the terminal. He was wearing a hooded sweatshirt that covered up his drummer's arms. He was carrying a single duffle bag. It appeared as though he hadn't showered or shaved that morning. Basically, he was a dead ringer for a man without a plan.

I was living in circles and frustrated by the fact that life was asking me to make the same decisions over and over again, as if I hadn't gotten it right the first time. I was more certain than ever that Joe's Costa Rica proposal was nothing more than a remake of that last scene where Mickey. The student knew it, too.

"But you chose *not* to go with Mickey," I reminded her.

"I know. Biggest mistake of my life."

The student viewed her New York decision as a mistake, but from where I stood, it was the absolute right thing to do. What if I were living in New York right then and had never had a legal career? Things would probably be even worse than they were, with the sole exception that I would still have my grandmother's blender.

When would she learn what I had learned—that Mickey was a nothing but a blender-thieving idiot? That Joe was no different? That the whole Costa Rica situation was guaranteed to end badly?

But then it hit me: although she was the eternal student, she was done learning.

And I was her answer to the essay question on the final exam.

"I can't believe it," I whispered. "I actually figured it out."

"What?" she said, nervously eyeing Joe's approach.

"I have the advantage, you know—since I used to be you." She looked to the ground where she shuffled the steel toe of her Doc Martens against the linoleum flooring. "The reason why you want me to go with Joe is because that's the only way you get to stick around."

"Huh?"

"You ceased to exist when you left Mickey to study for the bar exam. The attorney took your place."

"I—"

"I know it was hard to turn your back on the promise of romance and adventure and everything you have always held most dear, but I'm telling you, it was the absolute *best* decision you ever made."

"But it wasn't—"

"It was! You sacrificed yourself for me and the attorney and everyone in between and everyone hereafter."

"Here he comes," the teenager gasped.

I squeezed the student's hand. "And you'll do it again," I instructed. "We both will."

A single tear rolled down her cheek as she looked at Joe, but she released her hold on my hand and took a step backwards.

"Sam, you came!" Joe said when he reached us. I could hear the student's muffled sobs behind me.

I nodded. "Yeah," I said, "but I just came to give you a going-away present." It was a ridiculous answer given the fact that I was wearing a backpack the size of a blue whale. Still, I held out my hand. My fingers shook as I handed over the keys to the Vespa. "It's parked outside by the bike racks."

"What?" Joe asked, clearly confused and disappointed and everything in between. "How am I supposed to get it to Costa Rica?"

I shrugged. "You'll figure something out."

"Don't you need it?"

"Not anymore."

I turned around and walked briskly towards the exit, the three ghosts rushing to keep up. I walked through the automatic door with the teenager and the little girl, but the student paused on the other side of it. By now the tears were pouring down her cheeks, and the teenager was also sobbing.

The door closed between us. I waved at the student and she waved back.

I turned around and headed for the parking lot.

"Wait!" the little girl cried. "What about the other one?" The teenager sobbed some more.

"She's not coming," I explained, turning back towards the terminal to make my point.

Indeed, she was already gone.

The little girl didn't seem to understand, but she continued on with the teenager and me as we commenced the very long walk back to Jack's house.

✻

Chapter 16

GYMNASTICS

WHEN THE REMAINING GHOSTS and I finally got home, we dumped the large backpack in the dining room with everything else that was nothing but a sour reminder of something long past. The pack fit right in with the stacks of china and the piles of paperwork I had generated with Alex. Jack didn't ask what happened to the "trip." He didn't even get off the couch.

"Is that you Sam?" he yelled from the den.

"Yeah."

"Welcome back."

"Thanks."

Having removed the heavy pack for the first time in hours, I suddenly felt so light I swore I might just float away. Instead, I walked up the stairs and got straight into bed, with my shoes on and everything. It was sheer exhaustion and the accompanying laziness that prevented me from taking off my shoes. But sometimes laziness can be a lifesaver.

It was noon when I got in bed on Monday. And it was noon Tuesday when I first considered getting out. I laid there for an awfully long time weighing "in" versus "out" and I must admit that "in" might have won had the darn shoes not been so uncomfortable and so impossible to kick off without sitting up and untying them. Also, I hadn't forgotten the student's sacrifice and my implicit promise to her that I, too, would begin to act with consideration for the greater good despite any momentary discomfort.

Also, I missed her.

We all missed her, in fact. The younger ghosts looked very relieved when I finally got up.

"So what are we going to do now?" the teenager asked.

"I don't know," I said. "What do you want to do?"

As it turned out, there were a world of possibilities between Commerce and Costa Rica, a world that I had failed to consider until Costa Rica had actually been ruled out.

"What do you want to be when you grow up?" I asked the little girl.

"A trapeze person in the circus," she said without hesitation.

"Fair enough." I turned to the teenager. "And what about you?"

"Ummm, I haven't decided yet. Probably a teacher."

"Really?" I asked, surprised. "I didn't remember that."

"Or a beautician," she said. Unfortunately, I did remember that one.

"And I also want to be a gymnastics girl," the little girl said.

"Too late," the teenager huffed.

"What do you mean too late?"

"You have to be discovered when you're like four years old or something in a village in Romania."

The teenager had also wanted to be a gymnast every time the summer Olympics rolled around. But at age fifteen, she realized she was about the same age as most of the gymnasts and it was too late for her to take up the sport.

"I'm afraid she's right," I said, shaking my head. In truth, I was somewhat fearful of the thought of myself in a leotard after seven months of Sarita's Sunday dinners anyway.

After the passage of three days, the little girl had forgotten all about her athletic aspirations.

"Where's Disneyland?" she asked. In addition to pestering my ghosts about their life's ambitions, I had also asked them where they would like to live.

"In California," I said. "Not too far from Los Angeles, where I spent a summer."

"Good. Let's move there and you can work at Disneyland."

The teenager scoffed again. "What? As a street sweeper?"

"No, she'll dress up like Cinderella and take pictures with kids and sign their books. Because you know what?" With this, her voice dropped to a raspy whisper. "It's not the real Cinderella at Disneyland. It's just someone playing pretend."

"Too late," the teenager said again.

"What do you mean?" I asked.

"Duh, you're way too old to be Cinderella," she shot back.

"Well maybe she can be the wicked stepmother," the little girl offered.

"Who on earth wants the wicked stepmother's autograph?" the teenager asked, clearly disgusted.

"Umm…"

"I hate to break it to both of you," I said. "But nobody wants Cinderella's autograph anymore, either. They want Ariel's or Belle's or Jasmine's or Mulan's."

The ghosts looked at me as if I had gone positively insane. "*Who?!*"

But I had bigger worries than what popular Disney character my apparently aged features would permit me to play. Although the idea of a "fluff" job was initially tempting, I had been around long enough to know that such a job didn't exist. It took hard work to be a trapeze artist, and I'm sure an eight-hour shift in Cinderella's hoop skirt under the California sun was no thrill ride, either. I had been too spoiled by working from the comfort of Jack's dining room to adjust to something as purportedly "fluffy" as the ghosts desired.

"I know! Why don't you be in a rock n' roll band?" the little girl asked a week or two later as we were flipping through the cable channels and momentarily landed on a music video.

"I can't. I don't play any instruments," I said.

"But you like the drums."

"She likes drum-*mers*," the teenager corrected.

"I once liked them," I admitted.

"Well then you can be the singer," the little girl suggested.

"But I can't sing," I said, my mind immediately snapping to the long-lost time when I fit in the front of a grocery cart and sang about jam. "I mean, I don't sing."

"You should probably keep it that way," was the teenager's advice, and I was glad to take it. The idea of singing for a living was positively nerve-wracking to me. I was willing to admit that a little bit of singing might be therapeutic, but supporting myself off it was another issue entirely. Again, my present job had pampered me by never requiring me to go out of my comfort zone. Perhaps said pampering had been to my detriment.

Over the next several weeks, the ghosts and I continued to carve out our future by process of elimination. Travel writer. Restaurant critic. Dog trainer. Science professor. Jet pilot. Humanitarian. Most of the jobs momentarily put on our list were almost immediately crossed off due to the fact that they simply didn't pay enough. For some I was overqualified, whereas others would have required me to essentially start over in college and get another three degrees. I didn't have the talent, skills or training necessary for most of them and the acquisition of said talent, skills and training was either humanly impossible (professional basketball player) or practically so (astronaut). Some jobs required foreign language abilities that I did not possess. Others required psychic powers that I wasn't confident I had despite my ongoing communication with the undead. And many involved far more sequins than I was generally comfortable wearing.

In the meantime, I continued to work remotely for Alex. The only difference was that, after the Fourth of July and Costa Rica incidents, the latter of which he was possibly unaware, we didn't talk much. Or ever. Instead of a morning phone call, he sent me a morning email, responding to my evening email, which I sent the night before. Similarly, his weekly visits had been replaced by weekly FedEx exchanges. It was unfortunate timing as Jack's vegetable garden was positively overflowing by that point. Without Alex to take it off his hands, Jack started pawning the surplus off on Sarita and the usual neighbors, none of whom he particularly liked. I tried to do my part by helping him pull weeds. I even experimented with canning the tomatoes, which was a true labor of love as it required no less than twelve calls to Sarita in the process. Say what you will about my aunt, but she is a canning goddess.

Also on the goddess list: Starene, whose afternoon talk show had recently debuted. Starene was billed as an ordinary person giving other ordinary people common-sense advice. In her infinite wisdom, Starene recognized the best way to give said advice was to call people idiots for daring to have the kind of deep-rooted emotional scars that would, say, cause someone to end up in one physically abusive relationship after another.

"Maybe you should go work for her," the little girl suggested.

"Yeah, you've always liked her," the teenager said, wrinkling her nose. "Maybe you could be her assistant, or just be there to make sure that her hair gets brushed out more than once a week."

"Maybe…" I said unconvincingly.

You see, as much as I admired Starene, I had a feeling she would be a bit of a bear to work for. She had a tendency to yell and call everyone an idiot, even when their idiocy was somewhat justifiable. By contrast, Alex Martin had never called me an idiot despite the fact that there were a million reasons why he could. But Alex Martin was far more likely to dish out assistance than insult.

"Is Alex ever going to come back?" the little girl asked.

"I don't know."

"But then we'll never finish the ramp and we'll never jump the gulch," she pouted.

"Oh gag me. I'm so sick of hearing about that stupid gulch and gravity," the teenager said. "Technically, gravity is what's keeping us all grounded," the teenager said. "Otherwise we'd be bouncing around chasing glasses of milk and the whole wide world would be a mess."

"But you're still afraid of it, aren't you?" I asked.

The teenager took offense. "Of course I'm not afraid of it. I'm just... annoyed by it sometimes."

"Like when?" the little girl asked.

"Like that one time with Libby, at the dance."

Yes, the dance. It was a Sadie Hawkins dance and, therefore, a little less formal. People wore jeans instead of taffeta. There was group dancing instead of slow-dancing. At one point, things got crazy enough (for Commerce, mind you) that kids started jumping off the stage and crowd surfing.

"What's crowd-surfing?" the little girl asked.

The teenager answered authoritatively. "It's when people dance in a pack and then a person will jump off the stage backwards and land in the crowd and the other people will all catch him and stuff and pass him around."

"That sounds like fun," the little girl said.

"Well it wasn't fun for Libby," I said.

"She should have known better," the teenager shot back. "I don't know why she even tries these things. If she knew what was good for her, she would avoid the spotlight."

"What happened to Libby?" the little girl asked.

The teenager rolled her eyes. "Like I said, everyone was crowd-surfing and it worked for everyone but when Libby got up there and tried, somehow she jumped straight onto the floor."

"How come? Did she jump in the wrong place?"

"No, that's just the thing and I've been thinking about it for a long time. She jumped straight into the crowd, but they kind of parted at exactly the right point and she dove right into the ground and all I remember was her long skinny legs all flinging in the air as she asked someone to help her up but nobody did. But the thing was, there were a *lot* of kids in that crowd and yet they *all* scattered when she jumped. And at first I was all, maybe they don't like her and were like, ew, I don't want to touch Libby Billingsley, cause there were a lot of people at that school I wouldn't have wanted to touch, and so maybe everyone moved a little bit out of her way. But then I thought about it some more and the people who moved would have bumped into other people but that's not what happened. *Everyone* moved. And I began to wonder if maybe some of them had spread the word and it was planned. And then I began to wonder if maybe the whole crowd-surfing thing was planned just to play a scam on Libby."

"Gee," I said, sarcastically, "I wonder who would have planned something like that..."

"*Melissa!*" the little girl hissed.

"Are you kidding?" the teenager asked. "Melissa doesn't have time for stupid tricks like that. There were a million kids there—it could have been any one of them."

"Yeah, but how many of those kids had enough clout to coordinate a million of them?" I asked.

The teenager brushed off the suggestion. "It's not Melissa's style. Anyway, that's why I'm so mad at gravity."

"Why, because you were embarrassed when people found out you were the cousin of the girl who crashed while crowd-surfing?"

"No! I'm not as conceited as you think—I was embarrassed for Libby, okay? She had a concussion and Aunt Sarita made her wear a neck brace for two weeks just in case she had an injury the doctors hadn't found and that only made it worse because when people saw Libby in the neck brace it was like they were reliving the whole thing all over again and they would just bust up laughing at the sight of her."

"And what did you do?" the little girl asked. "Did you beat them up?"

"No, I didn't 'beat them up,'" she said. "That's what you don't get. That's what nobody gets—including Aunt Sarita and Libby. That would have just made it worse. Calling any sort of attention to her always made it worse."

"Maybe it wouldn't have mattered to her to 'make it worse' so long as she knew someone out there was supporting her," I said. "Did you ever think of that? Did you ever consider that maybe, after a certain level of humiliation, things couldn't really get any worse?"

"I did think about that, but every time I thought it couldn't get any worse, it did." She pulled her knees to her chest and buried her chin in them. "Anyway, if it weren't for gravity, I wouldn't have had to think about any of it at all."

The little girl narrowed her eyes into slits. "But that was the kids' fault," she said cautiously, "not gravity's."

"Can't it be both their fault?" the teenager asked.

"I would have just beaten all those kids up," the little girl claimed with total confidence.

"Then you would have had exactly as many friends as Libby," I said.

"So what? I'm not friends with meanies anyway."

"So I totally pour my heart out to you on gravity and all and now you're switching sides?" the teenager asked, with more than a little whine in her voice.

"Well, I'm sorta confused," the little girl admitted. "But which one of you thinks gravity is the bad guy again?"

The teenager raised her hand.

The little girl smiled. "Then I'm on your team. And you can help us jump the gulch."

The teenager flopped back on the pillow with dramatic aplomb. No matter how hard she tried, she couldn't rid the little girl of her gulch-crossing fantasy. I decided to toss her a bone by letting her fulfill her fantasy of being a beautician. The only problem was that we didn't have the requisite supplies.

"Can I borrow the truck for an hour or two, Dad?" I asked Jack. "I need to run some errands."

"Sure," he said, fishing the keys out of his pocket. "Are you going by the Garden Center?"

"I can if you need me to."

"Will you pick up two bags of organic potting soil for me?" He pulled out some money for the soil, as if he hadn't done so much for me that year that I owed him a thousand bags of potting soil. "A friend's got me experimenting with it."

A friend was clearly code for Alex—and why shouldn't it be? Nobody was a better friend than Alex. Too bad I blew it and he was just my boss now. But I was glad Jack still considered him a friend. Jack could use a few more of those.

"So what happened to the scooter, Sam?" Jack asked as he handed me the money. "I noticed it wasn't in the garage."

"I gave it away," I shrugged. "I think I finally outgrew it."

The corners of Jack's mouth turned up. If it were on any other face, it wouldn't count as anything—but on Jack's, it was definitely a smile.

"Good," he said.

"Yeah, I guess I'm going to have to be a big girl now and buy an actual car," I said.

"You probably should. But take your time."

I hadn't a friend in the world except for two ghosts and my own father, but I felt embraced and loved as I drove the old truck through the tree-lined highway that afternoon. As we passed at high speed, the bright sun intermittently broke through the branches like a strobe light. Like ice cream and too much dancing and many of the world's most wonderful things, it was absolutely divine while simultaneously giving me a bit of a headache.

Our destination was one of those everything stores, and the nearest one was located in the outskirts of Sherman Valley. Once there, the teenager dutifully pored over the fashion magazines before we headed to the makeup aisle. She was fulfilling her promise to ensure that my makeover was relatively current. In the meantime, the little girl perused the nearby toy section.

She picked up a particular box and became enraged. "Look at this!" she said, disgusted. "They changed Strawberry Shortcake!"

And indeed they had. The Strawberry Shortcake that the little girl had known and adored was elfin and wore a dress, a pinafore, mismatched striped tights and a huge shower-cap like bonnet in her wild yet wonderfully smelling hair. It was like *Little House on the Prairie* meets Candyland chic. Miss Shortcake lived in a tree with her cat and friends who dressed similar to her, but never in the same colors. There was some sort of pie theme going on with them, but I couldn't remember exactly what it was.

The "new and improved" Strawberry Shortcake was wearing what appeared to be jeans and a t-shirt. She had lost that "I'm living in a tree" innocence she once had. She looked like she just got off her job at the pretzel counter at the mall and was cruising for trouble.

"Things change," the teenager told her, clearly irritated at the interruption. At the same time, she couldn't get over the fact that teal eyeliner was now a rarity. "All the models' eye makeup is messed up."

"It's the smoky look," I told her. "It's been in for years."

"Gag me," she said under her breath. "It looks like they went to sleep without washing their faces."

Still, we finally settled on a new eye look and bought the products to match. It was drugstore rather than department store product, yet it was a definite improvement on the decades-old war paint I had occasionally worn over the last several months.

We got home and the teenager worked her magic. "You really are good at this," I told her after admiring the end result. It wasn't too heavy or overdone, but it gave the impression of a woman who actually cared about her appearance. It was a long time since I had seen such a woman in the mirror, and it felt great.

"Are you sad that you didn't grow up to be a beautician?" I asked her. "They're called 'makeup artists' now, you know."

"No," she shrugged as she did a little touching up. "I actually think it's super rad that I ended up being a lawyer."

"You do?"

"Yeah. You have to be smart to do it and it seems pretty fancy and you get paid a whole lot of money. You also have a really cute boss who lets you work at home and do whatever you want," she added. "That really helps."

"But I quit my job at Wallace."

"So what?" she asked. "It was just a job, not your whole life. Just cause you quit a job doesn't mean you weren't good at it."

The number of double negatives in that last sentence was astounding, but not nearly as much as her brilliance. "So if you had to pick a job for *me* to do when I grow up…" I ventured.

She nodded, anticipating the rest of the question. "I would pick the one that you already have, for sure."

✳

Chapter 17

DEAD GIRLS' PARTY

Libby had a big date with Raul, so big that she felt inclined to buy a new dress for the occasion. Given our lifelong and, at times, arduous relationship, the level of flattery I experienced upon receiving her invitation to go shopping for said dress was both surprising and a little embarrassing. The latter emotion had nothing to do with Libby but rather my own starvation for human interaction. For the past two months I hadn't seen Alex—we communicated by email and only occasionally by phone. Of course, Joe was long gone and I hadn't heard from Melissa. I considered asking Alex for Mina's number at one point, momentarily convincing myself that I might even drive out to Portland to visit her, but given the nature of our last conversation regarding Mina, I never got the nerve. As a result, the only person I ever really hung out with was Jack. Well, Jack and the entire cast of all the *Law & Orders*, that is.

As I waited at the end of the driveway for Libby to pick me up in Uncle Stanley's old sedan, I looked down at my own mismatched outfit and wondered whether I was a qualified shopping companion. I was wearing an old t-shirt, a skirt, a really nice sweater to compensate for the early fall chill, yet flirty sandals that held onto the last wisps of Oregon's Indian summer. I shrugged my shoulders and decided to focus not on the incongruous nature of the whole thing, but on the lone fact that the sweater truly was quite nice. I also figured I was the best shopping companion dear Libby could find, as her choices were essentially me, her mother and Charlemayne from the call center.

But then Uncle Stanley's sedan pulled up and I saw Charlemayne was in the back seat.

Charlemayne was on the older end of middle-aged and had very yellow hair, the way white hair looks when one is still trying to dye it blonde. Charlemayne smoked about four packs of cigarettes a day, at least I assumed it was four packs based on her voice and overall aromatics. Like a lot of lifetime smokers, Charlemayne had leathery skin and her mouth was permanently in some sort of a circular pout, as if she were sucking on a cigarette, only it stayed that way even when she wasn't. Unfortunately for Charlemayne and her fellow tobacconists, it was not a very flattering look. Back when I worked at the call center, this pout instilled quite a bit of fear in me as I always felt Charlemayne was scowling, and so I went out of my way to try to make her smile until one time I finally did, and she laughed and bore her yellow teeth in the process and I vowed to never see her smile again. Apparently, most of the people in Commerce had taken a similar vow and so Charlemayne went around scowling all of the time.

Charlemayne held the same regard for her clothing as she did for her lungs. Everything was very brightly colored—I'll give her that. She was a vivacious dresser. But the brightly colored clothes only washed out her hair and emphasized her sour expression and sturdy figure, which were so much less bright by comparison.

During my tenure as a call center employee, which, by that time, seemed very limited and long ago, I figured out that Charlemayne was some sort of manager and had made Libby her protégé. I imagined that, in twenty years, Libby would resemble some sort of skinnier combination of Sarita and Charlemayne, as if the two strong-willed women combined into a waspy, faux-Goth offspring. Although I was well-versed in the rules of basic biology, it somehow seemed more possible that Sarita and Charlemayne would produce a child such as Libby than would Sarita and Stanley. You see, when other kids were kids, they would think about the purportedly romantic specifics that led to their own existence with the same reluctant curiosity that one watches a horror flick or looks at a car accident—there is a sick satisfaction to be found in thoroughly shocking oneself. Unfortunately, the little girl and the teenager weren't like other kids as their deceased mother was a magical character of sorts and the whole scenario seemed almost fairy-like. However, one day the teenager did let her mind wander to the anatomical encounter that resulted in one Libby Billingsley and she got the dry heaves. Then she felt really sorry for Uncle Stanley for having been so violated. She couldn't envision the actual act so much as she could see Uncle Stanley in the shower afterwards, crying and scrubbing his skin raw.

I thought about this and Libby's female role models as the car approached. I realized that despite the fact that my interest in personal appearance was on the rebound, I still had something to offer Libby in the shopping department. I had once been the impeccably-attired attorney, after all. It didn't matter so much what I was presently wearing as it mattered what I would wear if I cared a whit and hadn't turned into such a tightwad. And the imaginary outfit I conjured up was quite nice, or at least more than nice enough for a special date with Raul.

"What happened to the Geo?" the teenager asked. On her sixteenth birthday, Libby's parents gave her a brand new Geo Metro convertible, an almost unheard-of luxury for our town.

"She totaled that thing a long time ago," I said. Like most things in life, Libby would probably be good at driving if she weren't so darn distracted all of the time.

"She did?"

"Yeah. She rear-ended Curtis Sullivan as they were both driving into the school parking lot her senior year because she was busy watching the marching band rehearse in the vacant lot across the street. Everyone saw it happen."

"Figures," the teenager said. "How'd she ever live that one down?"

"She didn't," I said. "She just graduated."

The teenager rolled her eyes. Needless to say, she was apprehensive about spending the afternoon with Libby, but she wasn't about to turn down my invitation to tag along. She hadn't been to the Sherman Valley Towne Center since they remodeled it. It was a big day for her.

"It's too bad though," she said. "It was a cool car."

I laughed. "I know it's not your fault because we have this whole time-warp thing going on, but trust me, the Metro was not a cool car."

"Why not?"

"Well, for one thing, it's the type of car that gets totaled when you have a simple rear-ending fender bender in a parking lot."

"At least it was a convertible."

"For your information, I owned a convertible once. A Mercedes."

"So I've heard. Was it purple, like Libby's?"

"No. It was silver."

"Oh gag me. Silver is so boring."

I opened the car door and climbed inside. Luckily, the sedan was made back in the day of the bench seat, so the teenager was able to sit in the middle with her knees up to her chin.

"Hi!" Libby said. "I brought Charlemayne, too."

Charlemayne nodded at me from the back seat, where she was smoking out the open window.

"Hi Charlemayne," I said.

"Hi hon," she huffed at me in her raspy tenor voice.

Within the hour, Libby was wearing the perfect little black dress. It was strappy yet modest, and had a layer of tulle netting over the bodice with some black beading. Understated, but still dressy.

"It's perfect," I said.

A little black dress. Who hasn't heard that it's the perfect "big date" attire? Who doesn't have five? I know at least ten women who have made an entire wardrobe out of little black dresses. Everybody looks good in one.

"You look like you're dead," Charlemayne offered.

That's right—Charlemayne had never heard of the little black dress. Charlemayne had only heard of the little red dress or the little fuschia dress, only scratch the "little" part as Charlemayne kept trying to steer bean pole Libby towards the elastic-waistbanded section popular with people in Charlemayne's demo-graphic.

Sure enough, Charlemayne talked Libby into changing into a pair of purple silk pants and a matching jewel-toned caftan.

"Oh—it's goshawful ugly!" the teenager frowned.

"I know," I said under my breath.

"You totally have to talk her out of it. Even if it is Libby."

"I will," I muttered so the others wouldn't hear me, "I'm just waiting for a moment when Charlemayne is not around."

"That old hag? What do you even care what she thinks?"

I didn't want to confess to the teenager my worry that, if I acted like I knew the best thing to wear on a date, Charlemayne would challenge my knowledge of men and the whole conversation would devolve into some sort of competition as to who had more dating experience under her belt (or waistband, as the case may be). And I was more than a little worried that Charlemayne would win. I was pretty sure she had at least two illegitimate children, and while bas-tard kids might not be a medal one usually wears with pride, they sure serve as convincing evidence that one has a way with men.

"If only I had some bastard children, then I would speak up," I said to the teenager. "Besides, it's just not polite to critique someone else's taste in fashion."

"Really?" she said. "Because I thought it wasn't polite to let your cousin go on a date looking like she's on *The Golden Girls*."

Of course, that only made me think about how all four of the Golden Girls had more boyfriends than me. Especially Blanche—she was kind of trampy in an old lady way.

Eventually Charlemayne had to step outside for a smoke break and I got my moment alone with Libby. She admitted she liked the black dress better but was upset by its high price tag. I had to talk some fashionomics with her—about how she was getting more bang for her buck out of the dress than the purple outfit because she could wear it anywhere—with hose and strappy heels it was dressy, with flip-flops and a cardigan it was casual, and with a jacket and pumps she could wear it to work. She wrinkled her nose and told me she wore jeans to work. I told her that these days I also wore jeans to work and that the American workplace as a whole was moving towards a more casual environment, but in no instance would it move towards an environment where purple silk pants were acceptable work attire unless, of course, your workplace was in Branson, Missouri and you were the background dancer in an M.C. Hammer revue.

Libby finally relented and bought the dress. Never breaking character, Charlemayne simply shrugged her shoulders and said "Suit yourself, hon." Things were going great until we left the department store and I first saw them.

"Oh my gosh!" the teenager said. "Walk behind the others so they don't see you."

It was too late as they had already spotted us. It was Melissa and she was there with Chad Latham of Commerce High School fame and Phil or James or Abraham or whatever that guy who sometimes hung out with Joe was named.

"Okay, Plan B," the teenager said. "Walk up to them first and talk to them before they realize you're here with these two."

"Oh my gosh, is that Melissa Matthews?" Libby asked, too excited. They heard her, of course.

"Uh, yeah," I said. I waved at them.

"Plan C," the teen instructed. "Wave but keep walking."

But, as usual, the teenager was one step behind Melissa. The three were already approaching us. Melissa had that smirk on her face. It meant trouble.

"Fancy meeting you here," she said in a voice so sickly sweet that both the teenager and I knew we were doomed.

"Hi, Melissa. Hi . . . ," I said, waving at the other two, desperately trying to avoid having to call the one guy by name.

"Sam Green, is that you?" Chad asked, incredulous.

"Hi, Chad."

"I haven't seen you since high school."

"I know, and yet here we are . . . hanging out at the mall together, just like old times."

Chad seemed oblivious to the tension in the air.

"Is it true that you're a big shot Seattle lawyer now?"

"Say 'no,'" the teenager begged me. "Boys hate it when girls are smarter than them and you'll just make Melissa mad by showing off."

I laughed nervously. "Umm, I don't know about the 'big shot' part, and although I'm technically practicing in Seattle, I'm actually working from Commerce right now. But I am a lawyer."

"That's amazing," Chad said. Melissa's smirk turned sour at his excitement.

"What are you doing?" I asked him.

"I'm in real estate," he replied.

"Good choice," I said. "I can't believe how this area has grown in the last ten years."

"I got lucky," he agreed.

I looked behind me at Libby. She was pale as a ghost.

"Don't do it," the teenager begged me. "She'll be better off if you don't."

But I simply couldn't obey her. The teenager had always been willing to pretend that Libby did not exist, a kind of variation on playing dead only she was playing that someone else was dead. But Libby was standing right there and she looked so eager for them to acknowledge her and so I had to do it. "You guys remember my cousin Libby, don't you?" I asked.

"Of course," Melissa responded, barely able to contain the deliciousness of the moment. I realized that the teenager may have been right, and I might have done Libby a huge disservice by simply acknowledging her presence. Chad's excitement at seeing me had scared Melissa off from attacking me personally, but she desperately needed a dog to kick. Libby was that dog. She always had been.

Chad extended his hand, which Libby eagerly shook.

"I don't think I know you," he said.

"Of course you do," Melissa corrected. "Libby Billingsley is the girl who accidentally Maced her entire P.E. class on self-defense day."

"No!" Chad barked, as he burst out laughing.

"She's also the girl who peed her pants in chemistry when Mr. Alonso was testing everyone's water consumption limits—"

"I'm not sure that happened," I said.

"Oh yes it did," the teenager said, her arms crossed.

"Oh yes it did," Melissa said. "Didn't it Libby?"

"I didn't realize I had to go until—"

Chad cut her off by grabbing her hand. By now, tears were streaming down his face. "I just have to shake your hand again," he said, fighting to control his laughter. "You are a Commerce High legend."

Libby smiled nervously. She was also holding back tears, but not the laughing kind.

"Do you see what you did?" the teenager scolded me.

"You know what they say," I said, laughing nervously. "Better to live in infamy than die in anonymity."

"I've never heard that phrase," Melissa said curtly.

"Neither have I," Charlemayne piped in. She clearly disproved of the entire situation. She stood behind us with her hands on her hips, her lips pursed even more than usual.

"Besides," Melissa continued, "I haven't even gotten to the baton incident—"

"Don't tell me," Chad said. He was still laughing, but his words were surprisingly firm. "That's enough."

Then Chad stopped laughing, and for a split second, all the background noise was drowned out by the teenager's faint whimpering. I looked at her and saw that she was gripping the sides of her face like the melting man in that Edvard Munch painting or baby-faced McCauley Culkin.

Indeed, despite the gargantuan size of the room—the main concourse of a three-story shopping mall, after all—the electricity therein was suddenly so strong it was confining. I squinted my eyes to the point that I could no longer make out the details of the people in front of me. Only then did I see them.

The ghosts. The room was completely full of ghosts.

Only these ones were not mine.

Every shopper on every level was followed by at least three of them. At the kiosk in the center, the sunglasses vendor put on a bored and disinterested front as one of his ghosts wrestled the other to the floor in a headlock. There were ghosts of all ages and sizes. They were out of control and inconsolable.

And even the nameless guy had them, and Chad did too. Charlemayne was so old and experienced that she must have had twelve of them there. Half were in love with the father of her son, while the others pined for the dad of her much older daughter. There were four different Melissas staring at me, all of them adolescent, each one with a different expression on her face. One was cackling in a sinister manner, one was fixing her hair in the sunglass kiosk mirror and yet another was covering her eyes and ears and begging the real Melissa to stop.

But by far the scariest ghosts in the room were those belonging to Libby Billingsley. I recognized every one of them because I had once known them all. Each had her own look, but they shared one thing in common: the wailing and gnashing of teeth.

As quickly as they subsided, the real sounds of the room burst forward again. My eyes came back into focus and all but my own teenaged ghost were gone. Said teenager crumpled to the floor in exhaustion.

Chad reached out and pulled Libby into a giant bear hug. Her bean pole arms flailed around her, the right one still grasping her shopping bag. He planted a huge kiss on the side of her cheek.

"Thanks for making my day," he said to Libby, his voice bearing empathy learned since I had last seen him. "Like I said, it was a pleasure to meet you." He stood back and she was clearly in shock. He turned to me. "Great to see you, Sam." And then he looked at Charlemayne. "Ma'am," he said, while nodding his head towards her.

She grunted in response. We headed back to the parking garage.

I have always assumed that when you pick a bunch of people up at different locations before you drive somewhere, you should drop them off in the reverse order so that you essentially retrace your steps back to your own house. When it is done another way, things tend to get messed up, like that one time with Enid Thompson. But Libby has never been fond of logic or particularly cognizant of the "right" way to do things, and so she dropped Charlemayne off first.

Once we were alone, she spoke up for the first time.

"It's just not fair," she said.

I knew where she was headed, but I had not idea how to escape. I thought again of Enid. I almost expected Libby to ask me if I was going to Chad's party.

"What?" I asked. For Libby's sake, I played the conversation like a volleyball game, and set her up to drive it over the net.

"No offense, but you're a total loser right now," she said. She wasn't so different from Melissa after all—she was down and needed a dog to kick. I decided that after what she had just been through, I was willing to be the dog for a change.

"I know," I said. "My life's a complete mess."

"You barely have a job, you just started putting on makeup when you leave the house—"

"I know, Libby. What's your point?"

"Why is it that, even when you're at your lowest and you're rude and can barely carry on a conversation, people still like you better—things still work out for you?"

"Well, I would hardly call Melissa Matthews and Chad Latham and, er, that other guy 'people,'" I said.

"It's like no matter what I do, I can't escape the person I was in high school," she said.

For a split second, her words caused me to see them again—all the ghosts hovering around Libby. One of them was driving alongside us in a purple Geo Metro. She wasn't driving very well because she was too busy watching us. If she and her car hadn't been ghosts, they would have gotten in five accidents. Another of Libby's ghosts was crouched in the back seat, sobbing. Her pants were wet. Yet another was wearing a pirate patch over her eye. All the ghosts had bruises and scratches and were wearing crazy clothes. Their eyes were puffy from crying. Their faces were downcast for want of friends or parents who get it or a simple un-derstanding of why the world is so cruel. They were confused. They were completely haggard. They were haunting and scary.

"Stop the car," I told Libby.

"I'm not in the mood to be bossed around."

"Stop the car," I repeated. "I want to talk to you, but you can't listen and drive."

She didn't agree, but she obeyed. We got milkshakes at Roger's Roadside and drank them in the car in the parking lot.

"I want you to listen to me very carefully," I told her after I had a few shots of creamy, caloric chocolate in me. "I know I'm a mess right now, but I've learned a few lessons about life along the way."

"Okay," she said, still pouting.

"That girl you were in high school? The one with the baton?"

"Yeah?"

"You are *not* her anymore. She is a completely different person than you, and she disappeared a long time ago. Her only hope for survival is if you resurrect her through your thoughts—and believe me, she will beg you to do it if you so much as give her a fleeting thought. You *must* resist the urge."

Libby stared at me for a long time. I was already regretting my words, picturing her repeating them to Sarita verbatim, and Sarita calling Jack and repeating them to him.

"How did you know?" Libby asked.

"Know what?" I said.

"That it's like, clumsy high school Libby is a shadow following me around."

"I think we all have those shadows," I said, marking my words carefully to avoid any red flags that might end me in the looney bin.

"They're horrible," she said.

"Not always," I offered. "You might need them to bail you out if you ever lose yourself."

"No, I want to get rid of them. How do I do it?"

I thought about this for a minute. I felt like a doctor must feel when he prescribes medicine for what he *thinks* is the problem.

Still, I didn't want Libby to clue in to any doubt. I tried to speak with absolute conviction.

"Well, for starters," I said, "you can wear your new black dress on your date with Raul and allow yourself to feel beautiful the entire time." She smiled. "For another thing, you can now truthfully tell everyone you know that Chad Latham kissed you."

She laughed. "I couldn't believe it when he did that. I didn't know if he was being nice or making fun of me."

"I think he was being nice," I said. "I think he did it to make fun of Melissa."

"That's rich," she said smugly.

"One last thing," I said, knowing that this tidbit would never be passed along. "You can love your mother, because she certainly loves you. But seeing as you're a successful and competent adult and all, you can stop listening to almost everything she says."

Once Libby dropped me off and the old sedan pulled away, I turned to the teenager ghost and grabbed her by the shoulders.

"Thank you," I said.

"I don't know why you're thanking me," she said. "You never even listen to me, even when I'm telling you things for your own good."

"I'm thanking you for being you," I said.

"What are you even talking about?"

"For the first time in a long time, I feel very lucky. If I'm going to have to have a bunch of ghosts haunt me, I am really, really glad you're one of them."

She kicked her Keds in the dust. "Then do me a favor," she said.

"What?"

"Tell me the deal about stinkin' Dan Polanski already."

And so I did tell her, and in doing so I had to relive her horror at the realization that her own best friend—nay, the person to whom she had devoted her entire life—would steal her precious drummer boy just to spite her.

"She did what?!" she gasped.

"She stole Dan. As payback for your being nice to Enid."

"Did they, like, kiss and stuff?"

"Uh, this was junior year . . . . Let's say they at least kissed."

"What?!" she said, and dropped to her knees. She fell back onto the grass and put her head in her hands.

"This is exactly why I didn't want to tell you," I explained.

"I can't believe that's it," she said.

"That's it? You mean you aren't horrified?"

"No, I mean, it's Melissa, what do you expect? And I've told you a million times, he was just some stoner I had a little crush on anyway, and just cause he was nice to me in that crazy art class where I really needed it. It's just, why did you stoop to her level?"

"How?"

"With Joe."

Now it was my turn to drop to the ground.

"I don't know," I sighed, arms wrapped around my knees. "He was nice to me when I needed it, too, I suppose. Why didn't you ever stick up to Melissa when she was making fun of Libby?"

"You don't remember how teenagers work," she said. "Saying nothing was the best way to protect her. The only problem is, Libby is totally clueless. So yeah, maybe sometimes I should have stuck up for her just so she would know I was willing to do it."

I nodded my head.

I stood up, brushed the dirt off my skirt, and headed toward the house. But the teenager stayed seated.

"You know who else has always been really nice to you?" she asked. "Like, even when you totally didn't deserve it?"

"Who?"

"Duh—Alex Martin."

"Fair enough," I nodded. "Are you coming inside?"

"No," she said, extending her legs and turning her chin toward the sun. "I think I'll stay out here and work on my tan."

"Suit yourself, hon," I said, instantly irritated with myself for picking up the phrase from Charlemayne.

I walked inside.

The teenager never followed.

✳

Chapter 18

BOTH REASONABLE AND PRUDENT

"Is she gone now?" the little girl asked me the next morning when we woke up.

"Yeah," I sighed. "She's gone now, too."

"Did she say goodbye?"

"No."

"That's rude. What did she say, then?"

"She just said she thinks I should like Alex." In fact, I hadn't been able to stop thinking about the teenager's parting advice.

"Oh, brother," the little girl groaned. "All she thinks about is boys and her friends and crying."

"She was silly that way," I agreed, all the while wondering why I hadn't realized what a catch a tall professional with a free t-shirt collection was all along.

"But I like Alex, too," the little girl offered. I was so relieved that the conversation had moved back to him. It was hard to keep the little girl on track most of the time. Of course, I knew the primary reason she liked Alex was that she was hoping he'd make good on his promise to help build us a ramp.

"How can you know someone but not know someone for nine whole years and then wake up one morning completely enamored?" I asked.

"What?" the little girl said.

It was going to be difficult getting used to having only her around anymore.

"What I mean is, how do I get Alex to like me again?"

"How should I know?" she asked. "I don't even like boys."

Point taken.

"I guess you'll just have to help me figure out what *other* people who *do* like boys would do."

"Huh?"

"For example, what would the attorney do?"

"Oh, I get it now," the little girl said. "That meanie would brush her hair and wear a necklace or something sparkly."

"Right. And what about the student?"

"She'd act real cool."

"Do you mean confident?"

The little girl furrowed her brow. "Confi-what?"

"Cool. We'll stick with cool. And the teenager—what would she do?"

"Probably cry."

"Well I don't think crying will work—"

Her eyes lit up. "I know—she would put on more makeup!"

"Bingo!"

"Bingo!" the little girl repeated. "Hey, that's the name of the farmer's dog."

"What?"

"*There was a farmer had a dog and Bingo was his name-o*," she sang.

"You're brilliant!" I said.

"What?" she asked. I had clearly lost her again.

"Do you want to go see the dogs one last time?"

Her eyes grew wide at the suggestion.

Jack readily lent us his truck for the venture, even though he couldn't quite mask his worry. The little girl sat in the front seat this time, watching the whole wide world whiz by the window.

When we were about twenty-five miles outside of Commerce, I figured it was best to call Alex to ensure he'd be home.

"Hello?"

"Hi, Alex. It's Samantha Green."

"Yeah, I know your number, Sam."

"Right. Listen, are you by chance working from home today?"

"I work from home every day."

"But you don't have any big errands planned or anything?"

"No . . . Why?" I could hear the blinking start on the other end of the line.

"Just wondering."

"Okay. Anything else you're 'just wondering'?"

"I am *so* glad you asked. As a matter of fact, I have always wondered exactly what kind of a person Bartholomew Richard Runyon, the Third was."

"Bartholomew *who?*"

"Bartholomew Richard Runyon, the Third—he went to your high school."

"Are you talking about Rick Runyon? How on earth do you know—"

"He goes by *Rick?* Ew. Never mind, then."

I hung up the phone and joined the little girl, who was still singing *B-I-N-G-O* over and over and over again.

Seattle was rainy as usual and the damp air made the smell in the condo overwhelming—like dust and Jello and unwashed hair. I tried my best to avoid breathing it or, even worse, recognizing it, acknowledging it, letting it wash over me.

The little girl tiptoed into the room behind me.

"There's ghosts here," she said.

"Just one besides you," I corrected. "But she's sleeping. We have to be careful not to wake her up."

The little girl nodded and, together, we made our way toward the walk-in closet.

Handbags, designer jeans, cropped jackets, lingerie, hosiery, jewelry, makeup, perfume—the cedar-lined mini-room was like the world's greatest boutique where everything fit and nothing cost anything. The bathroom was another cache of face creams, dental bleach and pricey makeup. Of course, the place was short on shoes as Alex had already brought most of them to Commerce, but I found a pair of impossible stilettos he apparently rejected as not being worth the trunk space that did the trick. The outfit was completed by the attorney's most designer of jeans, an old concert tee that belonged to the student and now nearly passed for vintage and a suit coat that, when separated from its matching skirt, resembled a wool motorcycle jacket. The little girl waited patiently as I painstakingly did full-face makeup for the first time in a long time, then buffed half of it away with a tissue until I felt like me again.

I grabbed one of the attorney's purses and switched the stuff out of the teenager's old one that I had toted around for months. I considered throwing the teenager's purse away because it had already been recycled once, but then I thought better of it and put it up on the shelf next to the designer bags before turning off the light.

The little girl and I opened the closet door and crept through the dark bedroom toward the hallway. Unfortunately, I wasn't used to walking in so high of heels and I half-tripped twice, catching my balance against the wall with a loud thud. But the form under the bedspread barely moved. Only a wisp of greasy hair dangled outside the covers.

The little girl and I decided to walk to Alex's apartment from the condo because we figured we wouldn't find parking over there and I needed practice walking in the heels. But the old plaid umbrella Jack kept in the truck didn't really match my snazzy outfit, and the peep holes in my stilettos left my big toes vulnerable to puddles. Intense blisters set in after only a few blocks and I considered taking off the shoes altogether but then I remembered how the last time I traipsed around Seattle I also looked like a crazy woman and I didn't want to get a reputation for such.

Finally, we limped up to Alex's building. I double checked the street number against that written on an old FedEx receipt from work before pushing the call button for his apartment.

"Yeah?" Alex answered.

"Top Ramen police," I said in a lowered voice.

"Sam? What are you doing here?"

"I'm here to inspect your pantry," I said, "Let's see how you're doing on your New Year's resolution."

He didn't respond. But he did buzz me in.

"You look nice," he said once we were in his apartment, watching me dumfounded as I looked through his cupboards and flippantly commented on the ample supply of soup, canned chili and macaroni and cheese. "Did you go shopping?"

"Sort of—in my own closet," I said as I finally gave up my search and sat down kitty-cornered from him at the secondhand kitchen table, which looked like it had been bought from an aging 1950s diner before it was demolished. "At the condo," I added.

"You went to the condo?"

"Yes. Are you proud of me?"

"I guess. Are you moving back to Seattle?"

"No," I said. "I'm putting it up for sale. Do you want to buy it?"

He blinked and looked down at table. "Not really."

"I'm sorry, I forgot," I said. "It's only a one bedroom, so there's no place for your roommate."

He smiled for the first time that afternoon. "I don't have a roommate anymore," he said, with a slight hint of pout.

"What happened?"

"He got married," he sighed. "Regardless, when I do get my own place I want a yard and trees so I can rake my own leaves for the first time in my life."

Without forewarning, he grabbed my knee under the table and held my leg still. I hadn't realized I had been swinging my crossed leg with nervous abandon until he stopped it.

"Stop kidding around," he said, his voice serious. "What are you doing here?"

My lip quivered as I started to answer. I hadn't expected that. But I knew that if it were the attorney, or the student, or the teenager in my place, her lip would be quivering, too.

"I'm just trying to do something both reasonable and prudent for once in my life," I explained, while thinking *albeit in a very Starene, ambush kind of way.*

I was expecting him to laugh or yell or even look bored, but I wasn't expecting him to flinch at this. "Why on earth would you want to do that, Sam? Don't you remember?"

And I did remember. I remembered all at once, like remembering what wet feels like once a tidal wave hits you. Through remembering, I understood the utter profanity of my comment.

Alex's *Shall we?* at the curb had stuck with me for forever. I remembered the student, sitting in the fluorescent-lit bar review classroom all evening long while a videotaped professor droned on about the Reasonably Prudent Person and how reasonable and prudent his every action was. And after taking copious notes wherein they memorized what the RPP would do in any given situation with any given occupation and any given special circumstances, all three hundred of her classmates packed up their laptops and gathered their phone-book sized study guides and headed out the door into the summer night air.

Including Alex.

The parking lot for the bar review course was across the street from the building where class was held and it was a very busy street. There was a crosswalk at a street light about two blocks down. Two blocks to the light and two blocks back to the parking lot was a *long* way to walk when you were carrying a laptop and four phone books. Especially when you could see your car just across the street.

The class got out late at night so there wasn't a ton of traffic. Regardless, the RPP would have carried his mountain of books down to the streetlight, waited for the signal to cross, looked both ways, crossed the street and walked back up to the parking lot. Then he would have been extra careful when backing his car out of the parking space. The RPP was always extra careful when driving in reverse.

But the student was tired that night and so was Alex. They were tired from sitting there for hours listening to a lecture on the RPP—a first year topic. It was like graduating from high school and then having to review your ABCs in preparation for an exam.

And so the student was exhausted and a little giddy as she stood on the edge of that curb with her three hundred classmates and looked across the street to her car.

And Alex came and stood beside her and held out his hand.

"Shall we, Samantha?" he asked, motioning toward the street.

The student turned to him and smiled. "I don't see why not."

"But what would the Reasonably Prudent Person do?" he pressed.

The student laughed at his naivete. "The Reasonably Prudent Person *does not exist*," she responded in her trademark matter-of-fact manner.

The student grabbed Alex's hand and together they stepped out into the street and jaywalked across it. Before long, the entire bar study class followed suit—people who were preparing to take an oath to practice the law were throwing caution to the wind en masse. Some of them ran haplessly with their laptops, while others dropped their phone books to the street in the melee. Soon, the traffic caught up with the class, but by then they were a large jaywalking mob blocking the street and cross traffic didn't stand a chance.

"The RPP is a construct," Alex explained, bringing me back to his kitchen, "a term of art, an average. But *we* are individuals with reasons and feelings and background. That prevents us from fitting the RPP mold."

I nodded, still a little light-headed at the memory.

Shall we, Samantha?

"Just do it," the little girl goaded from her spot across the table. "I won't watch, I promise. It's too icky." She headed down the hallway as I nodded again.

I reached across the table and grabbed the placket of his blue shirt. It was the one I had sewn the button on. Then, in one swift move, ripping the proverbial band-aid off, I pulled Alex slightly toward me by the shirt and kissed him soft and slow on the lips.

When I released my grip on his shirt, my hand was shaking. But Alex stayed put, leaning forward across the corner of the table, his weight resting on his left arm, so I took my shaking hand and touched his cheek, his temple, his ear. Alex's eyes stayed closed and he didn't pull away, but he didn't do anything either.

I kissed him again, and this time he let his right hand graze my knee and briefly touch my waist. He kissed me back for a marvelous ten seconds but then jolted away, taking a deep breath.

"What's wrong?"

"It's just—I'm still technically your boss, Sam," he blurted out nervously. He stood up and walked a few feet toward the refrigerator, rubbing his forehead with his hand and blinking like mad.

I stood up, too, at a loss. "You're . . . you're worried I'm going to *sue* you?"

"No, I—"

"For goshsakes, Alex, I'll sign a waiver."

I'll sign a waiver?! I repeated the words in my own mind with disgust. I could hardly think of anything less romantic to say, and yet there I was, unsuccessfully trying to make some serious moves on the guy, saying it.

But Alex laughed lightly, and looked up at me. The blinking had completely stopped. He looked straight at me, full eye contact and everything.

It was the first time in my life that I ever felt positively adored.

"Can we shake on that?" he asked, extending his hand.

"Sure," I shrugged, taking a few clumsy stilettoed steps over his chair.

But it was a trick, you see, and I should have seen it coming as I have known Alex Martin was a trickster since that first time I ever spoke to him, back at the on-campus interview for Wallace. When I got to him and grabbed his hand, he didn't shake it at all. Instead, he pulled me towards him and wrapped his hands around my waist and back and pushed me against the refrigerator and kissed me for a very long time. I circled my arms around his neck and held on. Eventually, we stopped kissing and just stood there, his arms tight around me, his head buried in the nape of my neck, and my fingers laced through his curly black hair.

We stood there for a very long time, just reveling in finally knowing each other.

It was pretty late at night by the time the little girl and I made it back to Commerce. I felt bad for having Jack's truck for so long and planned on apologizing profusely at the first available *Law & Order* commercial break. But when we entered the house, the television wasn't on.

"Something's different," the little girl said.

She was only six and she had crooked hair, but she had already proven her intuition. I walked through the entry towards the dining room. Jack was sitting on the floor where the piles of dishes had been all these months. He was staring at the opposite wall with a certain resignation on his face.

I looked to the wall. He had bought a new china cabinet. The dishes were inside. They looked out of place.

"New china cabinet, huh?"

"Yeah. Sarita helped pick it out and the guy delivered it today. Do you like it?"

"It's okay," I said. It was a little on the country side for Jack. It had fabric panels behind paned glass. "We can probably replace that floral with something else if you'd like."

"I'm not sure what I like. I kind of liked the dishes on the floor."

"I kind of liked the old cabinet," I offered.

He just sat there nodding for a second. "Me too," he said.

He took a deep breath and stared at the floor.

"Do you still think this house is haunted, Sam?"

"No," I said, shaking my head, "I don't. I was wrong about it before."

This wasn't the answer he wanted to hear. He wanted someone to validate that his old china cabinet was haunted by the spirit of my dead mother and that the new one, which wasn't haunted, only drove that fact home.

"It's been a crazy year for me, Dad. But out of the craziness, I've learned a thing or two."

"Such as?"

"Such as the fact that it is not places that are haunted—people are. Sure, places sometimes seem like they raise the dead when they're really raising memories of the dead, but trust me—ghosts follow the person, not the china cabinet."

He looked at me for a minute. Perhaps I had said too much. Perhaps I had let out too much crazy.

"Are you haunted by the ghost of your mother?"

"No," I said meekly. "I'm sorry. I wish I were. Maybe I didn't know her well enough. But honestly Dad, I don't think you're haunted by her either."

"Oh yes I am," he said with great conviction. "Twenty-five years later and I still can't move on. Twenty-five years and I'm still blown over by changing a piece of her furniture."

"Dad—"

"Yes?"

"Never mind. I don't want to offend you."

"Please Sam, there's no offense between us."

"It's just—has it ever occurred to you that you're not haunted by Mom? That instead, you're haunted by the man who loved her—the young man in love with a healthy woman who never foresaw the day he would be without her and therefore carelessly blew time with her into the wind like dandelion seeds?"

He put his head in his hands—that was all it took to conjure the little girl ghost to my side.

"That means he's sad," she reported.

She would know. She had seen that look before in her room, in the dark, when he thought she had already fallen asleep. She was only six, but she knew a grown man with his head in his hands was sad and not to be disturbed.

I had seen that look before, too. It was a year prior, but it might as well have been a hundred years ago. I could barely remember it. It was in the Seattle condo—my condo, I guess. It was during the year in jammies, towards the end, and I had not gotten out of bed for days. In what seemed like the middle of the night, I heard someone take the key out of the potted plant in front of the door and let himself in. A million thoughts raced through my sleepy head as to who it might be: the landlord, the police, a burglar, a rapist, the grim reaper himself. And then I decided I didn't care who it was. I was already dead, after all—what harm could they do?

But as soon as the door opened, a voice called out in the hall-way.

"Sam?"

It was Jack.

He came in my room. I realized it might not be the middle of the night after all, but rather the middle of the day, at least under the terms of waking peoples' time. I rolled over in bed and played dead.

The next time I woke up, Jack was sitting in a chair in my room. The blinds were still drawn but no light was coming through them. I couldn't think how long he had been there. My eyes adjusted to the dark and I dared to open them just a slit to see what he was doing. He was sitting there, with his head in his hands—the second worse time I had ever seen him do it. The gesture maximized the emotion he was willing to display. I was so ashamed at how I had let my entire life slip away. Still, I was incapable of doing anything but laying there.

Finally, he got up to leave.

"When you're ready to come home Sam, you just give me a call. Day or night."

And with that, he let himself out the door.

"Are you okay, Dad?" I asked him in the dining room, employing the words as a passive-aggressive means of begging him to take his head out of his hands.

"I am," he nodded. "But tell me one thing. If it's not your mother, Sam, then what is haunting you so terribly?"

I owed him an answer. I owed him so much more than an answer, actually, but an answer was all I could afford.

"Her six-year-old daughter."

✳

Chapter 19

GUMMY HAIR

P<small>LACES</small> AREN'T HAUNTED; PEOPLE ARE. I thought about this as I laid in the pink bedroom that night, staring at the gingham canopy on the bed. The little girl looked at me from the window seat.

"When are we going to go jump that gulch already?" she asked for the one millionth time.

"Tomorrow," I said. "On one condition."

"What?" she asked.

"You have to tell me how you got your crooked hair."

Her right hand instinctively jotted up and covered the mangy side, but at the same time she looked straight at me and lied. "Nothing happened," she said.

"Nothing happened," I mimicked. "I'm so sick of that answer. Nothing is not a sufficient excuse for anything."

It wasn't a fair argument, I know, as to date I had blamed everything and anything on nothing, whereas this was the first time the little girl had played the nothing card. I wasn't sure if the little girl learned the nothing blame game from me, or if I learned it from her a long time ago. We were the proverbial chicken and egg in that regard.

The little girl looked down at her shoelaces.

"Now tell me about the hair," I instructed.

"It started with the phone," she said.

"What phone?"

"The ringing phone. It woke me up."

The phone did ring. At first she mistook the sound for her daisy alarm clock, as if a six-year-old had any reason to set an alarm for anything. Disregarding this logical deficiency, she flapped her chubby hands around the nightstand in a drowsy effort to shut it off.

But little by little it dawned on her: there was no clock and there was no nightstand. In fact, she wasn't even in bed. She was in a sweaty heap on her bedroom floor, tangled in a mess of dress-up clothes and stuffed animals and half-eaten cheese slices she snuck in the night before because Jack had forgotten to feed her dinner.

Again.

So she stretched like a kitten. Her shoes were on. It was late afternoon and the sun was burning a hole through the curtains on her bedroom window. She felt like an idiot. Only babies took naps and she was no baby.

Her mouth was dry from sleeping with it open. She smacked her lips together and realized something was missing.

"The gum!" I cried out, remembering at last.

The little girl looked down again and pouted. "Yeah. The gum."

Back then, when the little girl thought of the gum, she jumped up and looked in the mirror of her pint-sized vanity. Her worst bad dream had come true—the gum was stuck in her hair and a hot pink, impossibly high-heeled Barbie shoe was stuck in the gum. She could hear her dad talking on the phone downstairs. As soon as he was off he would check on her and big trouble was bound to follow. Due to previous gummy hair catastrophes resulting from reckless chewing while napping, she had been forbidden to have gum altogether. Back in those days, she wasn't a big fan of rules. However, she was even less enamored of big trouble.

The only feasible solution was obvious. She grabbed the scissors off her art stand and cut away at the hairy pink chunk. But the scissors were safety scissors for kids and they weren't very sharp and so she had to keep cutting and cutting—moving closer to her head with each attempt. Long pieces of tangly hair fell to the floor. Finally, the gum fell too.

"Sammy!"

Just in time. She could hear Jack coming up the stairs. She took a last look in the mirror and—

Aaaah! The gum was gone, but so was a large chunk of her hair. She didn't think she had cut so much, but now there was a sorta small but kinda big bald spot on the right side of her head and the parts that weren't bald were all sticky-outy. Jack would see it for sure. And her room—her room was a complete disaster. If her mommy had seen it, she would have asked when the tornado hit. She was surely in the biggest trouble ever.

"Samantha," Jack called again as he appeared in the doorway. She put her hand over the bald spot to cover it and assumed her best poker face.

"What?"

"What are you doing?"

"Cleaning my room."

"Oh. Were you sleeping?"

"No." It was no time to admit weakness. Besides, he was the one who looked like he needed a nap.

"Well…," and here's where his voice got all creaky, which was really scary because he was generally a man of little emotion, "I'm afraid we've got to go."

"Go where?" She was beginning to lose feeling in her right arm, so she quickly switched the bald-spot covering responsibilities to the left which, admittedly, was an awkward position that partially obscured her view of him and, well, pretty much every-thing except her arm. But Jack didn't seem to notice. He stared down at the floor and rubbed his forehead with his hand, like he had a headache or something. Inspired, she looked at the floor and started rubbing her bald spot as if she also had a headache.

"Do you remember that talk we had, Sammy?"

At age six, the adults in her life had already made her painfully aware that listening to adults was not her strong point. She remembered vague details of several different talks, most of them involving her own trespasses into big trouble territory. But she had no clue which of these, if any, was "that talk."

"Yes."

"Well, it's time."

"Okay."

She was glad her mommy wasn't in the car because it meant she got to ride in the front seat and could put the bald part of her head against the window and away from Jack and give both her arms a rest.

She didn't normally pay attention to the way her parents drove because she assumed they were perfect drivers and she was usually preoccupied with staring out the window, looking for the kinds of landmarks that kids use to give them some sort of understanding as to where they are. But this time all the things outside her win-dow—parked cars, garbage cans, the retaining wall on the free-way—seemed to lurch dangerously close to her as Jack hugged the right side now and again. She kept looking at him to make sure he was awake. His eyes were wide open and he was looking directly at the road. Yet she felt like if she touched his arm, he would jump up the same as if she just woke him.

He held her left hand as they walked through the hospital, and she kept her right firmly planted atop the bald spot. She figured out that they were going to visit mommy, who was sick and in the hospital so the doctors could give her medicine and operations to make her all better so she could come back home and take care of them and the little girl wouldn't have to sneak cheese slices for dinner. The last time she visited the hospital, mommy let her eat the green Jello that came with her lunch. Maybe this time it would be the red kind, which was her favorite.

Her right arm was really starting to ache again, but she couldn't switch to the left because Jack was holding it. She tried not to think about it and concentrated on the Jello instead.

At the end of the hall, Grandpa walked out of a room. His eyes were puffy.

"Grandpa!"

Grandpa looked up and saw them, but he never answered the little girl. Instead, he put his hand to his mouth and started shaking a little.

"I'm afraid you just missed her, Jack."

Jack dropped the little girl's hand. "Oh . . . I . . . I shouldn't have taken the freeway. There was an accident. And all this traffic."

By now Grandpa was hugging him. "It's okay, Jack."

Jack nodded. His voice got all creaky again. "I think I'll go in there for awhile, all the same."

The little girl started to follow Jack towards the room, somewhat disappointed because it sounded like they had just missed seeing mommy and she had wanted to see her and had wanted the Jello. But Grandpa put his hands on her shoulders.

"Do you really think Samantha should go in there?"

Jack turned and looked at the little girl like he hadn't previously been aware she was standing there. Like he was wondering how she got to the hospital. "No, no—that would probably be a bad idea. Too traumatic. I shouldn't have brought her. I just thought she'd have a chance—"

Just then, one of mommy's nurses took the little girl's left hand and pulled her a step away from Grandpa. "I'll take her to get a snack. We've got some crayons at the nurses' station. You two take your time."

Finding herself led down the hall by her left hand once again, the little girl was regretting not switching off bald-spot hands while she had the chance. Her right arm was practically numb at this point. But now that Jack was acting so strange and his voice was so creaky, she *really* didn't want to aggravate him with the gummy hair problem.

She looked back at Jack as he entered that room. It was funny, because for a moment she thought she saw mommy lying on the bed in there before the door swung shut.

"What's the matter with your head?" the nurse asked.

"Nothing."

"Why are you holding it like that, then?"

"I have a headache."

"Well, I'm a nurse. It's my job to make headaches and boo-boos go away. Maybe I should look at it."

"No!"

The nurse set the little girl on an office chair at the nurses' big desk and then pumped a lever underneath it until she was high enough to reach the table, which was pretty fun. She gave her some old papers to draw on the back of, and a box of crayons that was missing the black.

"Do you want a snack?"

The little girl nodded eagerly.

"What kinds of snacks do you like?"

Truth be told, she would have settled for anything other than cheese slices, but she decided to go for the gold. "Do you have that kind of Jello that's cut into squares and in a little bowl and has foamy stuff on top?"

The nurse laughed. "You're in luck! We have tons of that kind of Jello here. What's your favorite flavor?"

"Red."

The little girl was beginning to like the nurse, and even trust her a bit, but when the nurse returned with the Jello she played a nasty trick on the little girl. The nurse *could have* put the little spoon in the bowl of Jello and handed it to the little girl in one piece—the little girl knew this, because that's how it was served when mommy had it. She also could have set them both on the desk in front of her, like a waiter does at a fancy restaurant. But instead she held out the bowl of Jello in one hand and the spoon in the other. Instinctively, the little girl reached out with her own two hands, exposing the bald spot in the process. It was brilliant.

The nurse smiled really big and giggled a bit, probably because her nasty trick had worked. "What happened to your hair, dear?"

"Nothing."

"It looks like you gave yourself a little haircut."

"Well, I had to. I got gum stuck in it." When she said this, the little girl felt like the nurse tricked her again. Sure, she'd already pegged her on the haircut, but somehow she got her to confess to the gum-chewing too.

"Did this happen today?"

"Yes."

"Did your daddy notice?"

"No. Don't tell him!" The little girl said this even though experience had taught her the futility of asking one adult to conceal her misdeeds from another, particularly a parent.

"Don't worry, I won't." The nurse stood above the little girl and ran her fingers through her hair, assessing the sticky-outy damage. Before mommy got sick, she used to brush the tangles out of the little girl's long, fine hair every night before she went to bed—a ritual so soft and soothing that it sometimes made her dizzy. But ever since mommy was in the hospital, the little girl's hair was only combed every other day by Jack—right after her bath and when it was sopping wet. He wouldn't ever use the no-tangles spray stuff, and his weapon of choice was one of his black old-man combs with the teeth too close together. It was a painful, even tortuous experience, and a part of their adopted routine they had both come to particularly dread due to the screaming and yelling and tantrum-throwing and tear-gushing that was bound to accompany it.

But the nurse knew how to touch hair the mommy way. Her motions were so rhythmic and calming that the little girl momentarily forgot about the Jello or the horsey picture she was drawing and limply sat there while Goosebumps sprouted on her arm. The nurse pulled a hairbrush out of her purse to gently work through the mass of knots. Like mommy, she knew to hold the hair firmly above the part she was brushing to relieve the pull on the little girl's head. She parted the little girl's hair far on the left side so that it fell over the bald spot on the right, and she braided both sides to hold the new division in place. She secured the ends of the braids with office-supply rubber bands from the desk drawer, and she even let the little girl pick the colors.

"There. Now you don't have to hold your hand up all the time."

The little girl smiled. She was beginning to like the nurse again despite her reputation as a trickster.

Jack never noticed her new braided hairdo, not even that night when they stopped by McDonald's. When they got home, he also didn't seem to perceive that the little girl's room was still a disaster. But he told her he loved her and, after tucking her into bed, he sat there on the pint-sized stool that went to her vanity for what seemed like an eternity, his head in his hands.

"Daddy, I have a question."

Jack looked up hesitantly, almost terrified at what the little girl might ask. The look in his eyes shook her faith a little, and for the first time in her life, she wasn't so positive that he would know the answer.

"Yes?"

"How come when you hold your hands up to your head for a really long time they start to hurt so much?"

At this, he relaxed his a bit. He coughed and finally got rid of that frog that had been in his throat all day. When he spoke, it was with his usual soft, matter-of-fact enunciation.

"Well, part of it is that the blood drains away from your hands…"

Uh-oh. That didn't sound so good. Panicked, she vigorously shook her hands underneath the covers to make sure they still had sufficient blood in them.

"…and the other part is just plain gravity."

The little girl held up her end of the bargain, and so the next morning it was my turn to make good on a promise that was as old as her crooked hair.

"Are you sure you want to do this?" Alex asked me.

"No. But yes," I said. I could tell I wasn't exactly selling him on my certainty.

"I mean, I think I've got the trajectory worked out, but I'm no physics expert. Science guys don't go to law school."

"Unless they want to practice intellectual property and be billionaires," I reminded him.

"I don't know. Didn't you always get the feeling in law school that the IP guys were outcasts from the computer and science industries?"

"Come to think of it, yes. But *why* were they outcasts? Perhaps the computer and science industries run their workplaces like reality television shows and those guys were voted off?"

Alex just smiled. "You're stalling, aren't you?"

"No—"

"Admit it."

"It's just that you said you knew how to do it, that you had done it before. But now you're scaring me with your 'trajectories' and whatnot."

"I told you I had built bike and skate ramps as a kid. Which we used to, say, jump the gutter on Spring Street. It was slightly smaller than, well, this."

And with that, he made a dramatic sweeping gesture towards the gulch.

The gulch seemed big again, as big as it seemed to the little girl back in the day. I decided it was a living thing that grew and contracted to match my mood.

I looked down into it. I estimated it to be as deep as a six-story building is tall. Sure, it wasn't fifty-five floors or anything, but six stories is enough to kill you, right? At the very least, "six-story fall" has paralysis written all over it.

I looked at the ramp Alex had built. Say what you will about him, but you've got to love a guy who's willing to spend three Saturdays fashioning a bike ramp for his girlfriend. You've also got to love a guy who takes three Saturdays to do it when one would have sufficed for most people. I thought back on all my drummers and couldn't imagine a single one of them building a bike ramp. First, most of them were not up on Saturday mornings due to the Friday night gig. Second, they could have easily injured their drumming arms—that is, their bread and butter. Well, their alleged bread and butter. Truth be told, I had never seen conclusive evidence of the same.

"How far across do you think it is?" I asked.

"Further than six feet. Past that, I can't really tell."

"Isn't there some sort of formula about distance and speed and to the nth power that we could plug these estimated numbers into?"

"I told you, I'm not a math guy. . . Remind me why you're doing this again?"

"Don't make me go over it anymore," I begged. "Like I said, it's an inner-child-needs-closure kind of a thing."

"Did Starene tell you to do this?" he asked. It was a playful insult. Starene's new daytime talk show had recently been revamped, wherein she dished out quasi-psychological advice to all sorts of women despite a complete lack of education or formal training that would qualify her to do so, and I was guilty of watching said daytime talk show on more than one occasion.

Still, I rolled my eyes. "That's about the most sexist thing I've ever heard. No, Starene did not tell me to do this. If Starene were here, she'd probably talk some sense into me, which is more than I can say for you."

He smirked. "Starene doesn't have to hang out with your inner child all day long like I do."

If only he knew. I looked over at the little girl ghost, who was doing cartwheels of glee through the tall grass. Her big moment had finally arrived.

"Do you want me to try it first?" he asked.

"No," I said. "If one of us is going to spend the rest of forever spoon-feeding the other, I would rather be the feedie."

"How considerate of you."

"Listen, I think I'm going to start riding from really far back so that I can pick up enough speed," I said.

"Okay," he said. "I'm going to stay here by the ramp with 911 already dialed on my cell phone and my finger on the 'talk' button."

It was the second sexist thing he said that day. Didn't he know that you were supposed to have 911 programmed into speed dial on the "9" position on your cell phone? Then I realized that only women cared about advice like that, and so the fact that he didn't know it was evidence that, like most men, he had never anticipated a violent personal attack which would require him to speed dial 911 and scream out his name and approximate location mid-struggle.

I shook my head thinking about this as I walked the bike to the back of the field. The little girl ran up alongside of me.

"Are you ready for this?" I asked.

"Am I ever!" she said. "You're going down, gravity."

"If this doesn't work, I don't want you to feel bad."

"Don't say that—you'll jinx it."

We walked and I realized that I had adopted a bit of her skip in the last several months. I realized that I was going to miss her. It was only then that it hit me that she would be going away.

"In a way, we already beat gravity," I told her.

"We did? How?"

"When you showed up in my apartment and kept poking me in the arm until I finally got out of bed."

"I wanted to walk the dogs," she reminded me.

"I know. And I'm so grateful for that."

I got on the bike and rode it as fast as I could towards the ramp. Like the gulch, the ramp had shrunk—I suddenly wondered not only if it could sufficiently launch me over the gulch, but whether it could even withstand the weight of me and the little girl's bike and our momentum.

"Here we go!" the little girl screamed.

She was right. There was no turning back now. As I rode towards the ramp I wondered why I should even care if I died, as a year ago I certainly wouldn't have. But now I had things, people even, to live for. What's more, I had already been raised from the dead—a luxury experienced by so few that I could hardly expect it to happen twice in one lifetime.

The bike hit the ramp and I leaned forward and pulled the handlebars toward me. For one second I dared to look below me as the gulch passed underneath. It looked exactly as the little girl had imagined it would so very many times so very many years ago.

"We're flying!" the little girl screamed. Or maybe it was me.

When I hit the ground on the other side, I did so with a thump. Months of riding the Vespa over Commerce's many potholes paid off as I was able to level the bike out before I went over the handlebars.

I grabbed at the brakes and then remembered that this was a little girl's bike and didn't have hand brakes. I kicked the pedals in reverse as if I had done it yesterday. The bike rolled to a slow stop.

I got off the bike and closed my eyes for a split second, preparing myself for the moment when I would turn around. I didn't want Alex to see me crying.

"You did it, Sam!" he yelled.

"I know," I said, my back still to him, my eyes still closed. I brushed away at my tears with the back of my hand.

"How does it feel?"

"It feels wonderful," I said, tears streaming down my cheeks. I pretended to fumble with the helmet. I was grateful the gulch separated us, that he couldn't run over and grab me.

"So what do you want to do now?"

I finally turned around. I didn't know if he could see the tears or not—tears that had waited so long to be shed that they had seemingly fermented inside my tear ducts. They burned as they splashed down my cheeks, burned so bad that I was sure they were leaving scars on my face and I would forever look like a girl who had just been crying.

"I don't know," I shrugged. "If you're willing to wait for me, I guess I'll just ride down to the bridge, cross over and come back to you."

He started laughing. "There's a *bridge*?!"

I laughed too. It was hilarious that I had risked life and limb when the bridge was only a ten minute ride away.

I opened my eyes, but I didn't have to look around. I already knew she was gone.

The ride down to the bridge was a quiet one. It was the first time in a very long time I had truly been alone. Self-analysis was begging to come through, but I resisted the urge to even think. I simply rode my bike.

Chapter 20

TODAY (REPRISE)

TODAY I AM WEARING "REAL CLOTHES"—at least the kind that you wear on a holiday when you plan on putting in an above-average amount of physical labor. My "real" outfit includes shoes (athletic shoes, but not the pair of running shoes that I wore into the ground), socks, jeans and an old law school sweatshirt. Unfortunately, Alex showed up wearing the exact same sweatshirt, so I turned mine inside-out so we wouldn't look like twins (or idiots).

Today we all helped Libby move into my Seattle condo, which is now her Seattle condo, as she bought it from me. I was a little worried that she couldn't afford it, but, as it turns out, eight dollars an hour plus several promotional raises over the years for going on eighteen years will get you pretty far so long as you (1) live at home with your parents the entire time and don't pay any rent, (2) drive your dad's old car and never assume a car payment or an insurance payment for that matter, (3) eat dinner every night at home and let your mom pack your lunch for work and (4) aren't a slave to fashion. Libby has done all of these things and, as a result, she amassed quite the little nest egg while I was out paying rent and buying drinks for Mickeys and their drum kits.

Libby and Raul both transferred to the call center's regional headquarters in Seattle. Raul is in Boston for the next two months receiving corporate training. When he gets back in March, he and Libby will get married. Aunt Sarita's impossible excitement at her daughter's forthcoming (if unforeseen) nuptials has been slightly dampened by her tsk-tsking that "March is not a good time for an Oregon wedding."

Today Alex drove Libby all over Seattle, pointing out the best coffee shops, the best bars, the best music stores, the best dry cleaners, the best Asian market, the best place to buy pizza, the best place to get pancakes, the best place to hail a cab, the best route from the condo to her job, the best route from the condo to the airport and the best awning in all of downtown to duck under when the rain gets unbearable. Libby, who doesn't even know what an Asian market is, took copious notes on a tourist street map the entire time. I sat in the backseat of the car and smiled, so happy for her. She had lived in Seattle for less than twenty-four hours and already she was an insider for the first time in her life.

Today I didn't want Alex to upstage me, so I introduced Libby to the only person I knew in Seattle anymore, the crazy lady upstairs. She's no Charlemayne, to be sure, but I think she and Libby will get along fine or at least get together to watch reality television shows or at the very least will do each other the favor of calling the cops if they hear a loud thud or a scream. You should have heard Aunt Sarita butter up the crazy lady by oohing and aahing over all her royal couple memorabilia. Aunt Sarita is very worried about Libby and I think she wants to go home thinking someone is looking out for her daughter in the big city. It is overbearing as usual, but it is also kind of touching. After a lifetime of being convinced otherwise, today I decided the two are not mutually exclusive.

Today Alex and Jack and the Billingsleys also helped me move out of the condo. Everyone complimented the nice Italian furniture. Sometimes it is fun when your old things are new again.

Today I realized that not all drummers are musicians. As much as it is hard to admit you are self-absorbed, I have finally come to recognize that I'm a bit of a lead guitarist. For convenience's sake, I will blame it on being an only child. The reason I crave drummers is because I need someone behind me, helping me keep time through my crazy freestyle solos so that I can seamlessly jump back into the song when I'm ready. That someone is Alex. He is a drummer after all. You might say he's more like a Human Metronome, but I would prefer that you didn't.

Tomorrow Alex and I will take a practice test for our upcoming Oregon Bar Exam. We just spent an entire week reviewing torts, all of it involving our old friend, the RPP. We are hopeful we will both pass as we have already leased office space in Sherman Valley. The office space is in an old house. The rest of the house is for living. It is where we will be living.

We were going to call the name of our firm Martin Green, but then we thought better of it. First, we researched it and found there are a million other firms named Martin Green and we couldn't get a domain for our website that was at all relevant to the name. Second, it sounds like a sole practitioner—like there is some schmuck named Martin Green who wants to give you a legal tip or two. Then we tried switching it to Green Martin, but that doesn't work either, as it sounds like the name of a garden shop or Mr. Green Jeans or like sole practitioner Martin is green with envy over something, and you'd hate for people to assume it's the fact that the competition does better legal work, which is just not true. After all, we are good lawyers. We are the best lawyers we know.

Today Alex and I are engaged to be married. I know it sounds ridiculous, but it was the issues with the firm name that necessitated our betrothal. We were talking about the firm name one day and I just said, "Why don't I just marry you and change my name to Martin and then we can call it Martin & Martin or Martin-squared?" And I was just joking, of course. I've been working on joking. But apparently I'm still off in the execution as Alex thought I was serious and immediately took me up on the offer. Let me tell you, accidentally proposing to someone is probably one of the most embarrassing things you can do in your life. But it was too hard to backtrack, and so I didn't bother. And it doesn't sound romantic, and yet somehow it was.

Aunt Sarita said she was surprised I was changing my name as she always took me for a hyphenator. Mind you, I have no problem with women who hyphenate their names. I am sure they do it for a variety of reasons. But the only reason I would see to hyphenate my name is to avoid losing my identity somehow. After the past year, losing myself is the last thing I'm worried about. The knowledge may have been painful to come by, but I can definitely say I know who I am, and it has nothing to do with a name.

Today there is only one ghost in my life. She is underweight. She has bags under her eyes although she sleeps all the day long. Her hair is uncombed. Her skin is pale. She smells like bed-sweat and Jello. She is mute in both voice and thought, but despite the fact that I know she'll never so much as speak to me, she is by far the scariest ghost I have ever seen.

This ghost wears nothing but jammies.

I almost didn't recognize her when I walked in the bedroom of the condo for the first time, although I had anticipated her presence there for weeks. It was her ragged jammies that gave her away.

Today a part of me hopes this ghost will stay in her bedroom in the condo, where the memory of her resides, where I feel she belongs. But the rest of me knows all too well that ghosts haunt the person rather than the place. This is okay—today I need her nearby to remind me how far I have come.

Today I realize that I am nothing more than tomorrow's ghost. In a way, it robs my sense of self to know I'm always changing; at the same time, it provides incentive to have the best today possible so I can have a positive influence on tomorrow and, if needs be, shake some sense into the living.

As of today, I have waged a million wars against gravity and I have lost every one. But today I won the battle.

Today is New Year's Day, you see.

And today I got out of bed.

Breinigsville, PA USA
05 December 2010
250694BV00001B/64/P